D0509019

V for
violet

ALSO BY ALISON RATTLE

The Quietness
The Madness
The Beloved

V for violet

ALISON RATTLE

HOT KEY BOOKS

First published in Great Britain in 2016 by
HOT KEY BOOKS
80–81 Wimpole St, London W1G 9RE
www.hotkeybooks.com

A CIP catalogue record for this book is available from the British Library.

ISBN: 978-1-4714-0381-1
also available as an ebook

This book is typeset in 10.5 Berling LT Std using Atomik ePublisher

Printed and bound by Clays Ltd, St Ives Plc

Hot Key Books is an imprint of Bonnier Publishing Fiction,
a Bonnier Publishing company
www.bonnierpublishingfiction.co.uk
www.bonnierpublishing.co.uk

Down in a green and shady bed,
A modest violet grew;
Its stalk was bent, it hung its head,
As if to hide from view.

And yet it was a lovely flower,
Its colours bright and fair;
It might have graced a rosy bower,
Instead of hiding there.

– Jane Taylor

Battersea, London
1961

The Beginning

I was born above our fish and chip shop on Battersea Park Road, at the exact moment Winston Churchill came on the wireless to announce the war was over.

Nobody saw me come into the world. Nobody saw me land on the newspapers that had been laid out under Mum's bottom and across the mattress to protect it from stains. Even Mum missed my birth, she was so busy cheering along with the rest of them. The rest of them being my dad (Frank the Fish), Mrs Rice the midwife, my sister Norma and a motley collection of neighbours who'd come in to listen to Mr Churchill, because they didn't have a wireless of their own. Mum had insisted on taking the wireless into the bedroom with her when the first pains started, so of course it stood to reason that everyone else crowded in there too.

It was a while before anyone saw me lying there, all goggle-eyed and gasping for air. 'Never felt a thing!' Mum said, when Mrs Rice finally turned her attention back to the goings on between Mum's legs and exclaimed out loud at the sight of me floundering around on the bloodied pages of the *Evening Standard*.

Violet, they called me.

V for Violet

V for Victory

Most people don't remember the moment of their birth. But I'll never forget it. One minute I'm cocooned in a delicious warm, safe darkness, dreaming of nothing in particular. The next, I am being squeezed so tightly that my soft little ribs pop. Then the shock of cold and wetness and a terrible burning as my first breath inflates the delicate tissue of my lungs. Then white, aching light and the stink of stale fat and newspaper print (although I couldn't have put names to the things I was smelling then, of course).

Once my eyes had blinked a few times and got used to the new sensation of brightness, I looked around. And there they all were; blurry faces turned towards the small box on the dressing table.

Advance Britannia
Long live the cause of justice
God save the King

Those were the first words that crackled down the tiny coils of my newly unfurled ears. The voice of the British Bulldog. I'm lucky they called me Violet. They could have given me a really stupid name, like Winnie or something.

Anyway, there I was, a tiny pink creature, star-fished in the middle of the bed, blinking and breathing and waiting for somebody to pick me up and love me.

The Hero

There's a photograph standing pride of place on the mantelpiece in our front room. Mum dusts it religiously every day. The frame is an ugly, heavy thing, made from carved oak. It reminds me of the coffin they buried our neighbour Mr Dennis in last year. Which is quite funny really, because the face staring out from the centre of the 'coffin frame' is of a dead person too.

It's my brother Joseph. He looks like a proper bobby dazzler all done up in his battledress. The collar of his jacket is buttoned tight around his neck and his cap is balanced very dashingly on the side of his head.

He looks as though he is swallowing a smile; trying to be all serious when really he just wants to fool around. In the photograph, Joseph is only nineteen. There's the trace of a pale moustache along his top lip and twinkling stars in his eyes

I never met him. He went missing in action before I was even born. Norma told me once that no one had ever heard a scream like the one that came out of Mum's mouth on the day the telegram was delivered. It was like her soul had been ripped from her insides, Norma said. But then Norma has always been prone to dramatics.

* * *

The telegram is on the mantelpiece too, in a tortoiseshell frame. I remember when I was younger I used to worry about the poor tortoise who had been robbed of its home so its shell could be cut up and polished and stuck up there on our mantelpiece. I asked Norma to teach me to knit so I could make little blankets for all the naked tortoises so at least they would be warm at night. 'You really are a ninny, Violet,' she said to me. 'Only you would think of such a thing.'

When I got older and learned to read, I forgot about naked tortoises. Instead, every time I read the telegram my tummy went all squirmy. At first, I thought it was sadness making me feel like that. But as I got older, I realised the feeling was something much worse.

From Wing Commander D. A. Garner
Royal Air Force Station
Kirmington
Lincolnshire
4th August 1944

Dear Mr and Mrs White
May I be permitted to express my own and the squadron's sincere sympathy with you in the sad news concerning your son Sergeant Joseph White.

The aircraft of which he was the Flight Engineer took off to attack Trossy St. Maximin Constructional Works, near Paris, on the 3rd August 1944, and nothing further has been heard.

You may be aware that in quite a large percentage of cases aircrew reported missing are eventually reported prisoners of war, and I hope that this may give you some comfort in your anxiety.

Your son was a most proficient Flight Engineer and his loss is deeply regretted by us all.

Your son's effects have been collected and will be forwarded to you in due course through Air Ministry channels.

Once again please accept the deep sympathy of us all, and let us hope that we may soon have some good news of the safety of your son.

Yours very sincerely
Donald A. Garner

Mum talks about Joseph every day. Even though it's been over sixteen years since he went missing. When she picks up his photograph she always breathes on the glass first before she polishes it with her cloth. Then she kisses the glass, right where his face is, and the ghost of her lips blurs his features. I don't know why she bothers to polish it at all.

Mum reckons that Joseph was the best son anybody could have wished for. The best *child* anybody could have wished for.

I always wondered why she bothered having me if that was the case. I asked Norma about this once. It was when she still lived at home and worked in the chippie, so I must have been about nine or ten. She was getting ready to go out and I stood and watched her glue a pair of false lashes to her eyelids and smear some Max Factor, Coral Glow across her lips.

'You were a mistake, Violet,' she said as she backcombed her hair. 'You were conceived out of despair and grief.' One thing you can say about Norma – she doesn't mince her words.

I don't like to think of Mum and Dad 'doing it' because of *grief* and *despair* (I don't like to think of them doing it at all!). It must have been a very snotty affair. I know what Mum's like when she cries. It makes me feel sick to think of it, it's so disgusting.

I bet when Mum found out she was pregnant at her time of life, she thought a miracle had happened. I bet she thought that Joseph was coming back to her again. I remember though, that when Mrs Rice, the midwife, eventually scooped me up from the mess on the newspapers and plonked me into Mum's arms, there was a long silence. That was disappointment. Even then, only minutes old, I knew that.

I think about Joseph a lot. It's hard not to with Mum going on about him all the time. I imagine him in his plane, flying high in a clear blue French sky, the skin on his face stretched tight and white with determination. I imagine the thud and shock of light and noise as his plane is hit by German bullets. What was he thinking as his plane spiralled to the ground? What picture did he have in his head as he was blown to smithereens? How many bits of him were scattered across the French countryside? Did anyone ever find a piece of him? A leg, an arm, a foot still in its boot? And who would have known that any of those bits belonged to Joseph?

Nobody ever did find him though; he was declared 'presumed dead' in August 1945. I was three months old. Mum never put that particular letter in a frame. But the news turned her milk sour and I had to make do with rubber teats and formula after that.

It's hard being the replacement for a hero. I never met my brother Joseph. But I hate him all the same.

I've always been able to see things that other people don't see. For example, I'm the only one who seems to notice that Mr Harper the park keeper, whose face has lost its grip from his skull, likes to look up little girls' skirts when they're playing on the swings. But nobody would believe me if I told them.

I know when people are lying too. I can see it in their faces. When a fib flies from their mouths, a curtain is drawn across their eyes. It happens a lot. People lie all the time. Mostly about things they don't even *have* to lie about. For example, Mum is always telling people she is 'fine, thank you' when they ask how she is. Why doesn't she just tell the truth? Why doesn't she just say, 'I'm very sad, if you must know. And I think I will be for the rest of my life'?

I know how a person is feeling inside just by looking at them. For example, even when Mum is laughing at something Dad has said to her and is patting him affectionately on the shoulder, I know that inside she is hating him for giving her the life she has. But she wouldn't thank me for pointing it out. And I know that although my sister Norma pretends to be irritated by babies and small children and says she loves her job at Fine Fare, I know that inside she is boiling with rage at having to work and is desperate to get pregnant.

My head is full of all sorts of brilliant stuff. I know that people suffering from Moebius Syndrome can't smile or move their faces, that people with Apert Syndrome have webbed feet, and people with Blue Rubber Bleb Nevus are covered in patches of blue skin. If you were really unlucky and were born with all three conditions, you'd most probably be mistaken for an alien and would be taken away at birth to a secret government laboratory where you'd be dissected and slivers of your tissue would be stuck onto tiny glass slides and be peered at by scientists who smell of cleverness and Bunsen burners.

I know that male and female rats can have sex up to twenty times a day. I know that a human being will definitely walk on the moon one day, and that there are over a hundred different words for camel in the Arabic language.

I know all these things because I read a lot. Once a week, I go to the library on Lavender Hill and borrow six books. I would borrow more if they would let me. I read every type of book I can: science books, history books, poetry, encyclopaedias and novels. I'm quite clever for a girl; I even passed the 11 plus. Not that it made any difference. I always knew that as soon as I left school I'd end up here in the shop with Mum and Dad. It's not like I had a choice or anything.

There's other stuff I know too. For instance, even though I've never had a boyfriend, I know that falling in love and marrying doesn't always make you happy. Look at Mum and Dad. Look at Norma and Raymond.

I told Norma once that she'd married the wrong man. Not that Raymond, her husband, is wicked or nasty or anything like that; he's just so dull and flat. And he's got these weird eyes that pop out of his sockets like marbles. Norma thinks it's romantic that she met him at the funfair in Battersea Park.

'He swept me off my feet,' she likes to say.

But he didn't. He worked on the Helter Skelter and all he did was hand her a mat to slide down on, and asked her out for a drink afterwards. I think she only married him so she didn't have to work in the chippie any more. She should have waited. She could have married someone loads nicer than Raymond. He's a taxi driver now (he's not clever enough to be a proper cabbie. His brain's not big enough for all that 'Knowledge') and there's no fizz to him, and I know Norma is a fizzy type of girl. Or she used to be before she married Raymond. She didn't like it when I told her this though. 'Shut up, Violet,' she said. 'What do you know about anything? You're only sixteen, for God's sake!'

Oh, and that's another thing. I know that *God* doesn't exist, and people who think he does are delusional; but you have to be polite and not criticise their beliefs and every time you write the word God, you have to use a capital letter, but if you ever have to write the word fairy or goblin or ghost, you don't.

'Violet!' said Mum in her most horrified voice, when I mentioned this to her one day. 'You can't go around saying things like that!'

From the way Mum's lips pulled together, like she'd been sucking on a lemon sherbet, you'd have thought I'd said FUCK, which is apparently the worst word a human being can utter according to Mum. But I think there are much worse words, such as 'get your apron on, Violet,' fish suppers and bloody, bloody chips. I don't know why Mum gets so worked up about things like that. It's not like she even goes to church or anything. And I don't believe for one second that she still thinks God exists. If he did, how could he have let her son die? How could he have let thousands of young men die? How could he have let millions of Jews be murdered? If God does exist he must be the evilest thing in creation. Worse even than Hitler.

11

I get really pissed off with being told what to say and what to think; as if I haven't got a mind of my own. I'm sixteen now. I'm not a child.

There's a new song that's been playing on the wireless recently. I always stop what I'm doing and listen to it whenever it comes on. It's sung by a girl called Helen Shapiro and she's only fourteen. It's called *Don't Treat Me Like a Child*. I've memorised the lyrics. They capture exactly the way I feel. That just because I'm only in my teens doesn't mean I should be treated like a child. I've got my own dreams and opinions, and I've got my own mind. I'm not a little girl any more.

I'm not daft enough to think the song was written just for me. But it's nice to think there's somebody else out there who feels the same way that I do. I know me and Helen Shapiro would be really good friends if we were ever to meet. Anyway, I always sing along really loudly whenever her song comes on, just to make my point.

'Turn that bloody racket off, Violet!' Dad shouts. 'And get your apron on. There's customers waiting.'

I wish he wouldn't speak to me like that. One day I'll show him. One day I'll show them all. I'm not going to be stuck in this shop for ever, you know. I'm not going to spend the rest of my life stinking of salt and vinegar and cod and chips.

I'm not going to be invisible for ever. I'm not going to be a shrinking Violet for ever. I'm going to do something to get myself noticed. One day it will be my photograph up on the mantelpiece.

Toffee Apples and Liquorice

I'm in the kitchen ripping up newspapers for Dad. As usual. It's Friday, our busiest day, and he'll need a stack to get through an evening of wrapping fish suppers. My fingers are smudged with ink and the stink of lard from the fryers has already melted into my clothes and hair. I've chipped four buckets of potatoes and I'll probably have to do another before the day is out. I'm pig sick of bloody chips. I look up at the clock above the sink. It's nearly five o'clock. Dad'll be sliding the bolts of the door open in a minute and they'll all be in for their six of chips.

Then Mrs Robinson will sidle through the door, her eyes darting guiltily from side to side as though she's just walked into a betting shop or something. She'll whisper her order for five large fish suppers with extra salt and vinegar, then she'll slip out the door again with her head bowed low and the parcel of fish suppers clutched tight to her chest. Mrs Robinson only has herself, two kids and a husband to feed. She eats the spare supper herself, on her way home. Not because she's greedy or anything, but because Mr Robinson is always making fun of her wobbly chins and big bum. Eating that secret supper is the only way Mrs Robinson can feel better about herself for a minute. If I get to serve her, I always slip some batter bits in the last packet, the one that will be at the top of the parcel; the one that I know she'll eat herself. There's only me that sees all of this, of course. Everyone else thinks the extra supper is for the Robinsons' dog.

Norma and Raymond always come round for their tea on a Friday night, after the shop's shut. It's always a fish supper of course and we have to eat it at the kitchen table, all together, like a proper family. Mum lays the table with plates and knives and forks. She even puts a folded napkin next to each plate, like we're posh or something. Who's she kidding?

There's nothing worse than having to eat a plateful of fish and chips after you've spent all evening shovelling mountains of the stuff into newspaper parcels. We have the leftovers. The chips are bitter and blackened around the edges and the fish is dry with soggy batter.

Actually, it's not true that there's nothing worse than stale fish suppers. There's plenty of worse things.

Listening to Norma pretending to be all grown up isn't much fun. I know she's been married for over six years now, but I don't know why that means all she has to talk about is the price of butter and the latest recipe she cooked for Raymond. She never used to be so boring. I don't know why putting a ring on your finger means you have to become a different person. I'd feel sorry for Raymond if he wasn't such a drip.

Another thing that's worse than eating a stale fish supper is having to look at the empty place across the other side of the table. It's been there my whole life, whenever we sit down to eat. There it is. The chair with no one in it. The gaping hole.

The place that can never be filled. Joseph's chair. The son who is never coming home. *Look at you all*, the chair says. *Filling your faces, while bits of me are rotting in the ground all over the French countryside*. It's enough to make anyone lose their appetite.

But worse than all of that. Worse than any of it, is remembering what Jackie said earlier when she popped her head around the door, all breathless and in a hurry.

'Can't meet you at the usual time tomorrow, Vi,' she said. 'Me and some of the girls from Garton's are going to see that new film, *Breakfast at Tiffany's*. But, I'll see you after, at Ruby's Café. Yeah?'

She didn't even bother to look guilty.

Jackie's my best friend. I've known her for ever and she's the only person who has ever stuck by me; the only person who has ever really got me. If I close my eyes I can see pictures in my head of all the special times we've shared; a bit like a photograph album, I suppose. In the first photograph, me and Jackie are only four. We're spinning our skipping ropes fast; slap, slap, slap on the pavement. We're singing loudly, hoping not to be the first to trip on our rope.

Fatty and Skinny went to bed
Fatty let a fart and Skinny went dead
Fatty called the doctor and the doctor said
If Fatty lets another fart we'll all be dead!

In the next photograph, me and Jackie are five. We're holding hands as we walk through the school gates for the first time. I'm not excited. My tummy has been aching all morning and

I need a pee. But I don't know where to go and I don't know who to ask. Then, suddenly, before I can stop it, there's hot liquid running down my legs. I want to cry. I tug on Jackie's hand to make her look at me. She stops and turns and I manage to whisper in her ear. Without saying a word, she leads me around a corner and behind a row of dustbins.

'Take your knickers off then,' she says, as she pulls her own down and steps neatly out of them. They are snowy white with a small pink bow sewn onto the waistband. I wriggle out of my soggy pants and Jackie whips them out of my hand and stuffs them into her coat pocket.

'Quick, put mine on,' she orders.

I do as I'm told. Jackie takes my hand again and we walk back around the corner and into a classroom that smells of Plasticine, pencil shavings and new leather shoes, and everything is okay again.

Another photograph, and it's a bright sunshine day in the playground. Marjorie Black is chanting in my face. 'Ugly Fish! Ugly Fish! Speccy four-eyes! Speccy four-eyes!'

Jackie throws a stone at her and it slices through the little witch's cheek. We stand and watch as Marjorie wails and blood drips on to the collar of her daffodil-yellow dress. Jackie's not allowed out to play with me for days after. The world is scary and empty without her. It feels like loneliness has swallowed me up whole.

I can flick through the pages in my head to one of my favourite photographs. Me and Jackie are eight and it's the best day ever. They've stopped rationing sweets! We go to Miss Suttie's sweetshop and buy a toffee apple and liquorice laces, black and shiny as tar. The toffee cracks in my mouth and the apple is sharp and crunchy. I've never tasted anything so delicious. The liquorice is so sticky that when Jackie smiles at me she looks like an urchin with rotten teeth. On the way home we stop and watch some boys messing about on a bombsite. They shoot at us with their sticks, so we poke out our liquorice-black tongues and show them our knickers.

Another favourite photograph is from my fourteenth birthday. Jackie's given me a present wrapped in pale blue paper. 'It was the nearest colour I could get to violet,' she says. I open it slowly. It's a silver letter V on a thin silver chain. It's the best present I've ever had. Jackie fastens it around my neck then she pulls down the collar of her school blouse and she's got one too. Only hers is a letter J of course. She looks at me seriously. 'We must never take these off,' she says. 'Never. Or our friendship will be broken.'

There's some photographs in my head that I don't like to look at. Like the one of me and Jackie walking out of the school gates for the very last time. Jackie has her arm linked through mine and she's chattering away like mad. 'That's it, Violet,' she says. 'Proper grown-ups now, we are!' She undoes her tie and yanks it from around her neck. Then she skips along the road swinging the tie above her head like a lasso. 'Yee ha!' she shouts. 'Freedom, Violet! Freedom!'

I try to join in. But my tie hangs limply in my hand and my skipping is half-hearted. The truth is, I don't feel grown up at all. I want to be excited and happy. I want the future to be a bright golden road stretching out in front of me. But all I feel is scared and disappointed – and jealous.

Jackie's going off to work at Garton's Glucose factory, as a sugar packer. I want to go there too, but Dad won't hear of it. 'Going to work in a factory!' he explodes. 'When there's a perfectly good job for you here? I don't think so, young lady.' He wags his finger at me. 'Family comes first. You know that.' His face slams shut, like a prison door. And I know that's that. No golden road. No bright future. Just buckets and buckets of potatoes and cold, wet fish.

'We'll meet up every night,' Jackie promises. 'And we'll still have Saturdays. And money to spend now, too! Think of the shopping we'll be able to do. And all the dancing! It'll be fantastic, Violet! You wait and see!'

I smile a tight little smile. I don't want to let her go. I don't want her to go out into the world without me.

In every photograph in my album, Jackie's much prettier than me. She's sort of light and dainty. Everything about her is small and neat and in exactly the right place. She has china doll lips, a nose that turns up at the end just the right amount and eyes like Marlene Dietrich. If she was a cake, she would have been made by a master baker. He would have chosen the best ingredients and weighed and sifted and stirred as carefully as he could. He would have baked the cake for not one minute more or one minute less than was needed and then spent all day icing it to perfection.

I'm more like a plain old sponge cake with a bit of jam in the middle. But I don't care. Because Jackie's the sort of girl who'd much rather have a piece of sponge than the fanciest cake in the world. That's why I love her. And that's why I don't want to lose her.

Jackie lives with her nan, Brenda, round the corner from us on Speke Road. She hasn't got a mum or dad, and she doesn't like talking about it either. Jimmy Green found that out back in junior school when he teased her and called her an orphan. His black eye lasted a good couple of weeks. Jackie's not an orphan. But she might as well be. She told me once that her mum died giving birth to her and that not long after, her dad ran off with a leggy blonde. It wasn't until ages after that I realised Aleggy Blonde wasn't actually the name of someone, but was a *type* of someone. 'I'm only telling you, cos you're my best friend,' Jackie had said. 'But I don't ever want to talk about it again.'

I don't blame Jackie for not wanting to talk about her parents. Neither of them are ever going to come back. I feel the same about Joseph. I hate it that Mum goes on and on about him all the time. What's the point? Joseph's never coming back either. So why can't she just shut up about him? Sometimes, I wish I could give *her* a black eye.

Thinking too much about Jackie makes my throat hurt. I love her more than my own sister, but something horrible is happening to us, something is changing and it's making my heart shrivel with sadness. It's like when a stone is thrown at a window. At first there's just a small pit of a hole with a barely-there crack and you hope and hope that it's not going to get any worse. But then the crack begins to spread and spider out. Then more cracks appear and they grow wider and deeper and suddenly, in front of your eyes, the glass shatters and comes crashing down in long pointed shards that could pierce your heart and kill you. That's what's happening to me and Jackie now. I'm just holding my breath and waiting for my heart to be pierced by our broken friendship.

The shop door jangles and I jump.

'Violet!' shouts Dad. 'Where the hell are you?'

I sigh. Here we go again. Another joyful Friday evening. I gather up the pile of newspapers and take them through to the shop. The fryers are already bubbling and spitting. Dad's face is already red and shiny and Mrs Robinson is already standing at the counter with her purse clasped in her hands.

It's busy this evening. I'm glad. There's no time to think about Jackie. It's just smile and greet, smile and greet. Scoop of chips. Large cod or small? A shake of salt, a dash of vinegar. That'll be two and six please. By the time the last customer has rattled the door closed behind them (Mr Carver – I gave him the meanest piece of cod because he's a mean old bugger; always shouting at the kids around here) my hair is sticking to my forehead and my apron is covered in grease where I've been wiping my hands down it all evening.

I just want my bed now. I want to close my bedroom door, draw the curtains tight and shut out the whole world. I want to settle back on my pillows and pull the blankets over my knees. I'll keep the light on, but I'll push my dressing gown against the bottom of the door, so when Mum comes up the stairs she won't see the strip of light and yell at me to, 'Switch that off, Violet! We're not made of money, you know!'

Then I'll pick up my book and find the page with the corner turned down. It's a new book, by an Irish writer called Edna O'Brien. I had to order it in especially from the library and it took ages to arrive. The book's been banned in Ireland. There's been a right old uproar. The priest that lives in the same village as Edna O'Brien even burned a copy. I wanted to read it to see what all the fuss is about.

Miss Read gave me a funny look when she saw it in my weekly pile. Her ink stamp hovered over it. 'Are you sure your parents will be happy for you to read this, Violet?' she asked.

'They don't mind what I read, Miss Read,' I said. 'And besides, I'm sixteen now.' I glared at her. Perhaps I shouldn't have been so rude. But it worked anyway, although she brought the stamp down so hard I thought she'd break it. The book's called *The Country Girls* and it's about two best friends, Kate and Baba. They're just like me and Jackie. They share each other's secrets just like we do. Although me and Jackie never took our knickers off and tickled each other. Perhaps that's why they banned it in Ireland.

'Here,' Dad grunts at me. 'Take these out back before your mother starts hollering.' He shoves a tray, stacked with the evening's leftovers, into my hands. It's heavy. I groan, but more from the thought of the evening ahead than from the weight of the tray. Kate and Baba will have to wait.

Mum's bustling about, buttering bread and making sure Norma and Raymond have enough tea. 'Oh good,' says Norma when I put the tray down on the table. 'We're starving.'

'All right, Violet?' asks Raymond.

He's got a new jumper on. It's the colour of English mustard and the stitches are loose and baggy around the collar. I reckon Norma's been knitting again.

Mum puts the plate of bread and butter in the middle of the table and starts to share out the fish and chips onto the

21

waiting plates. Norma picks up her napkin and spreads it out on her lap. I snort. 'Didn't know we were dining at The Ritz,' I say under my breath.

Norma looks at me sharply. 'So, Violet,' she says. 'Got yourself a boyfriend yet?'

'Why would I want one of those?' I say. I pull a face at Raymond. 'I might end up having to get married and then my life would be over.'

Norma sniffs and carefully picks up a chip from her plate with her red-painted fingernails. 'Just wondered,' she says. 'Only I thought you and your friend Jackie did everything together.' She pops the chip in her mouth and slowly licks her fingers.

'What do you mean by that?' The words are out before I can help it and Norma's lipsticky lips curl into a smirk, just like I knew they would.

'Only, we saw her the other night, didn't we, Raymond?'

'Who?' he says. He shakes a flurry of salt all over his supper. 'Pass the vinegar, will you, Violet?'

'Jackie,' says Norma, as I slide the vinegar bottle across the table. 'We saw Violet's friend Jackie the other night, didn't we? Coming out of the dance hall. With some fella all over her, don't you remember?'

'Oh, yeah,' says Raymond. He drenches his fish with vinegar. Norma's eyes light up with triumph. My cheeks burn. She might as well have slapped me in the face. *She's* like vinegar, I think; she sours everything.

Mum joins us at the table. 'Jackie's got a boyfriend, has she?' I can almost see her ears waggling. 'You never said, Violet!'

'I don't have to tell you everything,' I mumble. I can't eat now. I feel odd, as though someone has shoved their hand down my throat and is trying to pull my heart out. It's like I've been told the worst news ever.

'You all right, Violet?' says Norma. 'You've gone all pale. You want some vinegar on those chips? Hey, and look. Like my new earrings? Raymond bought them for me.'

I look down at my plate. There's oil congealing in the folds and bubbles of batter. 'I'm not hungry,' I say. I stand and push my chair back. 'I feel sick. I've got to go to the bathroom.' I hurry to the door.

'Nice to see you, too!' Norma shouts after me.

'Cow!' I hiss at the staircase walls. It's cold in the bathroom and smells of mildew and Mum's damp girdles that are hanging over the bath to dry. I take off my glasses and splash my face with water. When did Jackie start going to dances? Since when has she been interested in fellas? And when did she stop sharing her secrets with me? I swallow hard.

She's bored with me, I think. I'm not exciting enough for her any more. I'm just the dull girl from the chippie, the girl with no future. I put my glasses back on and study my face in the mirror, but there's nothing there worth describing. Pale skin and a splatter of freckles. Plain and ordinary; nothing too big and nothing too small. Nothing to notice. And all of it framed by frizzy brown hair and a pair of National Health specs. I remember walking home from the optician's with Mum, on the day I got my first pair of glasses. I was only four. I remember Mum tugging on my hand and telling me to hurry up because I was dawdling. But I wasn't dawdling, I was looking around in wonder. It was like someone had polished the whole world. Everything was so bright and clear and shocking. It was the first time I saw that trees had leaves, that the pavement had cracks and that Mum had wrinkles on her face. It was a miracle.

But then Norma went and ruined it all in her usual fashion. 'You do know, don't you, Violet, that men seldom make passes at girls who wear glasses?'

She's always been a cow.

I pull my glasses off again and rub my face dry with a towel. I rub hard, wishing I could rub out my features and find a new set of prettier, more exciting ones underneath. It doesn't happen, of course. I look just the same, except now my skin is a horrible shiny pink. I should have seen it coming with Jackie. I should have known I was never enough for her. I'm usually so good at knowing what people are thinking.

'Violet!' yells Mum from downstairs. 'We're waiting for you. Norma and Raymond have to go in a bit.'

Good, I think. Let them wait. I lock the bathroom door. If anyone comes up, I'll make retching noises and pretend I'm really ill. I sit on the toilet lid and watch the tap dripping. Mum doesn't shout again and no one bothers to come up. I don't know what's worse; if I'd been forced to go back down, or being ignored like this?

Plink, plink, plink. The leaking tap is getting on my nerves. I've never thought about it before, but looking at how the drips of water have stained the enamel a dirty yellow, I realise that the tap has been dripping all my life. I count how many plinks there are in a minute. Thirty. Then I try and work out how many drips there might have been since I was born. It's

24

a long, complicated sum and I have to keep starting again at the beginning. Before I can work out the answer, it suddenly strikes me that Joseph would have known this dripping tap too. He probably had his first shave in this sink. He would have washed his hands in here for the last time, before he went off to be killed in the war. For some reason that makes me really sad and I have to lift my glasses to wipe my eyes.

A door bangs downstairs and I hear Norma thanking Mum for a lovely supper. 'Bye, Violet!' she shouts up the stairs. 'Hope you feel better soon!'

'Good riddance,' I say under my breath. I dart from the bathroom and across the landing to the safety of my room. All I want is to be left alone with my misery.

The Country Girls is lying on the floor next to my bed. I read a few pages, but the more I read the more I realise that Kate and Baba's friendship isn't the perfect thing I thought it was. Baba is a bitch and a bully and Kate lets her get away with it. Baba is mean and spiteful and poor Kate begins to lose everything. Now her mother is dead; drowned in a river. I throw the book back on the floor. I want to climb into the pages and over all the words to find Kate and tell her that *I'll* be her friend and she doesn't have to put up with being pushed around any more. I wanted their friendship to conquer the world, like I wanted me and Jackie to conquer the world. But Baba isn't true and loyal and neither, I realise, is Jackie.

Mum pokes her head around my bedroom door. 'You all right, Violet? Me and your dad are off to bed now.'

I've got the blankets pulled up to my chin, so it's easy to pretend to be asleep. I just keep still and make sure my breathing

25

is deep and regular. I can feel Mum hovering for a moment, probably trying to work out if she should come and stick her hand on my forehead to check if I'm properly ill or not. She obviously decides against it, because I hear the door close and a short while later the water pipes banging as she begins the nightly rinse out of her stockings.

I close my eyes and try to ignore the knot that's growing tighter and tighter in my tummy. I wonder what Jackie is doing right this minute. Is she out at another dance without me? Why didn't she ask me if *I'd* like to go to the cinema tomorrow? Have I even crossed her mind at all tonight? The noise of Dad thumping up the stairs interrupts my thoughts. There's the creak of bedsprings as he sits down to take off his boots. Mum says something to him and he grunts in reply. There's the chink of Mum's pot of cold cream as she puts it back on her dressing table. Then the usual groans and murmurs as they settle themselves down to sleep. It's the same sounds every night. Nothing ever changes. They're the sounds which have always comforted me and sent me to sleep. But they don't help tonight.

Instead, after it's all gone quiet, I'm filled with a horrible empty feeling. I think of the room next to Mum and Dad's. The room which used to be Joseph's. It's horrible and empty in there too, even though it's still full of his stuff. Mum's never been able to bring herself to change a thing in there. His bed is still made up, the blankets smoothed and pulled tight. His old feather pillow is still dented in the middle where his head used to rest. I bet if I could bring myself to look, there'd even be a stray hair or two. There's a small wardrobe in the corner of the room, and all his clothes are still inside; there's woollens folded on the shelves and some shirts and a couple of pairs of trousers hanging, all neat and pressed. It's stupid and ghoulish and a waste of a room. Even Mum only goes in there to dust these days.

I used to sneak in when I was younger, just out of curiosity. I'd rearrange the tin soldiers on the windowsill and look through the pile of dusty comics under the bed. There was a razor and a piece of mirror on top of his chest of drawers. And inside the drawers there were a few yellowed vests and a couple of balls of socks. I suppose he must have taken all his pants to war with him, cos there's none in there. The room smells funny too, like sweaty feet and mothballs. And I always felt like I had to be quiet, in case I woke someone up. I took Jackie in there once, after she'd nagged me for an age.

'Oh, Violet,' she whispered. 'I can feel him, can't you?' She walked slowly around the room with her head cocked to one side. She ran her hands across the bed. 'I think he's watching us, Vi,' she said. She picked up the razor from the chest of drawers and turned it around in her fingers. When she put it down I had to move it slightly, back to exactly where it had been before she touched it. I remember feeling irritated with her, but I didn't know why. Then she walked up to the wardrobe. 'Shush,' she said. 'He's trying to tell us something. Can you hear?'

Even though I knew she was only mucking about, the hairs on the back of my neck prickled. She reached out her hand towards the wardrobe door. 'Shush,' she said, again. And for some reason we both held our breaths. I could hear the clock

27

ticking, from all the way down in the front room. And suddenly, I felt my brother. Like *really* felt him. He was in the room with us. He was watching us, making sure we didn't mess anything up. He didn't want us in there. The feeling was terrible. It started in the pit of my stomach and spread all through my body, until my fingers and toes were tingling.

Suddenly, Jackie pulled open the wardrobe door. 'Boo!' she yelled. 'He's in here, Violet! He's in here!'

I screamed loudly. And the shirts and trousers swayed on their hangers. I thumped Jackie on the arm. 'Idiot! You nearly gave me a heart attack!'

'Your face!' Jackie spluttered. 'So funny. So funny!'

I never went into Joseph's bedroom again. But sometimes in the quiet of the night, the thought of that graveyard in the middle of the house knocks on my brain like an unwanted visitor.

Breakfast at Tiffany's

'You'd best be back by four, or I'll have yer guts for garters!'
Dad shouts across the shop as I jangle the door open and step
outside. It's Saturday morning and it's freezing. Crisped-up
leaves are hurtling along the pavements and the wind is
swirling up the dust from the old bombsite opposite. I hold
my coat tight around my throat as I hurry up the High Street
towards Ruby's Café. I keep my head down and watch my
feet scuffing the pavement. Jackie won't be on her own.
They'll all be with her; her new friends. The Sugar Girls. I
don't want to meet them, I feel sick at the thought. But it
would be worse not to see Jackie at all. I'm like a pet dog, I
think; hanging around patiently, waiting to be thrown any
old leftover scraps.

It's been three months now since we left school. It wasn't
too bad to begin with. I'd still run round to Jackie's most
nights, after my shift in the shop had finished. We'd sit round
the kitchen table drinking tea, while Brenda clattered about
in the sink, and Jackie would tell me all about her day. 'It's
the early mornings that are killing me, Vi,' she'd say, yawning
loudly. 'And only two toilet breaks all day! Can you imagine?'

I nodded solemnly. I felt sorry for her. But inside, I was glad she wasn't having a good time without me. She looked different already. She'd changed her hair without telling me. It was backcombed and stiff on the top of her head.

'What've you done to your hair?' I asked.

She smiled, all pleased with herself. 'Nice, isn't it?' she said, patting it carefully. 'You should try doing something different with yours, Vi.'

'Makes you look older,' I mumbled.

'Yeah?' she said, smiling again as though looking older was a good thing.

Soon, she started talking about other girls at the factory. Sharon said this and Pauline said that. 'Sharon reckons you can get pregnant if you let a fella touch your boobs. And Mary! Oh, Vi, you'd like Mary. She's a right laugh. She says she's done *it* already. But standing up against a wall, cos it's safer that way.'

I didn't think I'd like Mary at all. She sounded like what Mum called a fast piece. A girl who'd come to no good at all. I didn't like the sound of any of them, and every time Jackie mentioned a new name it was like she was stabbing me in the heart.

'I wish your dad would let you leave the chippie and come to Garton's,' Jackie would say. 'You'd love being a Sugar Girl, Vi. I know you would. I miss you.'

That was the first time she lied to me. The curtains came down in her eyes. I saw them, as clear as anything. She didn't really miss me. She just thought she should say she did.

Now, Jackie lines her eyes with black kohl. She looks like she's been in a fight and lost. She wears hip-huggers and skinny rib jumpers (while I still dress like Mum.) She's been going out to dances too, and this morning she went to the Granada without me.

As I weave my way around the Saturday morning shoppers on the High Street and dodge the prams and a gang of boys carrying a broken go-cart, I picture Jackie and her new friends piling out of the Granada. I bet they all linked arms and giggled and oohed and aahhed over beautiful Audrey Hepburn, the star of the film. But I bet they don't know any of the things that I know about her.

1. For a start, Audrey Hepburn is far too skinny and could do with eating a few bags of chips.
2. And even though she's that skinny, she's got huge feet. Size ten.
3. She can speak five different languages.
4. She had to stand by and watch some of her family being shot by the Nazis.

I lift my eyes from the pavement. I can see Ruby's Café in the distance now. The windows are steamed up, which is annoying because I want to see where everybody is sitting before I go inside. I want to prepare my face, to arrange my features so that I look like I don't care if they are all in there or not.

But I can't do that now. I'll have to open the café door and look around the room first. And one of them is bound to see me come in and there'll be nudging and winking and then they'll go all quiet when I walk over to their table. I know I'll go red. I know I will. I can feel my cheeks burning already.

I put my hand up to check my hair. It feels a lumpy mess where the wind has stirred it up, like a bowl of porridge. I pull my fingers through it uselessly. I open the café door. A rush of warm dampness hits me in the face, and the smell of fried eggs, burnt toast and cigarette smoke curl around my nostrils.

I hear them before I see them. Jackie's lemon-sharp giggle cuts through the grease in the air, and there's another sound of hoarse, confident laughter that makes the palms of my hands sweat.

They're over in the corner, squashed around a red Formica table that's covered in mugs and crumb-scattered plates and a glass ashtray balancing a tower of fag ends. There's four of them, including Jackie.

None of them look round. They're too interested in each other. I have to walk right up to the table and tap Jackie on the shoulder.

She turns round. 'Oh. Hi, Violet,' she says.

The others stop talking. For a long, awkward moment all I can feel are their eyes, sliding up and down me, judging the scruffy pumps on my feet and the blue cotton slacks that Norma passed on to me when she got bored with them. Suddenly, I can't imagine why I ever thought they'd look good with my old white blouse and the lemon cardie that Jackie's nan knitted for me last Christmas. I pull down the hem of the cardie, as if it will make it look any better.

'You going to sit down?' says Jackie. 'Here.' She shuffles across her seat and pats the small space left beside her. I balance myself on the edge of her chair and nod to the three girls who are still watching me.

'Oh,' says Jackie, suddenly remembering her manners. She flicks her hand at the other girls. 'This is Pauline, Sharon and Mary.' She turns to me. 'And girls . . . this is Violet.'

They all smile quick, stiff little smiles and I notice how they are all wearing the same shade of lipstick, like strawberry jam smeared thickly across their mouths. 'Anyway,' says the one called Sharon. 'Like I was saying. Do you think if I pinned my hair back like this . . .' She grabs the ends of her dark shoulder-length hair and pulls it back from her face. '. . . And if I flick my eyeliner out at the edges . . .' She widens her eyes and blinks slowly. '. . . Do you think I might get mistaken for Audrey Hepburn?'

'In your dreams!' The one called Mary hoots with laughter. She has pale, down-to-her-bum hair and a dainty nose that twitches like a rabbit's. She's the one that has already done *it*, I remember. I scrutinise her face, looking for any tell-tale signs. She's got lovely skin. Really white and clear and pearly-looking. Her eyes are huge and when she blinks her lashes touch the tops of her cheeks. But there's no obvious sign that she's done *it*.

I laugh to myself. What did I expect? A big badge pinned to her chest that says, *Warning. Spoiled goods. Keep clear*?

'You all right?' says Jackie, nudging me. 'What's so funny?'

'Nothing.' I say brightly. Everybody's staring at me now. Expecting me to say something. 'Erm . . . Did you know,' I mutter, 'that Audrey Hepburn had to watch as some of her family was shot by the Nazis?'

Jackie frowns. 'And you think that's funny?' she says.

I've embarrassed her. I didn't mean to, but I have. And the stupid thing is, it's me that's blushing. It's my face that's burning up and it's my stomach that's gone all sick and fidgety.

33

Jackie turns away from me and takes a big swallow of tea. The other girl, Pauline, pulls a face at her as if to say, who's your friend?

She's got mean eyes. Like a blackbird. I have no idea why Jackie would want to be friends with her. She seems like a right stuck-up cow. I imagine Pauline flat on her back in the middle of the café floor, with me sitting on top of her, pinning her down. I grab handfuls of her perfect beehive and pull it all apart until she looks like she's been dragged through a hedge backwards. 'I'm sorry, Violet,' she sobs. 'I'm sorry for being such a horrible person. I'll try harder from now on, I promise.'

Of course, I'd never do anything like that, but it helps to imagine that I might. It's like when you think about a teacher or a policeman sitting on the toilet with their underwear rumpled around their ankles. It makes them less scary somehow.

They're all talking about a dance now. A 'work do' next Saturday night at Garton's. 'You going to be wearing your red dress?' Sharon asks Mary. 'Cos if you are, I won't wear mine. I'll wear my green.'

'But I was going to wear my green!' says Jackie. 'You know I bought it specially.' Her voice is pretend cross.

A layer of sadness washes over me. She likes these girls well enough to use her pretend cross voice. I've never heard her use it with anyone else but me and her nan. And worse than that, I don't know anything about her new green dress.

'Why don't you all come round to mine next week?' says Pauline. 'Bring all your clobber with you and we'll have a try-on session.'

They all coo like a flight of happy pigeons. I'm obviously not included in the invitation. They chatter on and there's nothing I can say to join in. So instead, I think about all the words I know for groups of birds: a murder of crows, a parliament of owls, a kettle of nighthawks, a company of parrots, a watch of nightingales, a pitying of turtle doves, and my favourite: an unkindness of ravens.

Jackie used to love it when I told her things like this. 'You're so clever, Violet,' she would say. 'I don't know how you have room in your head for things like that!' Another layer of sadness washes over me. I'm thick with it now, like the grease from the chip fryers.

'I've seen him making eyes at you!' Pauline is saying to Jackie.

'He doesn't!' Jackie protests. She wriggles her bum around and pushes me right to the edge of the chair. I have to hold on to the table now, to keep my balance.

'I bet he'll ask you to dance again!' says Pauline. 'I bet you'll get off with him!' Her voice rises to an excited squeal.

'I will not be getting off with Colin Trindle,' says Jackie, firmly. 'I'm a good girl, I am.' She giggles, and the sound of her happiness turns my stomach.

I don't know her any more.

The old Jackie was never bothered about dresses and dances. The old Jackie was never bothered about fellas. We were going to do all those things one day, of course. But we were going to do them together; one day in the future. But somehow, and I don't know how, Jackie's future has arrived before mine.

I stare at each of the Sugar Girls in turn. I can see Mary's future already. Before too long she'll be pushing a pram up the High Street, her stomach all fat and swollen with another baby and there'll be old lady varicose veins winding up the back of her legs. And Sharon's never going to look like Audrey Hepburn, no matter how much make-up she slaps on her face. And Pauline's too mean to ever amount to much. She'll probably end up as the type who has affairs with married men because no man will actually want to marry her. I thought Jackie was better than all this.

'What you looking at?' says Pauline. She brushes at her face with her fingers. 'Have I got something on me or what?'

I quickly look away. I don't know what I'm still doing here. Jackie hasn't said two words to me. I listen to them all giggling and talking over each other, like they all belong together. Like they're all part of the same pack. I try to remember what a group of girls is called. A gaggle? A giggle? A huddle? I don't think it's any of those. But I know what it should be. If it was my job to come up with collective nouns, I know what I'd call this lot.

A bitch of girls.

A bloody bitch of girls. I wish I could tell Jackie.

I stand up suddenly and in my rush I knock the table and a splash of tea slops from Mary's cup. She tuts and scowls at me.

'I've . . . I've got to go,' I say. I look down at Jackie. 'I've just remembered I've got to meet someone.' I don't want her to think she's the only one with a life.

Jackie looks up at me. 'But Vi, you've only just got here,' she says. 'You haven't even had a cuppa.' She narrows her eyes. 'And anyway, who are you meeting?'

I shrug. 'No one you know.' I turn to go. I need air. I can't breathe in here.

'Come round one night,' Jackie shouts after me. 'I haven't seen you properly for ages.'

But before I can answer, her attention drifts away. She doesn't want to miss what Pauline is saying. She raises her hand towards me as though she is shooing away an annoying wasp and then she leans back towards the bitch of girls. Pauline doesn't bother to lower her voice. 'She's weird. All that staring. What's that about . . . ?'

I shut the café door behind me, harder than I mean to, and as I stumble out onto the street I crash into a man wearing a buttoned-up overcoat. One of the buttons digs into my cheek. 'Watch where you're going!' he barks. I swing around and a cold blast of wind slaps me in the face, bringing with it the burnt toast stink of the sugar factory. The stink is always worse in the cold.

I hurry back down the High Street, pretending I have somewhere important to be. Someone important to meet. But I have nowhere to go and no one to meet. I didn't know you could be lost in a place you knew so well. And I didn't know how hard it was to breathe with a broken heart.

Battersea Park is quiet. I don't know how I've ended up here. There's a few dog walkers, huddled inside thick coats, striding along the pathway in front of me. There's two dogs tugging on a stick. One of them has long, floppy ears like a spaniel, and the wind keeps blowing them into the dog's eyes. But it doesn't care. It just shakes his head and carries on tugging at the stick. I find my way to the old pump house and walk around the crumbling walls. Thick stems of ivy have twisted their way through gaps in the bricks and covered the old windows. I think of Sleeping Beauty locked away in her castle. I breathe in the cold air. It smells a bit like Joseph's old room, of dust and damp and sadness. I don't like it here. It feels all wrong.

Leaves swirl around my ankles. I kick at them angrily. Suddenly I'm in the playground. There's not a soul here. The swings are jerking unevenly on their chains as though they are being rocked by ghost children. I crawl into the space under the slide. I'm ten years old again. There's a bed of dried leaves on the ground. I sit down and pull my knees to my chest. It's quiet in here and still, apart from my heart hammering against my ribs.

I look above my head to the underside of the slide, where the wood is rough and full of splinters. I squint my eyes, searching. When I find what I'm looking for, I reach out my hand and touch the faded carving.

Jackie + Violet = friends for ever

I remember the day Jackie carved it. We were ten and had been playing around in the park all day. It was summer and our skinny legs were brown and mud-scuffed. From out of nowhere, a black cloud had parked itself in the sky over the playground and before we knew it, fat drops of rain were bouncing off our skin and soaking into our thin summer blouses. We ran squealing into our little hideout under the slide. Brenda had packed us a lunch of bread and cheese and apples which we unwrapped and ate as we watched the world outside being blitzed by raindrop bombs. We were safe and cosy in our shelter. We had each other and nothing else mattered. It could have rained for ever for all we cared. Jackie had a penknife in her pocket and after she'd sliced up our apples she reached up with the knife and began to dig into the wood above our heads. 'There,' she said when she'd finished. She turned to look at me. 'You and me, Vi. For always.'

And it was. Until now.

I scrabble around on the ground until my fingers close around a small stone. Then I use the stone to scratch at the words, over and over and over again. And even when the words have completely disappeared, I keep scratching and scratching at them until my fingers ache as much as my heart.

I can tell something's happened as soon as I walk in the door. The air feels different – full of something other than chip fat and Dad's fags. It sounds different too. I can't hear Mum going on at Dad like she usually does and the wireless isn't on either.

Instead, there's a strange sound coming from the kitchen. It might be crying, I'm not sure. I stand outside the kitchen door for a moment, trying to decide if I should go in and interrupt whatever it is, or go straight to my room and ignore it.

I don't really want to be alone in my room though. Not yet anyway. If I go there now, I might never want to come out again. I need something to take my mind off Jackie. I need someone to put their arms around me and tell me everything will be okay. Fat chance of that. Can't remember Dad ever cuddling me. I suppose Mum must have done when I was little, but we're not that kind of family. No one's really into the touchy-feely, love-dovey stuff.

Jackie would have made everything okay again. Jackie's always been good at hugs. Ironic that the only person who

39

could make me feel better is the person who's made me feel so bad in the first place.

I open the kitchen door. Mum lifts her head up, startled. She looks terrible. Her face is all blotchy and her eyes are pink and watery, as though she's been peeling onions. She's got something in her hands. It looks like a piece of paper of some sort. But when I glance towards it, she crumples it up and pulls it towards her and hides it under the table. Dad doesn't even look at me. He's got his head in his hands.

'What's wrong?' I ask quickly. 'What's happened?'

Dad stands up suddenly. He pushes his chair back so hard that it knocks against the dresser and the cups rattle on their hooks. He's furious. I can tell by the way his lips have turned white and his eyes are cold and glazed like the eyes of the dead fish that are piled in buckets of ice out back. He crashes out of the kitchen and slams the door behind him.

'You're . . . you're back early,' Mum stammers, her voice all tight and croaky.

'What's the matter?' I ask again. My stomach's gone all swirly. Someone must have died, I'm sure of it.

'It's nothing to worry about, Violet. Really,' Mum tries to convince me. 'Just me and your dad having words, that's all.'

She's such a liar. Such a big, fat liar. She's drawn the curtains across her eyes tight shut.

'I don't believe you,' I say. 'Tell me what's happened. I know something has.'

'It's nothing, Violet. Just leave it now.' She wipes the back of her hand across her nose and sniffs. She takes a deep breath and stands up from the table. As she does, I notice her stuffing the piece of paper into the pocket of her housecoat.

'What's that then?' I ask. 'That's not nothing, is it?'

She glares at me. Her face hardens. 'I said. Leave it. It's none of your business.'

She walks across the room, but stiffly and awkwardly like an old lady. She stumbles and steadies herself on the back of a chair.

'Mum?' I start towards her, but she waves me away.

'Sorry, Violet,' she says. 'But I've really got to go and lie down now.'

As she leaves the kitchen, she seems to take all the air with her. It's as though the room is left as winded as me. I'm surprised that I can still breathe. I've never seen Mum and Dad like this before. Not like *this*. They've always nagged and gone on at each other, but I've never seen Mum cry because of it. And I've never seen Dad so angry before. I try and imagine what can have happened.

1. Somebody's dead and they don't want me to know.
2. They're getting a divorce.
3. Mum's really ill and she's going to die.

But nothing makes sense.

1. If someone had died they would tell me, surely? I'm sixteen, not a baby.
2. They're too old to get a divorce. And besides Mum would die of the shame.
3. Mum can't be ill. I would know if she was. And Dad would be sad, not angry.

41

As I climb upstairs to my room, I hear Dad banging around, heaving sacks of potatoes in from the yard. He'll be shouting at me to peel them before too long. I close my bedroom door and look at my hands. I turn them over so I can see the backs of them. They're like old women's hands, all dry and wrinkly. They're ugly, with stubby nails still full of potato dirt. Perhaps I should have tried harder. Perhaps I should have cared about keeping my nails filed all neat and tidy and painting them pearly pink. Maybe if I had, Jackie would still be my best friend.

I look down at Norma's old blue slacks hanging off my legs and I pull at the sleeves of the cardie that Brenda knitted for me. Maybe I should have cared more about these things too. Maybe instead of going to the library on Saturdays to choose books, maybe I should have caught the bus up West and pressed my nose against the windows of all the smart fashion boutiques. Maybe my greatest wish should have been to own a piece of Mary Quant. Maybe if I had tried to care more about stuff like that, then things could have stayed the way they were. And maybe, I could have sat in Ruby's Café with Jackie and the Sugar Girls and felt as though I really belonged.

Maybe it's not too late. Hope sparks in my belly. Maybe, I *can* try harder. It can't be that difficult to be like everyone else.

I flop down on my bed. I'll go round to Jackie's tomorrow. She never goes out on a Sunday. We'll sit at her kitchen table and Brenda will make us tea. Then we'll talk. We'll talk about everything. Just like we used to.

For a moment, I feel a bit better. Everything's going to be okay. But then I hear Mum making strange strangled noises in her bedroom and I remember that there's more to worry about than just Jackie.

Mum's still in her room when I finally force myself to go down to the shop. This isn't like her. She doesn't normally give in. She always just gets on with life and pretends that everything's fine. Something's definitely wrong. Something's really wrong.

'Mum okay?' I ask Dad carefully.

'She'll be fine,' he says. But, he won't look at me. He tips a bucket of chips into the fryer. 'Now stop asking daft questions and get your apron on.'

The evening passes in a blur. The shop windows are thick with condensation and every time the door opens, the soup of fog creeps in from outside, hanging on to the coat tails of every customer. It's a grey and miserable evening, and it matches my mood. Mrs Pearl from down the road comes in for her small piece of cod. She's got no teeth and must have to suck the flakes of fish into her mouth and mash them up with her gums. Mr Brogan comes in with his rolled-up fag stuck to his bottom lip. Mum doesn't like him because he's Irish, but I like the honey in his voice. When he talks it sounds like poetry. Then there's Mr and Mrs Rodgers. Her all sallow-faced and him with a huge dewdrop dangling and wobbling from the end of his nose. Then Eileen Carter with red lipstick on her teeth and another new baby on her hip, and then a girl whose face I remember from school but not her name. I smile at her anyway, but she ignores me and fiddles around with her bag while I wrap her supper for her like I'm her bloody servant or something.

Suddenly, a horrible picture comes into my head.

It's me in five years, ten years, fifteen years' time; I'm standing here in the same spot, wearing the same apron, serving up scoop after scoop of chips and the only thing that's changed is the date on the sheets of newspaper. For a minute, I can't move. I'm frozen in time. Then I shudder, like someone's walked over my grave.

'S'cuse me, love. You serving?'

I blink. And then blink again. There's a boy standing at the counter. My heart does a stupid flip-flop thing, and I don't know why, but my hands reach up to my hair to try and smooth it back behind my ears. The boy is wearing a leather biker jacket that looks hard and dangerous but as soft as fudge all at the same time.

'You all right, love?'

He's grinning at me.

'You was away with the fairies then!'

I open my mouth to ask what he'd like, but nothing comes out. I stare at his hair. It's dark and long with a waxed quiff that falls into his eyes. Blue eyes that are laughing at me. And cheekbones like James Dean.

'Sorry,' I mutter. 'What can I get for you?'

'Six of chips,' he says. 'Plenty of vinegar.' He taps his fingers on the counter and watches me closely as I wipe my forehead with the back of my hand before I bend to fetch his chips. When I straighten up and begin to pile his chips on to the waiting newspapers, he is still watching me. He is leaning close and he smells of cigarettes and petrol and warm beer. My insides feel all weird, like a dish of butter melting in the sun.

'Sixpence, please,' I say. I push the packet of chips towards him and hold out my hand.

He digs around in his jeans pocket. 'In here somewhere,' he says. He checks his other pocket. 'Nope.'

He's frowning now as he unzips a pocket in his leather jacket and rummages inside. 'Sorry,' he says. And he grins at me again.

I watch his lips change shape as he purses them in concentration. My insides are totally liquid now. I look away from his lips. It's rude to stare. Then – I don't know why I do what I do next – the words just come out of my mouth before I can stop them. 'It's all right,' I whisper. 'Don't worry about the money. Here, just have them.'

He looks up at me and his eyebrows flicker in surprise. 'I have got some,' he says. 'Just can't remember what bloody pocket I put it in.'

'Really,' I say. 'It doesn't matter. You can have the chips.'

He stares at me for a minute, like he thinks I'm joking or something. Then he reaches for the packet. 'Thanks,' he says. 'What's your name, by the way?'

'It's Violet,' I say quietly.

'Well, thanks, Violet.' He winks at me.

I swallow hard.

'See you around,' he says. Then he opens the door and disappears into the fog outside.

Suddenly, Dad's standing at my shoulder. 'You have a problem with him?' he asks.

I shake my head. 'No problem,' I say.

'Good,' he says. 'We don't want to encourage his sort in here. Bloody trouble makers. The lot of them.'

What do you know? I want to say. A leather jacket and a motorcycle doesn't make someone a bad person. But I don't say anything. There's no point. Because according to Dad, a leather jacket and a motorcycle is *exactly* what makes someone a bad person.

The shop's empty of customers now. I lean on the counter and try to stop my hands from shaking. I hear the roar of an engine from outside and it's like the roar is coming from inside me too. 'Thanks, Violet,' he'd said. 'Thanks, Violet.' I can hear his voice in my head as clearly as if he was still standing next to me. I don't know what's just happened. But I know that whoever he was, I'll see him again. I know that as surely as I know that the sun's going to rise tomorrow. And for the first time in a long time, I'm glad to be me.

Lost in the Amazon

It's Sunday morning, and Mum's back to being Mum again. There's sausages sizzling in the pan, hymns playing on the wireless and Dad's sitting at the kitchen table in his pyjama bottoms, vest and braces. 'One sausage or two? Mum asks me without turning around.

'Just one, please,' I say.

The sun's shining softly through the nets at the window and the smell of breakfast makes my tummy rumble. Everything feels as it should feel; normal and safe and boring. I imagine Jackie sitting having breakfast with her nan, their big, brown teapot on the table between them. I'll go round there in a bit and I'll ask Jackie to come shopping with me next weekend. I'll tell her I need her advice about what to buy. I need new stuff to wear, and she knows what'll suit me best. She'll like that.

I can't stop thinking about the boy from last night. I still remember the smell of him and the way his leather jacket stretched across his shoulders. Perhaps I'll tell Jackie about him too; about this new thing that's happened to me. Because that's what best friends do. They tell each other everything.

I sit at the table and the sun slants warmly across my arm. I smile at Dad as he spears a sausage, and he winks back at me. But then, as Mum puts a plate of breakfast in front of me and I look up at her to say thanks, I see, with a shock, that her eyes are all pink and puffy and her cheeks are flushed a deep and angry red, like the ketchup that Dad's got smeared across his plate. But I don't want to spoil my mood by asking questions again, and besides, I don't expect there'll be any answers.

I want to keep the morning perfect; as perfect as the fried egg that Mum has laid on top of a slice of buttered toast for me. I cut the end off a sausage and push it against the yolk. The thin skin wobbles promisingly. I push harder, and in an instant the yolk breaks, the yellow insides spill out and soak into the toast, and the beautiful shimmering egg is spoiled.

The back door at Jackie's is ajar and I don't think twice about walking in without knocking. 'Hello!' I call out. 'It's only me! Violet!' There's no one in the kitchen and no sign that anyone's eaten breakfast. 'Shall I put the kettle on?' I shout. There must be someone up, for the door to be open.

'That you, Violet?' Brenda shouts out from somewhere in the house.

I smile to myself. 'Yeah!' I shout back. 'You two are having a lazy Sunday!' I fill the kettle and turn on the gas. Then I swill out the old brown teapot and tip a handful of tea leaves inside. I fetch three cups and put them on the table along with the sugar bowl. I'm just pouring boiling water into the teapot and enjoying the dark perfume of the leaves, when the kitchen door opens.

48

'Hello, love,' says Brenda as she shuffles over to me in her slippers. 'Didn't expect to see you this morning.'

'Just thought I'd pop in,' I say. 'And have a cuppa with you both.'

She looks at me, puzzled. 'Both? You think I've got the milkman hidden away upstairs or something?' She cackles at the thought and pats the rollers that are tightly curled into her hair.

'You wish!' I laugh at her joke. 'No. Not the milkman. You and Jackie. Thought I'd come and have a cuppa with *both* of you.'

'But she's not back yet, love. That's why I'm surprised to see you. Didn't you stay out with them all?'

'Stay out where? With who?' As soon as the questions are out of my mouth, I groan. I wish I could snatch them back, but it's too late now.

Brenda pours tea into two of the cups. 'Oh, I don't know,' she says. 'Wendy's, was it? Or Pauline's? You know, one of her new friends from Garton's. They were all having a girls' night in or some such. Whatever one of those is.' She glances up at me before I have time to wipe the dismay from my face. 'Oh, love,' she says gently. 'Didn't you know about it?'

I force a smile. 'Oh, yeah. Yeah, of course I did. I couldn't go though. Too busy at the shop, you know. Forgot all about it!'

'Shame,' she says. 'Well, never mind. Don't expect you missed much. Sit and have your cuppa. She'll be back any minute.'

I imagine Jackie breezing through the door, her face all lit up and shining with secrets I know nothing about. I imagine how her smile will disappear when she sees me sitting at her kitchen table. She'll be nice enough. But I'll know what she'll really be thinking. *Oh, God. Not Violet. Not boring old Violet with her frizzy hair and hand-me-down clothes. Not dull old Violet who'd rather read a book than kiss a fella.*

'Actually,' I say. 'I can't stop. There's something I have to do for Mum. Sorry. Tell Jackie I'll see her some other time.'

Brenda opens her mouth, but before she can say anything, I've dashed out the door and I'm half walking, half running back home. My teeth are clenched together so tightly that my jaw hurts. I ball my hands into fists and I thump my thighs as hard as I can as I stumble along the pavement. I hate myself. I hate myself so much.

Idiot

Idiot

Idiot

I don't want to be boring and dull and left behind. I don't want to be stuck in a bloody chip shop. I don't want to end up like Mum and Dad or Norma and Raymond. I don't want to be stuck in the past like all the bloody people around here, who still talk about the war and let their kids play on the bombsites. I don't want to care about what Jackie does, or who she does it with. I want to be doing it all *with* her. I want the boy from last night to come back in the shop and lean across the counter towards me again, so I can taste the beer on his breath as he kisses me. I want him to grab me by the hand and pull me out of the shop. I want to climb on the back of his motorcycle and wrap my arms around his waist and rest my cheek on the soft leather of his back, and I want him to speed me away, faster and faster until all I can feel is the wind in my hair and the rush of promises.

I'm back outside the shop now. I stop and uncurl my fists. I peer through the window at the Sunday emptiness inside and the ghost of myself standing behind the counter. I rest my forehead against the glass and think about Mum and Dad. Perhaps they've only just realised that they married the wrong person? Or perhaps they just don't love each other any more? You can't love the same person for ever, surely? Unless that person's dead of course. Like Joseph. Perfect bloody Joseph.

Perhaps it's all to do with money. Perhaps the letter Mum tried to hide was a massive bill they can't afford to pay? Perhaps they're going to have to get rid of the shop? I let my breath slowly cloud the glass. Could that be it? I can't imagine what would happen if we lost the shop. It's all Dad's ever done. He *is* Frank the Fish. He couldn't be Frank the Builder or Frank the Rag and Bone Man or Frank the Anything Else. That's why Dad's so angry and Mum's in such a state. It all makes sense. I use my sleeve to polish my breath from the glass. If I'm right, it would be the worst thing in the world for Mum and Dad. But even though I know this, I can't help smiling at the thought that it would be the *best* thing in the world for me.

I walk away from home towards Battersea Park. I shove my hands in my anorak pockets and walk quickly along the pavements. The High Street is deserted; the shops shuttered and locked. There's a Blue Riband wrapper blowing along the road and a couple of beer bottles left discarded in the gutter. I catch sight of my reflection in the window of Woolworths. A wild-haired skinny thing in a scruffy anorak and a pair of jeans that lost sight of my ankles months ago. I turn away quickly.

I should go to Norma's. She'd love it. She lives for visitors. Any chance to show off the latest addition to her home. Last time I went she wouldn't shut up about her new refrigerator; it's got a freezer drawer where she can keep packets of fish fingers. And the time before that it was all about her new washer dryer. It was the happiest day of her life when she realised she'd never have to go to a launderette again.

If I was a good sister I'd go and see her. If I was a good sister I'd sit down with her and share a pot of tea and I'd ooh and aah over all her fancy new things. I'd let her pretend to me that her life is great and that her new refrigerator and washer dryer have made her happy. But I'm fed up with pretending. It's all a lie. Norma isn't happy. She hates her life. All she wants is a baby. Even though she won't admit it, I know it's true. I can see the sadness inside her. She's aching to be pregnant, but it's just not happening. I kick out at a broken piece of brick that's lying on the pavement in front of me. I watch it skitter into the road and break into even smaller pieces.

I should *want* to go to Norma's. She's my big sister. I should be able to tell her about Mum and Dad and she should be able to tell me not to worry, that everything's going to be fine. But Norma's not exactly good at dealing with problems. She gets her knickers in a twist if the milkman delivers her gold top instead of silver top. She'd go nuts if I told her about Mum and Dad, and then she'd probably tell me it was all my fault. Neither of us are very good at being sisters.

The sky's grown dark. It's getting colder. I zip up my anorak, shove my hands deeper into my pockets and walk faster. There's a warning growl and a flash of lightning, then the sky opens and fat drops of rain pound down onto my head and shoulders and bounce off the pavements. I quickly pull my hood up. I could be at Norma's in two minutes. She'd have a go at me for leaving wet footprints on her clean kitchen floor, but at least I'd be warm and dry. But I'm not far from the park either. I can see its canopy of trees just across the road and I know straight away where I'd rather be.

I walk under the tunnel of trees that skirt the edges of the park. It's like having my own giant, green umbrella. The rain's still pattering down above me, but it's soft and muffled now. I imagine I'm lost in the Amazon rainforest. I imagine there are tribes of chattering monkeys swinging through the branches above me and poisonous snakes lurking in the undergrowth at my feet. I eat exotic fruits and chop down giant leaves to build shelters to sleep in at night. I am an expert at survival and when, months later, I am eventually found and rescued, I'm flown home on a specially chartered aeroplane and when I land in England there's a crowd of journalists waiting to meet me and take my photograph. I'm on the front page of every newspaper. LOST HERO RETURNS. I'm even on the wireless, and the whole of Battersea tunes in to hear me tell my story. Jackie boasts to everyone that I've always been her best friend. Mum and Dad tell the papers that I'm the most brilliant child any parent could wish for and my boyfriend (I haven't decided on his name yet) lifts me onto the back of his motorcycle and rides off into the distance, leaving everybody behind to stare after us in wonder.

I'm so caught up in my story that I'm dismayed to see a couple sitting on a bench up ahead. There's no benches in the Amazon rainforest. I'm about to turn around, so I can be alone again, when the colour of the woman's headscarf catches my attention. It's a bright kingfisher blue. Mum's got one just like it, that she wears for best. I don't know why I do it, but I quickly step back into the shadow of the trees. I look at the couple again. I can't see the man because his back's facing me.

I stare at Mum.

Her lips are moving as she leans in to talk to the man. I can see from here that she is wearing red lipstick. Mum never wears lipstick. I watch as she lifts a hand to stroke the man's face. She laughs. Then she takes the man's hands in her own and holds them in her lap. I feel like I've been caught stealing money from Dad's wallet. My heart's doing the jitterbug and my hands are actually sweating.

It should be the easiest thing in the world for me to shout out, 'Hey, Mum! What are you doing here?'

But I can't. It would be like barging in on her while she was in the bathroom. My brain's not working properly. It's like someone's stuffed my head with cotton wool. I can see that it's Mum there, cuddling up to a man, who is definitely not Dad. I can see her as plain as can be. It's Mum and it isn't Mum. Not the Mum I know anyway.

Mum calls up that supper's ready. I've been in my room ever since I got back from the park, with my head buried in *The Country Girls*. Kate and Baba have left their village and gone away to a convent school. The convent is a grey stone building that's run by nuns. The nuns are mostly silent but very strict. Kate and Baba have to sleep in a dormitory with loads of other girls. The convent is a cold and miserable place and the food they have to eat is so disgusting that they have to sneak in cake and eat it late at night under their bed sheets. But Kate gets on with it all better than Baba. She's cleverer than Baba for starters. She makes other friends and Baba's bullying doesn't bother her as much. I don't think Kate needs Baba as much as she used to. She's growing up and finding her own way.

I think my life's like that convent right now; empty and miserable, with me just waiting for something to happen. Kate might not need Baba as much as she used to, but I still need Jackie. Especially now, since Mum's lost her head. I need someone to talk to, but there isn't anyone left.

Mum shouts up the stairs again. I tuck the book under my pillow for later, and take a deep breath. If Kate can get on with it and make the best of things, then so can I.

I watch Mum closely as she butters bread and empties a tin of fruit cocktail into three bowls. She's been careful to wipe off the lipstick but I can still see the faint stain of it in the corners of her mouth. She doesn't look guilty, not one bit. In fact she looks really happy. Her face is soft and relaxed and the smile crinkles around her eyes are deeper than usual.

Dad looks the same as ever; like he's got a stick up his bum. He's dipping his bread and butter into his tea, leaving pools of yellow grease floating on the surface. It's his favourite thing, but because Mum thinks it's a disgusting habit she only lets him do it on a Sunday as a special treat. He's got the thick crust of the bread folded in half and he grunts with satisfaction every time he takes a soggy bite.

I swirl a spoon around in my bowl of fruit. Mum's given me the cherry as usual. There's only ever one in the tin. I don't know why. I don't know what's so special about it. It doesn't even taste like a cherry. And it's definitely not the colour of a real cherry. It's a bright plastic red, the colour of the lipstick Mum was wearing in the park. I eat the chunks of pear and peach in my bowl, but I leave the cherry floating all on its own in a puddle of syrup. 'You can have it,' I say to Mum when she nods towards my bowl and raises an eyebrow.

She picks the cherry up with her fingers and pops it in her mouth. She smiles at me and then for the first time in my life I catch a glimpse of how she must have looked when she was a young girl. She's pretty as a picture. She hums a tune to herself as she clears the dishes from the table. Dad shakes out his newspaper and leans back in his chair to read it.

I can't believe they're behaving so normally! As though nothing has happened. Dad must know what's going on, surely? That's why they were arguing yesterday. It was nothing to do with money or getting rid of the shop. He must have found out somehow that Mum's got a bit on the side. He must have found the letter; a love letter perhaps? The one that Mum tried to hide from me yesterday. Maybe Mum promised Dad it was all over and he has no idea that she went out today to meet this man again.

I watch Dad licking his fingers as he turns the pages of his paper. What would he do if I told him what I'd seen today?

I clear my throat. 'Dad?' I say.

He peers over the top of his paper.

'Dad . . .' I begin again.

He lowers the newspaper onto the table. 'Spit it out,' he says.

But, before I can say anything, Mum sits down next to me and stirs some sugar into her tea. She smells of Lily of the Valley soap, cold cream and happiness. I watch as she lifts her cup to her mouth. She's done her hair differently, I notice. It's not as tightly set and stiff with lacquer like it usually is. It's soft and shiny and she's tucked a loose curl behind her ear. I've never seen her like this before. If someone asked her, this very minute, how she was, she'd reply 'fine, thank you' like she always does, but this time she'd be telling the truth.

Mum's such a stickler for doing the right thing, it's hard to believe she'd actually have an *actual extra-marital affair*. I remember all the fuss last year when our doctor had an affair with one of his patients, Mrs Johnson. When Mr Johnson found out, he stormed down to the surgery and punched Dr Harvey so hard in the face that he broke his nose. Dr Harvey and his family had to move away after that, because none of his patients would take their complaints to him any more. I sometimes see Mrs Johnson walking to the shops with a basket over her arm. She always looks like she's about to cry. And she's lost all her colour. She's like an old pair of curtains, all washed out and faded. I feel sorry for her. It's not her fault she married the wrong man before she fell in love with the right man. And now she has to be miserable for the rest of her life.

I glance sideways at Mum again. She's got a faraway look in her eyes and she's still stirring her tea like she's forgotten what she's doing. Everyone says it wrong for married people to have affairs, but it can't be wrong for Mum to have some happiness for once in her life.

Dad's staring at me. 'Well?' he barks. 'Come on. What do you want? I haven't got all day.'

I can't give Mum away. Of course I can't. So, instead I just ask, 'Anything interesting in the paper?'

He frowns. 'Give me a chance to bloody read it first,' he snaps. He hides behind the pages again, like a grumpy old tortoise retreating into its shell. *Sod you*, I think. I jump up from the table.

'I'll do the dishes for you, Mum,' I say.

'Oh, bless you, Violet,' she says. 'I might go and put my feet up for a minute then.'

When I go into the front room later, she's asleep in her chair. Her chin has dropped onto her chest and she's whistling softly through her nose. Must be exhausting being in love at her age, I think. I look at her hands resting in her lap. I can't believe they've touched another man's face and held another man's hands. It's odd, but when I look at her now, I see two different people. There's Mum, who's always just been my mum, in her housecoat and slippers, with her arms in the sink or up to her elbows in flour. Mum, who still says 'night, night, sleep tight, watch the bed bugs don't bite' and is always telling me to 'speak the Queen's English' if I ever say 'ouse instead of house.

And then there's this other woman, who looks just like Mum, right down to her wrinkled stockings and varicose veins, but who is a complete stranger to me. I don't know this woman at all. I don't know what she's thinking or feeling or what she dreams about at night.

My eyes slide to the pocket at the front of her housecoat. If I'm really careful I could slip my hand inside and pull out the letter or whatever it is she's hiding in there. I could find out right now what her big secret is. I hold my breath and tiptoe towards her. I stretch out my hand, but just as my fingers reach the pocket opening, Mum grunts in her sleep and shifts around. I pull my hand away and freeze. Her eyes flick open.

'Violet?' she mumbles. 'What is it? Can't I even snatch forty winks in peace?'

'It's nothing,' I say, turning away from her. 'It doesn't matter.'

But it does matter. Of course it matters. I just can't tell Mum that.

Private Detective Stuff

It's Wednesday afternoon. The dead part of the day. Dad's having a nap in the front room, along with the rest of the world it seems. I've swept the shop floor and given it a once over with the mop, ready for opening later. The whole place smells of lemons now. I stare out of the shop window. Even the street is empty and sleepy. There's no kids out playing and everyone's front doors are closed.

I still haven't seen anything of Jackie. Part of me has been waiting and hoping that she'd pop in one evening. Just poke her nose round the door and say, *Hi, Vi. Long time no see. Fancy doing something on Saturday?* But of course, she hasn't.

I wish we'd had a row at least. Something big and bad with loads of swearing. A huge, walloping argument, where we'd screamed at each other and said hateful things.

Bitch!

Ugly cow!

Scrubber!

At least with an argument there's a chance to make up afterwards. There's a chance that one of you will say sorry and the whole thing can be forgotten about.

But there's never been anything to argue about. All there's been is a kind of slipping and loosening. Like a pair of tightly knotted laces that came undone without me noticing and then tripped me over.

I finished reading *The Country Girls* last night, but it didn't give me any answers. Kate and Baba ended up being expelled from the convent for writing a disgusting thing on a picture of the Blessed Mary. They moved to Dublin then, to learn how to live and drink gin. But they became like strangers to each other, just like me and Jackie.

Maybe that's what growing up is all about? You grow too big for playing with dolls, you grow too big for your favourite dress, and maybe you just grow out of your friends too.

I carry the mop bucket back through to the kitchen. Dad's snoring rumbles like distant thunder from the front room. I pour the dirty water down the sink and am just wondering where Mum is when she hurries into the room. 'Just popping out,' she says, knotting her headscarf under her chin. She's got the kingfisher-blue one on again.

'Oh,' I say. 'Where you going?'

'Just nipping to the shops,' she says quickly. 'Won't be long.'

I stare at the back of her coat as she walks out of the door. It's her Sunday best one. I've only ever seen her wear it to funerals before. It's usually at the back of her wardrobe covered in mothballs. She can't seriously think that no one will notice her wearing it. And she can't be stupid enough to have forgotten that it's Wednesday. It's half-day closing. There won't be any shops open.

I count to one hundred and eighty. Then I grab my anorak and close the door carefully behind me so as not to wake Dad.

61

I peer out onto the road, looking quickly in both directions and I just catch sight of Mum disappearing around the corner at the end of the street. I hold back for another minute before I begin to follow her. It's tricky, keeping her in sight and staying as far back as I can, all at the same time. But it's exhilarating too; like riding on a roller coaster. My stomach lurches into my throat every time she slows her pace and I think she's about to turn round.

She walks right down the High Street without even pretending that she thought the shops were open. Once, when she stops to cross the road, I dart into the doorway of Chester's the grocer's and stare through the window at the faded packets of Bird's Custard powder.

The further away from home she gets, the faster Mum starts walking. The park's right up ahead now. She starts to run, in little bursts, but then she checks herself, rolls her shoulders back and walks at a more dignified pace. She's desperate to get to where she's going, that's for certain.

It's easy to get closer to her, now we're in the park. I slink into the trees and weave in and out of the shadows. I'm getting good at this private detective stuff. I even hear her panting a little as she hurries along the pathway towards the bench. I knew she was coming here. Stands to reason they have their own little meeting place, away from prying eyes. A secret tryst for secret lovers.

He's already waiting for her. I flatten myself against a tree, then I take off my glasses and polish them on the sleeve of my anorak. I don't want to miss a thing. The man stands up as Mum walks towards him and he holds out his arms to her. She walks right into them and he folds them around her. I forget for a moment to even look at him, I'm so stunned by the sight of Mum melting into the embrace of another man. But then they move apart, and as they turn to settle themselves on the bench, I see his face for the first time.

Bloody hell! I was expecting someone like Dad. Someone grey and battered around the edges. Someone old. This man's not old. Not Dad old, anyway. He's got a thick dark beard and dark hair that's all messy and touching his shoulders. He's got so much hair in fact, that there's not a lot of face left to see. But I can tell he's younger than Mum. Old people are blurry, smudged-out versions of their younger selves, but this man is solid and clear. He's all shiny and bright like the front cover of a magazine. He's not dressed like an old person either. He's wearing a black donkey jacket and a pair of blue denim jeans.

They sit close together, like they did the last time, with their heads almost touching and their fingers entwined. I wish I had a listening device like a proper detective, so I could hear what they are saying to each other. Are they planning on running away together? Does he know about Dad? Does he know about me? And who is he anyway? Where the hell did Mum even meet him? She never goes anywhere.

Suddenly, I hear voices. I turn round, and there's a couple with a pram walking along the path towards me. I step away from the tree. I don't want to look like some weird Peeping Tom. I bend down quickly, pretending to look for something in the grass. The couple don't even notice me. They're too intent on babbling and cooing to the baby in the pram. I don't recognise them. They've never been in the shop at least. Lucky for Mum,

I think. How would she explain it if one of our customers saw her canoodling with another man in Battersea Park? I can't understand why she meets him here. It's not exactly hidden away.

I stand up again and peek around the tree. The couple with the pram are a way down the path now and Mum and the man are hugging each other again. At least, Mum has her face pressed against his shoulder and he has his arms around her. It looks like he's comforting her or something. I've got that strange feeling again. I know it's my mum over there, but this is the first time I've ever *really* seen her.

I shouldn't be spying on her, I know that much. She'd die of shame and embarrassment if she knew I was here. I feel grubby. I want to go home and fill the sink with warm water and scrub myself all over with a flannel. And I want to get home before Dad wakes up. For some reason I don't want him to be on his own when he finally stirs and grunts and opens his eyes. He deserves a cup of tea at least.

I steal a last glance at Mum. She's dabbing her eyes with a hankie now. I'd love to know why she's crying, but I can't exactly ask her. Instead, I creep away, back towards the entrance to the park. There are more people milling around now. I nervously check their faces, hoping I don't recognise any of them. Not for my sake, but for Mum's. Luckily there's no one familiar.

I can't stop wondering why Mum's crying though. I think about it logically. There can only be a certain number of reasons.

1. She's told Donkey Jacket Man that it's all over between them, and she's saying a painful goodbye.
2. She can't cope with the guilt of cheating on Dad.

3. She's agreed to run away with Donkey Jacket Man and she's crying at the thought of having to tell me and Dad and Norma.
4. Donkey Jacket Man has told her it's all over between them, and she'll never see him again.

Whatever the reason, none of it looks too good for Mum.

I trudge the rest of the way home. I can't believe that now, finally, when something so crazy, awful, exciting and terrible has happened, I've got no one to share it with. Now, when my life has been shaken up, stirred and turned completely upside down, there's not one single person I can talk to about it all. A secret like this is a horrible thing to hold on to. It's a life-changing secret; too big for one person to carry. I can already feel it filling me up to bursting point. I imagine myself growing bigger, my skin stretching as the secret inside me grows bigger. I imagine my head ballooning and my lips growing tighter and tighter as I struggle to keep the secret inside.

When I get home, Dad's already awake. He's sitting at the kitchen table sorting out his betting slips. 'Where've you been?' he asks. 'And where's your mother?' He flicks his ash into a saucer and takes another drag on his fag.

'I just went out for some fresh air,' I say. 'And I think Mum did too. 'Spect she'll be back in a minute.'

Dad laughs. 'Fresh air?' he says. 'What, in Battersea? You'll be lucky.' He pats his slips into a neat little pile and places them in the middle of the table then he grinds his fag out in the saucer. Mum'll go mad. She hates it when he does that. It's not like there isn't a perfectly good ashtray on the windowsill. Dad yawns loudly and stretches his arms above his head.

'Want a cuppa?' I ask.

'Yeah, go on then, love. Why not?' he says.

As I fill the kettle, I picture Mum walking back up the road. I imagine she's dried her eyes properly and taken a good few deep breaths. She'll be dragging her feet, not wanting to come home but knowing that she has to. She'll be preparing herself to tell Dad the terrible news. She might have her case packed and ready and hidden under the bed.

Or maybe not. Maybe she won't say anything. Maybe she's hoping that Dad's still asleep, and she's got a cover story ready just in case he's not. I hope she doesn't tell him she's been to the shops. I hope she's realised by now that was a stupid thing to say on a Wednesday.

I fill the teapot with boiling water and put it on the table to brew. Dad likes tea you can stand a spoon up in. I fetch his cup and the sugar bowl and put them in front of him. 'Thanks, Vi,' he says. He smiles and winks at me. He can be nice, Dad can, especially when it's just the two of us. But I wish he wouldn't be nice now. It makes this, waiting for Mum to come home bit, even harder. I feel like I'm waiting for a catastrophe to happen, for a bomb to explode in the middle of the house. I feel like all our lives are about to be blown to pieces and scattered all over Battersea.

But nothing happened. No explosion. No tears. No shouting, no screaming. Mum just walked through the door, took off her coat and scarf and poured herself a cup of tea. Dad didn't even ask her where she'd been. For a moment I thought I'd imagined it all. Or that perhaps it was me that had been asleep in Dad's armchair and I'd dreamed the whole thing. It didn't seem possible, that after all I'd seen in the park, Mum could just stroll back into the house and pour herself a cup of tea as though the fact that she'd just met up with another man was the most ordinary thing in the world. She even yelled at Dad. 'Frank! What have I told you about putting out these disgusting things in my saucers?' She'd tut-tutted and stomped around the kitchen emptying Dad's fag ends in the bin and rinsing the saucer under the tap.

And now, I'm standing behind the counter in the shop, slapping a piece of cod onto some newspaper and wondering what the bloody hell is wrong with my parents.

It's busy for a Wednesday evening. Sometimes it goes like that. For no reason at all it's like every other person in the neighbourhood suddenly fancies a fish supper. There's a queue of customers snaking out of the door and as fast as Dad can fill the hot cupboard with freshly fried fish, I'm wrapping it up and handing it over the counter. Halfway through the evening, the demand starts to beat us and I have to apologise and tell everyone there'll be a ten-minute wait. I rush out the back to grab another bucket of chips while Dad mixes up another batch of batter. Nobody seems to mind. A couple of customers wander outside for a smoke while the rest shuffle around chatting amongst themselves. I fill the chip fryer again and take off my glasses to polish the steam off with the bottom of my apron.

And that's when I see him. At least I think it's him. I quickly put my glasses back on and push the loose wisps of hair off my face. It's definitely him. He's standing outside, at the back of the queue, leaning casually against the window. My stomach does a small flip and begins to sizzle, like the pieces of cod that Dad's just dropped in the fryer.

I knew he'd come back. I just didn't know it would be so soon.

I begin to serve again and as the till rattles with shillings and sixpences, the queue begins to move. He's in the shop now, and I serve people as fast as I can, until eventually he moves closer and closer to the front of the queue. 'Hey. Violet,' he says, at last. 'Remember me?'

I nod, stupidly. How could I forget?

'I wanted to settle up,' he says. 'And to say thanks again. You know. For the other night.'

I shrug. As though giving away free chips is something I do all the time.

'Anyway,' he says. 'Here's what I owe. And another sixpence for tonight's supper.' He presses two coins into the centre of my palm. They're still warm from where they've been in his pocket.

I clear my throat and begin to measure out his order. 'Open or wrapped?' I ask.

'Open, I reckon,' he says. 'I'll eat them while I'm waiting for you to finish, shall I?'

I'm not sure I've heard him right. But I feel my cheeks colouring anyway and I keep my head down as I douse his chips in salt and vinegar and fold the newspaper into a cone.

'I'll only wait if you want me to,' he says.

I want to be all cool and nonchalant, as though boys asking to meet me after work happens all the time. Bloody cheek, I want to say. But instead, when I look up to give him his cone of chips, all I can manage is a croaky, 'Yeah, okay.'

He grins at me and takes a bite from one of his chips. 'Later, then,' he says. His quiff flops into his eyes as he turns to walk out of the door and my heart flops around in my chest, like there's nothing left to hold it in place any more. 'Oh,' says the boy, just before he disappears out the door. 'My name's Beau, by the way.'

I quickly glance over at Dad. He's too busy refilling the hot cupboard with freshly cooked fish to notice who I've been serving. Which is just as well. He'd have a fit if he knew what I'd just agreed to do.

The last half-hour of the evening takes for ever to pass. But eventually, the final customer leaves and when I've finished wiping down and after I've locked and chained the shop door, I tell Dad I'm nipping round to Jackie's. He won't know any better, and Mum won't care less. She'll be too busy mooning over Donkey Jacket Man.

I run upstairs and change into some clean slacks and a jumper. Then, because I haven't got anything better to wear, I grab my old anorak from the coat hook before slipping out of the kitchen door. I can't believe I'm doing this. He won't be there. He won't have waited this long for me. He'll have just been having a laugh with himself. I bet he does this all the time; teasing girls like me and then leaving them to wait like idiots for him.

It's quiet out on the street, and cold. The air is fizzing with frost. It's a clear night with a sixpence of a moon and the seven stars of the Plough twinkling like a newly scrubbed saucepan.

I walk to the end of the road. My chest is tight with anxiety. It's hard to breathe. I've never been this brave before and I don't know if I can go through with it. But my feet carry on walking anyway and then I'm round the corner and there he is, waiting for me, leaning against his motorcycle, blowing smoke at the moon.

'Didn't think you'd come,' he says. 'But I guess you're not as good a girl as you look.' He pats the seat of his motorcycle. 'Fancy getting out of here for a while?'

I nod dumbly. I want to pinch myself, just to check I'm not dreaming.

He climbs on to the motorcycle and indicates with his head for me to climb on behind him. 'You'll need to zip that up,' he says, pointing to my anorak. I swear it's going in the bin tomorrow and on Saturday I'll go to the market and buy myself a proper jacket, just like the one he's wearing.

I slip easily on to the seat and find a place to rest my feet, then as he revs up the motorcycle's engine, I realise I've put my arms around his waist. And it feels like the most natural thing in the world.

There's a roar, the smells of oil, leather, smoke and heat, and then the world as I know it disappears in a blur of colour and sound and light. It's just as I imagined it would be, only a million times better. The rush of speed takes my breath away and the rush of wind tears the cloak of worries and cares from my shoulders. I feel lightheaded and free.

We head north, leaving the streaks of Battersea's streetlights far behind. We sail over Chelsea Bridge and I see the moon quivering on the surface of the Thames. As we speed along the black roads, the cold air makes my eyes sting. I press my face against the back of his jacket and I hear his heart thrumming as loudly as the motorcycle's engine. We pass the grand entrance to Victoria Station where some late travellers are humping suitcases into waiting taxis. We ride through Belgravia with the gardens of Buckingham Palace on our right and rows of posh five-storeyed houses on our left. Hyde Park Corner flashes past. We cross over Oxford Street and skirt around Regent's Park. I'm holding on to him so tightly, I can't feel my fingers any more. I close my eyes and it's like riding the Big Dipper. I'm ten years old again and I want to scream with fear and excitement.

We speed through St John's Wood and past Swiss Cottage, then, just as I think I'm about to lose my grip and be thrown back on to the road to break every bone in my body, the noise of the engine deepens and slows and the battering wind dies down to a breeze.

We've stopped, but it's a minute before I can move. All my muscles have locked. I wriggle my fingers and straighten my back, then I manage to slide from my seat and put my feet back on solid ground. I'm freezing and my legs are all wobbly. I watch as he climbs from the motorcycle and props it up against the nearby wall. He shakes out his hair and his quiff bounces back into shape. I don't want to even think about what *my* hair must look like. As he fiddles with his keys and a chain of some sort, I pick at my hair, trying to pull it back down around my face where the wind has frizzled it into stiff little tufts. I wipe my eyes and straighten my glasses. He turns around then and grins at me.

'Come on,' he says. 'What are you waiting for? Wanna see something really cool?'

'Yeah . . . Yeah. All right,' I say. As he walks off into the shrubby fields in front of us, I hear Mum's voice in the back of my head. *What the bloody hell do you think you're doing, Violet? You're in the middle of nowhere with a complete stranger, you stupid girl! You haven't got the sense you were born with!*

I ignore her and hurry after him anyway. He's striding ahead easily and his denim jeans are so tight around his legs that I can see the muscles flexing in the back of his thighs. If I look any further up, I swear my eyes will literally pop out of my head. *God, Violet*, I think. *Get a grip.* I swallow hard.

'Where are we?' I yell at him. 'Where are we going?'

'Hampstead Heath!' he shouts back. 'Parliament Hill. You ever been here before?'

'No!' I yell. 'What's so special about it?'

'You'll see. Come on. Keep up!'

I traipse after him. But it's harder to go faster than a determined walk because it's almost completely dark, the ground is lumpy and muddy and there's a tiny part of me that's actually a little bit worried. He could be an axe murderer after all. But it's too late now. I have to stick with him, because I have no idea how the hell to get home, and I don't want to get lost on my own all the way out here.

The ground's getting steeper, and I'm hot now, even though my breath is coming out in little puffs of toy train steam. I unzip my anorak. 'Is it much further?' I sound like a whining little girl.

He stops for a moment and when I catch up with him, he takes my hand. 'Need a little help, I reckon,' he says. And just like that, there's me, Violet White, hand in hand with a gorgeous fella. I wish there was someone here to see it. He pulls me up the hill, higher and higher and higher. His hand is all warm and soft. After what seems like an age, the ground starts to flatten out. We walk out into a huge open space and suddenly it's much lighter. The sky is like an enormous, glittering blanket wrapped around us.

'Close your eyes,' he says.

The hair on the back of my neck prickles. If he is an axe murderer, it's too late now, so I might as well do as he asks. I flinch as he puts a hand on my shoulder and then I do as he says and close my eyes. But there's no whoosh as the axe slices through the air towards me and there's no agonising pain as the sharp blade thuds into my neck. Instead, he just spins me around and around and around.

'There,' he says eventually. 'Now, open your eyes.'

I slowly inch my eyelids open. 'Wow!' I breathe, and I steady myself against his arm.

'Told you it was cool,' he says.

He's right. It is cool. Really cool.

It's like we're floating high above the city. It's all spread out below us. Dark shapes of buildings; office blocks, tower blocks and churches. There's so many lights; red, white, orange and yellow. They're flashing, twinkling and blinking at me.

'Look,' he says, pointing. 'There's St Paul's. And over there, the Houses of Parliament. Can you see?'

I nod. It's all so beautiful I don't want to speak. I think of all the people down there, scurrying around, heading for home. And the late-night office workers still sitting at their desks and policemen walking their beats and all the young girls dancing with their fellas. And all of them with their own cares and worries and dreams and their own pasts and futures.

'Best view in the whole of London, that is,' he says.

I think he might be right. I've never seen the city like this before. I never knew it was all so vast and fast and throbbing with life. It makes me feel tiny and insignificant. Like I really don't matter at all. Like I'm just a speck floating in the universe.

'Here,' he says. 'You want some?' He's pulled a bottle of beer from inside his jacket. He prises off the cap with his keys and then sucks quickly at the hissing foam. He hands me the bottle.

'Thanks,' I say. I take a mouthful of the beer. It tastes like warm metal. He takes off his jacket and lays it on the ground and we both sit down and pass the bottle between us.

This is his favourite place, Beau tells me. He comes here a lot. Just so he can get away from the crowds. Crowds bug him. He loves his motorcycle. It gives him a sense of freedom. Means he can escape from the world from time to time. He'd die without his bike. He likes to smoke too. He smokes properly, taking two drags at once and blowing the smoke through his nose. He offers me a cigarette from a battered packet. I've never had a smoke before, but I take one anyway. He cups his hand around a lighter and holds it to the end of my cigarette. I suck, like I've seen Dad doing, and my throat is filled with stinging smoke. I cough until my eyes water and Beau laughs at me.

'Virgin,' he teases.

V for Violet, I think. V for Virgin.

I tell him I wish I had a motorcycle too. That I'd like to escape from the world sometimes. I tell him how much I hate working at the chippie. I tell about some of the customers. About mean old Mr Carver and how I always try to give him the smallest piece of fish and about Mrs Pearl and her gums and about poor old Mrs Robinson who eats her extra fish supper in secret. Beau laughs at my stories. 'You're funny,' he says. And I feel all warm inside, even though I never meant to be funny at all.

When the bottle of beer is empty, we walk down the hill and climb back on to Beau's motorcycle. It's easier this time, I know what to expect. I relax against his back and let the bike move my body where it needs to go. Beau pulls over on Chelsea Bridge and buys me a coffee from the late-night stall. There are other fellas gathered there, all dressed like Beau with slicked-back hair and shiny motorcycles.

And there's a couple of girls too. They've got the same black leather jackets on and boots that are covered in chains and studs. Their hair is amazing. They've pinned it back behind their ears and teased the rest of it into exaggerated quiffs. They're laughing along with the fellas like they really belong. I stand next to Beau while he and the others rev up their bikes and talk about ton-ups and getting their kicks and pleasing themselves. With all the bikes growling so loudly around me, I feel like a lone deer surrounded by a pride of lions. But nobody attacks me. Nobody looks at me the wrong way or makes me feel like an idiot. One of the girls sidles up to me. 'Hello,' she says. 'What's your name, then?'

'Violet,' I reply.

'Nice name,' she says. 'So what do you do then, Violet? You got a job?'

I nod. 'I work in my Dad's chippie.'

'Nice one!' she grins. 'I love chips, me. So . . . you with Beau, then?'

'Yeah,' I say. 'Well . . . not *with* him. He's not my boyfriend or anything.'

She shrugs. 'Whatever. It's cool.' She smiles at me, a proper smile that reaches her eyes. 'You're not like the others he's brought here,' she says. 'You seem like a nice girl.' She laughs, then saunters off and drapes herself against the arm of one of the other fellas.

I sneak a look at Beau and watch him blow long curls of cigarette smoke from his nostrils. I wonder how many other girls he's brought here. The thought makes me feel weird and uncertain. I bet they were Rocker girls, all cool and pretty. I shiver as I wonder what he sees in me. I warm my hands on the paper cup of coffee. I take a sip. It's strong and sweet and exotic. It tastes of things I don't even know about yet.

The bikes are roaring loudly. The fellas are all sitting astride their machines with their denim thighs squeezing the flanks as though they're trying to control a herd of powerful horses. 'Hey, Violet!' Beau shouts in my ear. 'Time to go!'

We follow the other bikes along the bridge. Faster, faster and faster. My heart's in my throat. The wind's in my face and all thoughts of anything other than this moment fly from my head and sail over Chelsea Bridge and into the Thames. 'Yee ha!' I scream into the night. 'Yee ha!'

I'm having the ride of my life and I never want it to end.

I have no idea how late it is when Beau pulls up outside the chip shop. He keeps his engine purring as I quickly clamber off the bike. There's an awkward moment as I wonder if he's going to kiss me or not. He leans towards me and I breathe in sharply. But then his hand reaches out and he touches me gently under the chin. 'See you later, Violet,' he says.

'Yeah. See you,' I say. Of course he was never going to kiss me. Why would he want to? But then he winks at me and it's enough to give me goosebumps. He revs up his engine and disappears down the road in a burst of choking smoke. I stare after him. Did all that really just happen? Did such a good-looking fella actually notice me and speak to me and whisk me away on the back of his motorcycle? I pinch myself on the arm. It hurts, so I can't be dreaming.

I expect the house to be in darkness. Mum and Dad should have gone to bed hours ago. But as I walk round the side to the kitchen door I see a square of light shining on to the path. Hoping they've just left a light on for me to come home to, I open the door. I'm in a hurry to get to bed and think about the extraordinary evening I've just had. I want to think about the rush of the wind and the blood pumping through my veins as Beau flew us over Chelsea Bridge. I want to think again about the quiet of Parliament Hill and being alone with Beau at the top of the world. I want to remember the smell of the cold grass and the night air and the taste of beer and coffee. I want to remember Beau's voice and the feel of leather against my face and how his muscles tensed as he guided his bike around sharp bends and along dark roads.

But as I walk into the kitchen, Mum and Dad are both sitting there at the table. Mum's eyes are small and furious and Dad's face is grey with cigarette smoke. Mum jumps up from her chair. 'Where the bloody hell have you been?' she screeches. 'We've been worried sick! And don't you dare say you were at Jackie's. I went round there hours ago and they said they haven't seen you for days.'

'I just went out,' I mumble. 'Nothing to get your knickers in a twist about.'

Mum takes a deep breath. She's trying to keep calm. 'Out where?' she says. 'At this time of night?'

'None of your business,' I say. 'I'm sixteen. I'm not a baby. I'll go where I like.'

'Oi!' Dad shouts, leaning forward across the table. 'Don't speak to your mother like that! While you're living under our roof, we've every right to know where you've been!' He sits back in his chair and slides a newspaper towards me. 'It's one in the morning, for Christ's sake,' he says. 'And haven't you seen the paper today? If you'd bothered to read it you'd know why we were so worried about you.'

If I'd *bothered* to read the paper today? I can't believe he's just said that. Dad, who's never read a book in his entire life and only ever usually looks at the sport pages is having a go at me just because, for once, I haven't seen the paper today! I want to punch him. Right on the end of his ignorant nose. I look at Mum with her face all pink and pinched up with self-righteousness and suddenly I can't keep it in any longer. If they won't let me have my own secrets then why should I let them have theirs? Ignoring the newspaper, I turn to Mum.

'I'll tell you where I've been, if you tell Dad where you went today.'

There's a horrible silence. Mum opens her mouth and closes it again, like a fish drowning in a bucket of water. The ash that's trembling at the end of Dad's cigarette falls on to the table and neither of them move to brush it away. 'What does she mean?' Dad says quietly. He's looking at Mum and I know he means business because without even putting his last cigarette out properly, he's lighting another one.

I run out of the room, slamming the door behind me, and by the time I've got upstairs, they're already yelling at each other. Mum's crying. 'I had to see him, Frank. I had to see him!'

'You bloody promised me!' Dad shouts. 'I told you, just the once and never again! You lied to me! You bloody lied to me!'

'But, Frank. Please!'

'Does Violet know? Have you told her? Have you told Norma?'

I shut my bedroom door and throw myself on the bed. The shouting is muffled now, but not muffled enough. I pull a pillow over my head to drown the noise in feathers. Mum'll hate me now, and Dad probably will too. But I don't care. It's their mess, not mine. I don't want anything more to do with it. I've got better things to do. There's another world out there that I tasted tonight for the first time. And I want more of it. Because it tastes a whole lot better than fish and chips and salt and vinegar.

The newspaper is still spread out on the kitchen table where Dad left it last night.

GIRL, 15, MISSING

Police in South London are becoming increasingly concerned over the welfare of a fifteen-year-old girl who was reported missing over a week ago. Joanne Thomas was last seen on the evening of October 15th at approximately 7.30pm at a funfair in Battersea Park, where she was spotted talking to a man. She has since failed to return home.

Officers have described the girl as having shoulder-length blonde hair, blue eyes, of slim build and approximately 5ft 4 inches tall. When last seen she was wearing a white skirt, black jumper and a blue half-length coat.

Joanne Thomas? I recognise that name. A picture comes into my head of a pretty girl in the year below me at school. Not just ordinary pretty, but 'stare at in complete envy pretty'. The sort of pretty that gets a girl into trouble. And now it looked like she *was* in trouble. Big trouble. I remember she seemed a lot older than me, even though she was a whole year younger. But some girls are like that. Born with boobs, Mum would say.

Poor Joanne, I think. I bet the 'man' she was seen talking to was her boyfriend. They probably went too far and she got herself pregnant and now she and her boyfriend have run off together because they don't know what else to do. They'll have to come back home and get married though, whether they want to or not. It's the only way they'll ever be able to live with the shame of it all.

I'm puzzled. Is this why Mum and Dad sat up waiting for me last night? Because a girl's run off with her boyfriend and they thought I was out with a fella getting myself into trouble too? I'd be pretty narked if it wasn't partly true. I *was* out with a boy, but I wasn't getting myself into trouble. I'd never do that. Did they see Beau, then? Did they see me getting on his bike? I thought I'd been so careful.

Or maybe they think something else has happened to Joanne Thomas. Maybe they think there's a murderer on the loose. One that's prowling around the fairground preying on young girls. They'd have to think the worst then, wouldn't they?

There's no point in saying anything to them this morning though. They're not talking to each other and they're ignoring me too. Like it's my fault that Mum's got herself another fella. They've both got faces like statues. If they smiled or spoke the stone would crack and crumble and their heads might fall off.

Breakfast this morning is a bundle of laughs. It's like being at a funeral. Dad's all ashen-faced. He doesn't touch his eggs. He just slurps his tea and smokes his fags. There's so much smoke wafting around the kitchen, I wouldn't be surprised if a passing neighbour doesn't call out the fire brigade. And as for Mum – she takes one bite of her toast, bursts into tears and runs from the room.

And they're meant to be the adults.

I've still got to peel the potatoes though. Life goes on. The world still needs chips. Apparently. I imagine I'm cutting every chip for Beau. I have to make them perfect. No trace of skin and all of them an even length and thickness. I don't know when he'll come again and it doesn't really matter. Because I know he *will* come again, in his own time.

I counted out all my savings earlier this morning. I've got almost ten pounds. More than enough for a leather jacket. First thing Saturday, I'm getting the bus to Shepherd's Bush market. I'm going to buy some eyeliner too and some tight denim jeans. I want to look like the girl on Chelsea Bridge. I want to drape myself against Beau and look like I really belong.

I wonder what Jackie would make of Beau. Not that I care what she thinks. He's not the clean and tidy sort, that's for sure. Not like the fellas that work at Garton's. Beau wouldn't get all dressed up in a tie and suit to go to a dance.

Fellas like Beau make old women tut and shake their heads and cross the road to avoid them. That's why I like him, I think. He's not like most fellas. Just like I'm not like most girls. I pick out another potato from the sack next to me. Mum and Dad can't have seen me with Beau last night. Mum would have had a fit if she had. She'd think Beau was a bad sort straight away, just because he rides a motorcycle. But I don't care what Mum thinks either. Why should I? After what she's done.

Speak of the devil. Mum comes into the room and puts her hand on my shoulder. I stiffen and carry on peeling the potato in my hand. 'Violet, love,' she says. 'There's some things you need to know . . . obviously . . . after last night.' She sniffs and blows her nose.

'Uh huh,' I murmur, like I really don't care one way or the other. I concentrate on the potato. I'm trying to peel the skin so it stays all in one piece. I used to peel apples like this, with Jackie. If we managed to get the skin off all in one piece we would drop them on the floor. However they landed would spell out the initials of our future husbands. At least that's what Brenda would tell us. I'm thinking it would be quite difficult to get a spiral of potato peeling to land on the floor in the shape of the letter B.

'We need to talk, Violet,' Mum continues. 'I don't know what you know already . . . or what you think you know. But . . . well, it's only fair that Norma is told the truth the same time as you. She's coming here after she's finished work, and your dad and me have decided not to open the shop tonight, so . . . there'll be plenty of time for us to . . . sort everything out.'

My heart sinks. Shut the shop! Mum and Dad have never shut the shop. Dad's favourite boast is how he kept the shop going all through the war. Fish and potatoes were one of the few things not rationed. 'Did my bit to keep the country going,' he always says. 'Would've been a rum do if folks couldn't have had their fish suppers.'

If a war and even the Blitz couldn't shut the shop but Mum's announcement can, it's got to be really, really bad. It's got to be the worst thing ever.

Divorce.

The dirtiest word of all. A word that makes Mum's lips pucker like a prune. A word that's only ever whispered. I can't believe Mum would even consider talking about it, let alone do it! Sally Hayes was the only girl at school who came from a broken home. The only girl whose parents had actually *divorced*. Nobody was allowed to go to her house to play and she was never invited anywhere. It was like she had the measles or fleas or something else catching. Would Mum really do that to us? And would Dad really let her?

83

'So . . .' says Mum. 'You can have the afternoon off now. But don't go off anywhere, will you? Or, at least make sure you're back by five. I won't ask where you were last night. Just be careful though. Won't you?'

I drop the half-peeled potato back into the bucket. Splashes of cold muddy water land on my legs. *Just be careful.* Did she mean be careful of fairground murderers or be careful of something else? Be careful of boys who might want to take advantage of me? Or be careful of spotting your own mother in Battersea Park canoodling with another man?

Five hours is a long time to wait. It's a long time to wait for anything, but it's especially long if you're waiting to find out what your future might be. What will happen to the shop? Will Mum move out? Will I have to stay and look after Dad? Will I be stuck there for ever now? What will happen if the shop closes? Will I ever see Beau again? Will I have to go and live with Norma and Raymond and live on a diet of frozen fish fingers? Five hours is a long time to wait for all hell to break loose.

I take back my copy of *The Country Girls* to the library. Miss Read raises her eyebrows as I pass the book back to her over the desk. 'You should read it,' I say to her. 'It's brilliant.'

She sniffs and colours slightly and I know instantly that she already has read it. I smile to myself as I think of her tucked up in bed with her hair in rollers, a cup of cocoa at her side, a cat asleep at her feet and a copy of *The Country Girls* in her hands. I wonder if she blushed when she read the rude bits. Perhaps she's not such a stick-in-the-mud after all.

The hush and warmth of the library helps to quiet the thoughts that have been banging around in my head like flies trapped in a jar. I go to the Family Health section first, and after flicking past *Bringing up Baby*, *Life Saving and Water Safety* and *First Aid for Beginners*, I pull out a book called *The Good Housekeeping Marriage Book (Twelve Steps to a Happy Marriage)*. It's all about courtship, getting engaged, the Wedding, working wives, having children, managing money . . . there's nothing about the twelve steps to a happy divorce though. Not even one step to a happy divorce. It's such a terrible word it can't even be written down. I consider for a moment asking Miss Read if she knows of any good books on the subject of divorce. But I think she might throw me out. It would be like asking her if she knows any good books on the subject of

S. E. X !

I go to the reference section instead and run my fingers along the spines of the Encyclopaedia Britannica. I find VAN–VIR, and turn the pages until I find the entry, VIOLET. It says that there are over two hundred species of violets but that the flowers of the violet are solitary and irregular in form. That sounds about right. Next, I find BAR–BEC and read that BEAU as a name means beautiful, admirer or sweetheart, and that Beau Wilkes was a character in the book *Gone with the Wind*. I picture Beau on his motorcycle flying into the wind across Chelsea Bridge and I think that his mum must have known something about her son when she gave him the name Beau. She must have seen the spark of something in his baby-blue eyes and felt the stirrings of adventure in his tiny limbs.

I carry on pulling volumes of encyclopaedias off the shelf. I find DIO–DRO and read under DIVORCE that in the old days a wife could only divorce a husband for three reasons.

1. If he committed murder.
2. If he was caught preparing poisons.
3. If he violated tombs.

But a husband could divorce a wife for loads of reasons. He could even divorce her if she went to a fair or the theatre without his permission. I presume going to a park with a fair *in it* counted as the same thing. Hard luck, Mum. Dad could divorce you with just one click of his fingers. I pile the books on the table next to me. Miss Read looks across and frowns. She likes everything neat and in its place, but she can't say anything to me because even though she thinks the books belong to her, they don't. They belong to everybody.

Under SOU–STE, I learn that Steatopygia is the name for a really fat bottom. There's a certain tribe in Africa called the Hottentots who are famous for the size of their behinds. I laugh to myself when I think about Mrs Robinson and her five fish suppers. She's definitely got Steatopygia and she doesn't even know it. Miss Read sidles up to me. She's got the opposite of Steatopygia, whatever that is. She's got no bottom at all; her back just joins her legs in one long straight line. I wonder how she gets her knickers to stay up. 'Closing in five minutes,' she whispers, even though I'm the only person left in the whole library. She begins to pick up the encyclopaedias and slots them back in place on the shelf with efficient little thuds.

I wish I had thought to hide. I wish that earlier, when Miss Read had been busy stamping books, I'd crawled under the bottom shelf of the history section, tucked my arms and legs tight to my sides and made myself as small as possible until the last person had left and Miss Read had turned off the lights and locked the library doors. I could have stayed here all night then. I could have pushed some chairs together to make a bed and found an old coat in the lost property box to keep me warm. I could have gone into Miss Read's little room at the back where she makes herself hot drinks and eaten her packet of Lemon Puff biscuits for my tea. If I'd done all that, I wouldn't have to go home now and listen to Mum make a confession that will change all our lives for ever. I want to stay in this 'before' place for a while longer, because I'll never be able to come back to it again.

But it's too late. 'Off you go then, Violet. I'm locking up now.' Miss Read's not even bothering to whisper any more. It's getting dark outside. I thrust my hands in my anorak pockets and head down Lavender Hill and back on to the High Street. All the shops are closing now. I imagine Norma leaving Fine Fare, waving her goodbyes to the other till girls, buttoning up her coat, pulling on her gloves and hanging her handbag over her arm. She'll be wondering about what Mum wants and worrying about what Raymond's going to do for his tea, but she'll be click clacking along the pavements and checking her stockings for ladders at the same time. She'll go mad when Mum tells her the news. Norma can't cope with anything shocking; even bright colours give her a headache. Whatever happens, it's not going to be pretty, that's for sure.

I walk as slowly as I can. The last thing I want to do is bump into Norma. A couple of motorcycles whine past me, up the High Street. I immediately hope that one of the riders is Beau, but of course it isn't. I watch their backs as they disappear around the corner at the top of the street. They're not even wearing leather jackets. I try not to be disappointed. Beau could be anywhere. He doesn't have to walk, or wait for buses or trains. He can just jump on his bike and go wherever he likes. I wonder if he lives in Battersea and what his house is like and if I'll ever get to see it. He must have a family and . . . a life. What does he do when he's not stealing girls from chip shops and taking them halfway across London to see the view?

I'm home before I know it. There's a scribbled note stuck to the shop window that says, *Closed due to unforeseen circumstances. Open as usual tomorrow.* A man and a woman are walking away, grumbling to each other. 'Great. Bloody eggs on toast again then.'

I take a deep breath. It's time for Mum to reveal her *unforeseen circumstances*. Time for her to drop the bomb and blow our lives to pieces. I open the gate, but before I can walk through it, Norma comes clacking up to me. 'Violet,' she gasps, as though she's run all the way from Fine Fare, 'what's all this about then? What's going on? Why's the shop shut?'

I shrug. 'You'd better ask Mum all that.'

'But, everything is all right, isn't it? It's not like Mum to come and see me at work. And she wouldn't say anything. Just bought a packet of tea and told me to come straight here after I'd finished. Well, it'd better be quick, whatever it is. Don't want Raymond coming home and finding me not there. He'll be worried sick.' She pauses for breath. 'Oh God! That's it, isn't it? Someone's sick. Is it Dad? Is it Mum?' Her voice starts to quiver.

'Nobody's sick,' I tell her, as I follow her through the gate and round to the back door. 'We're here now. Just let Mum tell you.'

She pushes open the door. 'Mum?' she shouts. And then she stops, her hand still on the door knob. She's blocking the way in. I can't see past her. But I can hear the silence. It's like the world has stopped. Then Norma starts murmuring, 'Oh my God, oh my God, oh my God.' She drops her handbag on the floor and rushes into the kitchen. I step in after her. My heart's pounding and for an awful moment I expect to see blood splattered everywhere and Mum lying dead on the kitchen floor with Dad standing over her holding a dripping knife.

But instead, I can't make any sense of what I do see. Mum's alive, sitting at the kitchen table with a weird look on her face, like she's half laughing, half crying. Dad's nowhere to be seen. But, like a scene from some mixed-up, crazy nightmare, Donkey Jacket Man is sitting at the kitchen table too and Norma is clinging on to him for all she's worth, still sobbing, 'Oh my God, oh my God, oh my God.'

It's Mum who finally says something. Norma is beyond talking. She's gulping and hiccoughing and wiping snot from her nose on to one of Mum's tea towels. Donkey Jacket Man is smoothing her hair and whispering, 'I know, I know. I'm sorry, I'm sorry.'

Mum holds her hand out to me. But I don't move. I just keep staring. 'Violet,' she says gently. 'Violet. This is your brother. This is Joseph.'

Shattered Glass

I stare at the man sitting at the kitchen table. The same man that I saw Mum canoodling with in the park. The one I thought she was going to run away with. He's my brother? My dead brother Joseph? I can't make any sense of it.

'Violet?' says Mum. 'Aren't you at least going to say hello? Joseph's been looking forward to meeting his baby sister.'

Donkey Jacket Man untangles himself from Norma and looks across at me. 'Hi, Violet,' he says. 'It's good to meet you.'

I can't speak. Just because Mum's telling me this man is my brother doesn't mean I can suddenly love a stranger, or even *like* a stranger. He's still just the man in the park.

'Violet!' Mum hisses. 'Don't be so rude.'

'It's okay,' says Donkey Jacket Man. 'It's a shock. I know it is.' He smiles at me. It's an awkward sort of smile, like he doesn't know if he should be doing it or not. I don't smile back. My face won't let me. There's a thousand questions racing through my head, but the first one I ask is, 'Where's Dad?'

Mum nods towards the front room. The glow disappears from her face for an instant. 'He's in there,' she says. Then she puts her hand on Norma's shoulder. 'Come on, love,' she says. 'Sit down and have a cuppa. Calm yourself down a bit. I know it's the biggest shock ever. But look . . .' She cups Donkey Jacket Man's face in her hands and loudly kisses the top of his head. 'He's here. He's really here. Our Joseph has come back to us. He's come back from the dead.'

A shiver runs through me. Not a creepy shiver. He's obviously not back from the dead. He's not Jesus, is he? It's more of a 'this is too weird' shiver. A 'how do they know it's him' shiver? That it's *really* him? He looks nothing like the nineteen-year-old boy in the photograph on the mantelpiece. The one who's been dead for nearly seventeen years. The man sitting at the kitchen table has much darker hair for one thing. It's long and scruffy and he has a beard to match. His face is ruddy too, like he's spent his life working in the fields. He's broad and hard, nothing like the soft-looking boy in the photograph. And how can he not be dead, when there's a letter from the War Office to prove it?

I turn my back on them all and walk through to the front room. I need to see Dad. I need to know why he's not in the kitchen with everyone else. First thing I see when I walk in the room is that the photograph has gone. The mantelpiece is bare. Dad's sitting in his chair with his head in his hands. 'Dad?' I touch his shoulder. 'What's going on? Is that really Joseph in there?'

He doesn't answer for a moment. He rubs his face in his hands and groans, then he draws his hands up over his face and pushes them through his hair. He sighs and slumps back in his chair with his eyes closed. I see then that he's got the photograph in his lap. 'Dad?' I say again. I shake his shoulder this time. 'Dad? Tell me what's going on.'

'For God's sake, Violet!' he bellows.

I jump back.

'Can't you just . . . for one minute . . . just leave me . . .' He thumps the arms of his chair so hard that the photograph falls from his lap and lands on the floor. There's a crack and the sound of splintering glass. Dad bends down and picks up the photograph frame. He turns it over. The image of Joseph, so smart in his battledress, is now lost underneath the burst of shattered glass. 'That,' says Dad, stabbing his finger at the photograph, 'that is my son Joseph. That is the war hero.' His voice is quavering with anger. 'But, him in there . . .' He points towards the kitchen. 'He's not my son! He's a coward. And a deserter!' He spits the words out with such hate that flecks of his spittle land on my arm. 'How dare he come back here. How dare he show his face.' He's talking to himself now. He's forgotten that I'm here. But I've heard enough anyway. I'm beginning to understand.

A deserter. A deserter. The words echo around my head. My brother, the hero, is a deserter. My brother, the hero, didn't give his life for his country. My brother, the hero, didn't die in a plane crash over the French countryside. Parts of him aren't buried and rotting away in fields of corn. He didn't die at all. He wasn't ever a hero. He just ran away.

I slip back into the kitchen. Mum and Norma are huddled up close to Joseph, like they're scared that if they move too far away he'll disappear again. Mum looks up at me. 'How's Dad doing?' she asks grudgingly.

'Don't know,' I say. 'Not too happy though, is he?'

Mum's face hardens. 'Him and his stupid pride. How can he do it?' Her voice rises to a wail. 'How can he put his pride above his own son?'

Joseph leans in to pat her on the arm. 'It's okay, Mum. It was never going to be easy. I knew that. Just give him time. He'll come round.'

It's the strangest thing. To hear this stranger call my mum, Mum. He doesn't have the right to call her Mum. He lied to her for nearly seventeen years. He let her think he was dead. And for all that time she's been dead inside too, because of him.

'You're a deserter,' I say to him. 'Doesn't that mean you'll get shot?'

'Violet!' Norma gasps.

'Well, it's true, isn't it? Deserting the army is a crime, isn't it? You'll go to prison at least.'

'Stop it, Violet!' Mum glares at me.

'No. She's right.' Joseph leans back in his chair. The empty chair, I realise. The chair that has always been waiting for him. 'It was a crime,' he says. 'It still is, I suppose.' His voice has an odd burr to it. It's like a Battersea voice with an added ingredient. 'But good old Winston Churchill pardoned us all. All of us who chose disgrace over the grave, he found it in his heart to forgive us.' He says all this with a sneer, as though he never wanted to be forgiven. 'Twenty-fourth of February, 1953. The day I stopped being a criminal.'

'But that was eight years ago,' I say. 'Why didn't you come back then?'

'I couldn't,' he says. 'It's hard to explain. It's complicated. But I just couldn't.'

'Violet, please,' Mum says. 'Don't make him explain himself again. It's enough that he's back with us now. Give him some space.'

I look at her in amazement. 'So he can just waltz back in here after all these years, a brother I've never met, and I can't ask him where he's been?'

'In time, Violet. In time,' she says.

In time? I want to say. Hasn't seventeen years been long enough? Haven't I got a right to know where he's been and why? But I'm tired all of a sudden. And so angry. All the unanswered questions are giving me a headache. 'You're all crazy,' I shout. 'The lot of you. You're all bloody crazy.' Then I slam out of the back door and before I know it, my feet are taking me along the pavement towards Jackie's house. It's the only place I've got to go.

I pause outside her gate. There's a light on in the front room, yellow and hazy behind the nets. I stare at the window. I know every detail of that room in there, like it was my own home. There's the battered green sofa with lace antimacassars covering its back and arms, there's the china cabinet in one corner full of Brenda's flowery plates and cups and saucers that she keeps for best but never uses and there's the little wooden table with the wireless on it. There's the brown tiled fireplace with a mirror hanging over it and the brown and green rag rug in front of the grate with its dozens of scorch marks made by fallen coals. Then in pride of place in the other corner is the television set that Jackie persuaded Brenda to rent from Radio Rentals.

I miss being in that room. I miss squashing up on that sofa next to Jackie to watch our programmes. *Coronation Street* is her favourite, *Dixon of Dock Green* is mine. I've always fancied myself as a copper. I think I'd be really good at solving crimes with my knack of knowing what people are thinking and feeling. But fat chance of that ever happening.

Jackie always kept me up to date with the storylines when I missed the programmes because of working in the shop. I'm way behind now though and Dad would never get us a television set. Waste of money, he'd say. What's the point when we've already got a wireless?

There's shadowy figures moving about behind the nets. I imagine Jackie and Benda settling themselves on the sofa with a plate of biscuits. Would it be so bad if I went inside and joined them? I'm burning to tell someone about Joseph, and Jackie's the only one who'll understand that this is the most amazingly awful thing that's ever happened. She won't think I'm boring now. She'll want to know me again. She'll want to be in the thick of it all and when people find out about Joseph, she'll want to be able to say, 'Well, of course, I've known about it for ages.'

As I walk around to Jackie's back door, I feel like I'm dreaming. It's all so unreal. But even though I'm angry and upset and really pissed off, there's a part of me that's really glad this has happened. Because, the one good thing about my brother coming back from the dead is that Jackie will want to be my best friend again.

'You've got to be joking?' Jackie's all agog, just like I knew she'd be. She puts her half-eaten custard cream back on the plate and shuffles sideways so I can join her and Brenda on the sofa. 'I can't believe it,' she says. 'He's turned up, just like that? After all this time? Where's he been for seventeen years?'

'Oh, love!' says Brenda. 'Your mum must be beside herself!'

'I don't understand,' says Jackie. 'Where *has* he been? What's he been doing all this time? Did he lose his memory or something?'

'He didn't lose his memory,' I say. 'And I don't know where he's been. All I know is he's sitting in our kitchen right now, large as life.'

Brenda puts her hands over her mouth. 'Well I never.' She shakes her head in wonder. 'It's a bloody miracle. A proper bloody miracle!' There's silence for a minute as news of 'the miracle' sinks in. But then Brenda whips her head round and looks at me sharply. 'But why are you here, love? You should be home with your family at a time like this. Or was there something you wanted? Is there anything we can do?'

I shake my head. 'I just wanted to let you know,' I say. 'And to be honest, it's been such a shock, I just had to get out for a while.'

'Oh, love. Of course,' says Brenda. She stands up and brushes biscuit crumbs from her apron. 'Of course it's been a shock. I'm sorry, love. I'm so sorry.' She bustles to the kitchen. 'A drop of brandy is what's called for, I reckon. A drop of brandy all round.'

As soon as Brenda's gone, Jackie grabs my hands. 'Oh my God, Violet! This is crazy. I can't believe it. I just can't believe it!' Her face is flushed and her eyes are all huge and glittery. 'What's he like? she whispers. 'Is he all handsome and heroic? Can I meet him? I bet it'll be in the papers, won't it? I bet it'll be front-page news!'

I shrug. 'I don't know,' I say. 'It's probably best if it's not in the papers. It's probably best if nobody knows he's back, actually.'

'But, why? It's amazing. It's unbelievable. Like Nan says, it's a miracle!'

'I suppose so,' I say. But it doesn't feel like a miracle. It feels all complicated and messy and confusing. 'Could you do me a favour?' I ask her. 'Could you keep it a secret for now? Just between you, me and your nan? I don't think Mum and Dad would want anyone knowing just yet.'

Jackie nods, seriously. She's always loved secrets. 'Of course,' she says. She mimes zipping up her lips. 'Me and Nan won't say a word.' She leans over and hugs me. She smells sweet, of burnt sugar and hair lacquer and custard creams. 'I've missed you, Vi,' she says. 'But, I've just been so busy. Life's a whirl these days, isn't it?'

Brenda comes back carrying a tray with three little glasses of amber liquid. 'Here you are, girls,' she says. 'Get this down you.' We clink glasses. I shudder as the brandy burns my throat. But soon it begins to warm my insides and the familiar cosiness of Brenda's front room wraps itself around me. Brenda swallows her brandy and sighs. 'That's better. Nothing like a drop of the good stuff for shock.' She shakes her head. 'Still can't believe it, though,' she says. 'I remember him being called up like it was only yesterday. So proud of them all, we were. All those young men going off to fight for us.' She sips some more brandy. 'And so many of them never came back.' Her eyes glisten. 'Your mum must be over the moon. It's like all her prayers have been answered.'

I nod, thinking of how young and girlish Mum has seemed lately and how I thought it was all because of a man and because of love. And I was right in a way. She's got her first love back. She's got her perfect son back, when she thought she'd lost him for ever.

'And you really don't know where he's been?' Brenda asks. 'Or why he hasn't come home before now?'

'No,' I say. 'And like I said to Jackie, if you could just keep it all to yourselves for now . . . you know . . . until Mum and Dad sort things out . . .'

'Of course,' she says. 'You can trust us, Violet. You know you can.'

I smile at them both and they smile back with bright eager faces. I feel like I've given them some sort of unexpected gift. Something they didn't know they wanted but are really happy to have.

'So . . .' I say to Jackie. 'How's things at Garton's?'

She curls her feet up under her bottom and stretches her arms above her head. 'Same as always,' she says. And, just like that, things are back to how they used to be. Brenda switches on the television set and gets out her knitting and me and Jackie slope upstairs to her bedroom.

She shows me her new Dansette record player. It's bright red and cost her a whole month's wages. We lie side by side on her bed and listen to Billy Fury, The Everly Brothers, Ricky Nelson and Helen Shapiro. Jackie rolls on to her front and hangs over the edge of the bed to reach underneath it. She brings up a packet of Embassy cigarettes, a box of matches and an ashtray. 'Want one?' she says, waving the packet in front of my face. I slide a cigarette out and wait for Jackie to light hers before I lean in towards the match. I manage to inhale without coughing this time and it makes me think of Beau and how he laughed at me and called me a virgin.

Jackie tells me that she's been seeing a fella called Colin Trindle. He works in the packing department at Garton's. 'He's ever so nice,' she tells me. 'He kisses like a dream and earns seven pounds a week!' She lowers her eyes. 'If I tell you something, promise you'll keep it to yourself?' she says.

I promise her. And I get the old feeling back for a minute. The old, 'it's Jackie and me for ever' feeling.

'He asked me to do it, Violet,' she whispers. Then she puts her hand over her mouth like she shouldn't have said what she said, and looks at me with wide eyes. 'I've let him touch me,' she says between her fingers. 'You know. Down there.'

I don't know what to say.

'Are you shocked?' she asks.

I know what she's telling me, of course I do. And I am shocked. I'm completely shocked, and I feel sick too – with jealousy. It's another thing she's done without me. 'What was it like?' I ask, before I can stop myself. 'What will you do, you know, if he gets you pregnant?'

Jackie smiles a secret smile. 'It was lovely,' she says. 'Better than I thought it would be. And I won't get pregnant, cos if I decide to go the whole way, he's got some of those French letters.'

Now I don't know what she's talking about. What the hell's a French letter? But I don't want to look stupid, so I just say, 'Well, that's all right, then.'

There's a bit of an awkward silence. Then she asks me if I'm seeing anyone yet and I've half a mind to tell her about Beau. But I don't even know his last name and he only held my hand. He didn't even kiss me. And besides, he's still too shadowy. I can't let myself believe that he's real yet and I'm scared that If I talk about him it'll turn out that he's just a figment of my imagination. So I tell Jackie that no, I'm not seeing anyone and she says that in that case I've got to go with her to the next Friday-night dance. 'You can meet the girls from Garton's properly this time. And . . .' She winks. 'I'll introduce you to Colin.'

She gets up from the bed and begins to dance around the bedroom. She jerks her arms up and down and moves her hips from side to side like she's trying to shake a tail. 'Come on,' she says. 'Dance with me.'

I wish I could. But I feel too stiff and self-conscious. I can't let go of myself like Jackie can. I think I've always been like that, but I've only really noticed since Jackie went off into the world and left me behind.

'I'd better go,' I say. 'It's getting late.'

Brenda hugs me before I leave. 'You know where we are,' she says.

'Let me know when I can come and meet Joseph,' Jackie says. 'And don't forget the dance next Friday. No excuses!' She winks at me, wriggles her hips and starts singing Helen Shapiro at me . . . *Walking back to happiness, woopah, oh, yeah, yeah* . . .

As Jackie's wriggling around, I see a glint of silver around her neck. I put my hand to my own throat and feel the silver V nestling there; our matching necklaces, the symbol of our friendship. And if Jackie hasn't taken hers off, that must mean something.

I walk back home with Helen Shapiro singing in my head, but I don't walk back to happiness. Just to Mum sitting on her own in the kitchen cradling a cup of tea. 'Good of you to leave like that,' she says in her best sarcastic voice. 'You never even spoke two words to him.'

'What did you expect?' I say. 'Happy families?'

'Actually, yes,' she snaps back. 'That's exactly what I expect.' She digs around in her housecoat pocket, pulls out the piece of paper she's been hiding there and shakes it in my face. 'When I got this letter from Joseph, it was the happiest day of my life.' Her voice cracks. 'My boy's back, Violet. My boy's come home.'

I wish she wouldn't cry. Not for him anyway. She might be a pain sometimes, but I don't like to see her upset. I put my arm across her shoulder and try to comfort her. 'It's all right, Mum,' I say. 'Don't cry.'

'We should all be so happy,' she sobs. 'But your dad cares more about what people will think when they find out that Joseph deserted the army than the fact he's alive! And you don't seem to care at all.'

'Mum . . .' I say. I think about when I first saw her sitting on the bench in the park in her kingfisher-blue headscarf and her red lipstick. I remember how I felt when I saw her holding hands with a strange man. 'You've got to give us more time to get used to it all,' I say. 'When I saw you in the park with Joseph, I thought he was your lover. I thought you were going to leave Dad and run away with another man!'

Instead of her laughing at the idea and telling me not to be so daft, she whips her head around to glare at me. 'That's disgusting, Violet,' she spits. 'How could you have thought such a thing? He's your brother!'

She might as well have slapped me in the face. 'He's not my brother,' I shout back at her. 'He's a stranger. And he lied to you for seventeen years.' Mum's face flushes. 'You can't make me love him,' I say, before I slam out the room. 'You can't make me love a stranger.'

Bus Stop

It's Saturday. I've got a pocket full of pound notes and I'm sitting on the top deck of the number 49 on my way to Shepherd's Bush. Mum decided to talk to me again this morning, after ignoring me all day yesterday. She told me that Joseph is staying in lodgings until things settle down a bit. Which means, until Dad can bear to look him in the face. I'm not sure he ever will though. I saw the photograph, still in its shattered frame, at the bottom of the bin. The telegram and the tortoiseshell frame have disappeared too. What's the point in displaying a lie on the mantelpiece?

Mum also told me not to speak to strangers and to be home no later than three o'clock. They found that girl, you see. Joanne Thomas. They found her body yesterday. She hadn't run off with her boyfriend and she wasn't pregnant. It was much worse than that. She'd been raped and strangled. They found her in the old pump house in Battersea Park. Apparently someone had managed to break the lock on the door and drag her inside. When they'd finished with her they covered her body in dusty leaves and pieces of old brick that had fallen from the pump house walls. They hadn't locked the door behind themselves though, and a dog (a spaniel they said) had pushed his way through the door and when his owner found him he was already chewing on one of Joanne's shoes.

Now everyone's freaking out. At the bus stop, the air was thick with snatches of gossip. Someone knew her mother and from all accounts she was a good girl; quiet and sensible. Someone else had another opinion. Her skirts were too short. And why was she out on her own at the funfair anyway? A girl of fifteen shouldn't be out on her own in the evening. Have the police got any leads? Could the murderer be someone local? It couldn't be, could it? No one around here would do such a thing. People seemed to be talking about it like they thought it was her fault. On and on they went.

I was glad when the bus arrived to shut them up. But I still can't stop thinking about it. This sort of thing only happens to other people in other places. It doesn't happen around the corner from where you live. But it has, and now everyone's looking at everyone else in a different way and the funfair's been closed and the only people out walking in the park now are the police.

I remember being at the pump house last Saturday. I remember feeling that something was wrong. And it was. Joanne's body was already in there. There was a real ghost inside those walls. A Sleeping Beauty, asleep for ever. There'll be no prince coming to wake Joanne up. I shudder. I think about how she must have looked; her blonde hair all tangled with leaves and twigs and her white skirt all muddied and ruined. I imagine what it was like in there. Did the rain find its way through the gaps in the bricks and spatter down on her cold skin? Was it quiet in there and dark? Or did the sun filter through the ivy-covered windows to warm her body and did the faraway voices of children in the playground and the screams of riders from the funfair keep her company while she was waiting patiently to be found?

A horrible thought crosses my mind. I can't help it, but I'm thinking that at least Joanne will be remembered for ever now. Everybody knows her name and her photograph will be displayed pride of place on her parents' mantelpiece.

I wonder if I saw the killer that day without knowing it. Was he wandering around, bold as brass, all pleased with himself and with what he had done? I think about Mr Harper, the park keeper, and how he gives everyone the creeps with his droopy skin and yellow teeth and the way he looks up girls' skirts and always gets a funny look on his face if anyone kicks a ball where they shouldn't. Did he murder Joanne? Did he do those awful things to her before he put his hands around her neck and squeezed until she had no breath left? Or was it someone else? Someone who works on the funfair? Someone whose face is so familiar that I wouldn't even notice him?

I look around the top deck of the bus. He could be here now. He could be that man over there. The thin one sitting looking out of the window; the one with his hair cut so short you can see the pale skin of his scalp. Or he could be that one there with the bag of shopping on his lap or the one sitting opposite me chewing his fingernails. But it's Mr Harper's face I keep seeing. I've always known there was something not right about him. And I'm not usually wrong.

The bus pulls in and the cheery conductor announces we've arrived at Shepherd's Bush. I push poor Joanne and Mr Harper from my mind as I jump off the bus on to the pavement. The market's buzzing. I push through the crowds, past stalls piled high with fruit and vegetables and others hung with colourful shirts and denim jeans, and more stacked with cheap jewellery and second-hand books. The air is vibrating with the shouts of market traders and the chatter of shoppers. There's people spilling out of cafés and music blaring from open doorways. The air smells of fried bacon and new possibilities.

I wander up and down the market aisles with my hand in my pocket holding tight to the wad of pound notes. I spot the jackets on a stall way down the end. There are rows of them, black and gleaming like liquorice. The stall holder, a pale, stringy man with a neatly trimmed beard, looks me up and down as I finger the warm leather of the jacket nearest to me. 'Don't touch the goods unless you're thinking of buying,' he says sharply before turning his back. He clearly thinks I'm a fake and a time waster.

'How much?' I ask. That gets his attention and suddenly he can't do enough for me. He stands in front of me and cocks his head to one side, sizing me up.

'Right,' he says. 'Try this one first.' He slips a jacket from its hanger and hands it over to me. I take off my anorak and let it drop to the floor. I think of a snake shedding its skin. I look down at my old anorak, all shrivelled and washed out, and I kick it to one side. I slide my arms into the sleeves of the leather jacket. It's heavier than I expected; I imagine it's what a suit of armour must feel like.

'No. Too big on your shoulders,' the stallholder says. 'Try this one.'

The next one is perfect. I know it as soon as it folds around me. It's like it's mine already. I smell the soapy warmth of the leather and listen to how it creaks when I bend my arms. 'I'll take this one,' I say. It's £9 8s, but I don't even blink as I pull the notes from my pocket.

As I walk away, the stallholder calls after me. 'Hey! You forgot your coat!' He's waving my anorak at me.

'Keep it!' I yell back. 'It's all yours!'

I love it. I love this new jacket. I feel different already. I don't have to be a shrinking Violet any more; I can be whoever I want to be. I find a Boots the Chemist and spend ages choosing an eyeliner and a cake of mascara. After I've paid for them, I go to the underground public toilets on the Green. It stinks of bleach and stale pee down here and the big mirror over the sinks is cracked and stained. I polish a section with my sleeve until I can see my face staring back at me.

The eyeliner is in a small bottle with a tiny paintbrush. I take off my glasses and I carefully draw a thick line across each of my eyelids and add a little flick at the outer edges. I have to push my face really close to the mirror to be able to see properly. The lines are a bit wobbly, but not bad for a first attempt. Next, I spit on to the cake of mascara and mix it to a paste, then I brush the paste onto my lashes, top and bottom. I try not to blink until I'm sure it's all dry.

I look like someone else now. Older, like a 'don't mess with me' Rocker girl. Like the girls from Chelsea Bridge. But that might just be because I haven't got my oh-so attractive, blue-rimmed National Health specs on. I shove them away in my pocket, because although everything's a bit of a blur without them, at least my new look won't be ruined.

Back out on the street I realise that as people walk past me, they actually notice me. Some of them even turn around for a second look. I don't hurry along like I usually do. I don't stare down at the pavement. I walk slowly, enjoying myself. It feels like I've got all the time in the world. I can go wherever I want, when I want, and I can hold my head up high. Nobody can touch me.

I saunter to the bus stop. I imagine being back on Chelsea Bridge. I imagine Beau standing next to me, being proud of how I fit in with everyone else. I imagine how the other girls there might talk to me again and tell me their names. I want to see Beau again so much now, that I'm scared I might never see him again.

A girl with pointy boobs and a tight skirt bumps into me as she wiggles past. I'm about to say sorry, when I realise I don't have to any more. Instead I say, 'Hey, watch where you're going!' She opens her mouth to protest, but when she sees my leather jacket she mumbles sorry to *me* instead.

All the bright, mad colours of Shepherd's Bush whirl around me as I feel myself grow taller and stronger. I join the queue at the bus stop and tap my foot impatiently. I zip up my leather jacket, then unzip it again, enjoying the chunky sound of the metal teeth. Eventually the bus appears at the end of the road and everyone picks up their bags of shopping and shuffles forward. I find a window seat and pull some coins from my pocket to pay for the ticket. The conductor is joking with some passengers up front, so I gaze out of the window while I'm waiting for him and that's why I don't see the last passengers to board; the ones who were late and had to jump on the bus as it moved away from the stop.

That's why it jolts me when, just as the conductor has torn a ticket off for me, someone from behind coughs and taps my shoulder. I turn around and my heart jumps into my throat when I see Joseph sitting there looking all smiley and pleased with himself.

'Hey,' he says. 'I wasn't sure if it was you. You look different.'

I turn around to face the front again, too shocked to reply. What the hell is he doing here? The bus judders, it's slowing down, and for a moment I wonder if I should get off at the next stop. He taps me on the shoulder again. 'Violet?'

I freeze.

He leans forward to whisper into my ear. 'Violet. Please? Why won't you talk to me?' His breath is hot and smells of onions.

The bus stops. I could get off right now. There's no reason why I can't. I could jump off at the last minute and run for it. He wouldn't chase me, would he? It would look bad if he did that, and someone would stop him.

But I don't jump off. The old Violet would have done. But the new Violet is better than that. The new Violet is ready for anything. Passengers get off and others get on. There's an empty seat next to me now. I hold my breath. Then, as the bus starts rolling again, he does what I knew he would and he slides into the empty seat. 'You don't mind, do you?' he says.

I shrug.

109

'I couldn't believe it when I saw you. I . . . I was hoping we could talk. Go somewhere maybe? We could get a coffee or something?'

'No thanks,' I say. 'I've got to be back by three.'

He flips his wrist to look at his watch. 'It's only half one,' he says. 'Come on.' He nudges me gently. 'Let me buy you a coffee and I can get to know my little sister.'

'Bit late, don't you think?' I snap back. 'I'm hardly little any more.'

'Look,' he says. 'I know this has all been a huge shock . . . and with Dad being how he is . . . it's not easy. But it hasn't exactly been easy for me either, you know. Please, Violet. At least give me a chance to explain.'

He's wringing his hands in his lap. His skin is brown and dusty and there's a couple of scars, like white scratches, on the backs of his hands. There's dirt under his nails and a thick gold band on his finger. 'Are you married?' I ask.

He shakes his head. 'No,' he says.

I point to his finger. 'What's the ring for then?'

He twists the ring round and round, but doesn't say anything.

'You're not divorced, are you?' I ask, adding it to the growing list of dirty words about him in my head. Deserter, liar, coward, divorcee . . .

He laughs, like it was a stupid question. 'No. I'm not divorced. It's just complicated, that's all.' The bus judders and pulls over to the next stop. 'Come on,' he says, changing the subject. 'A quick coffee?'

I follow him off the bus and we walk in silence along Old Brompton Road. He swings his arms like he's marching. We come to a buzzy little café with tables on the pavement covered in red and white check cloths. 'This okay?' he asks. We sit at a table and I fiddle with a plastic rose that's been stuck into a green glass bottle as a table decoration. A waitress comes and Joseph orders two coffees. He chews his fingernails and taps his feet as we wait. When the coffee arrives he offers me the sugar first and then we stir our drinks like stirring is going out of fashion. After a while, when the silence between us is so tight it's painful, he clears his throat.

'Okay, Violet,' he says. 'Ask away. Ask me anything you want.'

There's only one thing I really want to know. I look at him and he looks back at me. There's no twinkling stars in his eyes any more and the skin around them is crepey and grey. He doesn't look like he's slept since 1944. I think of the photograph that was on the mantelpiece my whole life, the photograph of the shiny young boy, that's now in the bin, probably covered in eggshells and tea leaves. The photograph of the boy I could never be better than, no matter how hard I tried. The photograph that was, as it turns out, just a big, fat lie.

'Were you ever a hero?' I ask him. 'Even for just a second?'

He looks at me for a long time, then shakes his head. 'I never wanted to be a hero, Violet. I just wanted to live.' He digs a cigarette from out of his pocket and I watch as it takes him three matches to light it. 'I was a welder before the war,' he says, as smoke trickles from his nostrils. 'Did Mum and Dad ever tell you that? I used to work in the chippie, but Mum wanted something better for me. Dad wasn't too happy at first, but in the end even he agreed that he wanted his son to do more with his life than he had. I was glad about that. I had plans, you see. I was going to get my own garage one day, earn a good living, save some money. Then I was going to get out of London. Go to Kent or somewhere and see if I could rent a piece of land. I wanted to grow my own crops, keep some cows. Be a farmer of sorts. Does that surprise you? But then the war came and planted a black full-stop right in the middle of it all.

'Everybody was enlisting at the beginning of the war. It was the thing to do. And Dad encouraged me. He wanted his son to do 'the right thing'. We all thought it was so exciting at first. I decided to volunteer for the RAF. I liked the idea of working with planes. And I knew some stuff about engineering, with the welding and all that. I had to go to Sheffield to enrol. First time I'd been out of London. Made me think that I wouldn't mind travelling. I was glad the war had come so that I had the chance to see some of the world.

'I didn't have a clue, Violet. I didn't have a clue.' He grinds his cigarette out on the ground and immediately lights another one.

'I went somewhere in Wales for my training. I can't remember where now. It's all a bit of a blur. But we had lessons in a classroom on how to operate a plane. We all thought we were so clever. I made some good friends there. I thought I'd know them for ever. But they were all killed. One after the other.'

Our coffee goes cold as Joseph talks. He's like a gushing tap; the words just pour out of him.

'It was all like a game at first,' he says. 'Like when I was a kid, playing with tin soldiers. None of it was real. But the last time I came back home, just before I had to go and join my squadron, was when it all became real. The bombing had started, you see. The night-time raids. People were dying. Homes were being destroyed. It wasn't a game any more. And I realised I didn't want to go away to fight. I wanted to stay at home. I wished I hadn't signed up. But I had no choice then. And Dad was so proud of me.

'And do you know what I thought? I thought how unfair it all was. Why were there some fellas that were allowed to stay behind and I wasn't? All those lucky enough to be in reserved occupations. The miners, the teachers, the railway men, the dockers and the farmers. I was so envious of them all, and I was terrified. But I couldn't show it. I had to be a brave young man.' He sucks deeply on his cigarette and blows the smoke furiously into the air.

'I think most of us knew we were pretending to be brave, but nobody could say anything. On the train on the way to the barracks there were some fellas that were sick. They laughed it off and said it must have been all the drink they'd had the evening before to celebrate their last night of freedom. But I knew it wasn't. I knew it was the terror that they couldn't stomach. Because I'd been sick myself, only I'd done it quietly, on the station platform while we were waiting for the train. I'd bent down to pretend to tie my boot laces and I'd vomited quickly and silently down onto the tracks.

'The fear never went away. Never. It was like having a rat gnawing away at your insides, day in and day out. I kept thinking of all the things I could have done if I'd been allowed to stay at home. I could have driven ambulances, I could have worked in an ammunition factory, I could have become a teacher or I could have gone to Kent and grown vegetables to help the war effort. But instead, I was just another young body; a pig on its way to the slaughterhouse.

'You can't imagine what it was like, Violet. It was a nightmare. A never-ending nightmare that I couldn't wake up from. But then it got worse. The first time I flew in a plane I thought my insides would fall out. Every time we were called to a briefing and sent out on a bombing raid, I thought it would be my last day on Earth. Every few days someone wouldn't make it back. There would be another empty chair in the mess hall.

'The last bombing raid we did, I knew it was going to be a big one because we were told there was two thousand gallons of fuel in the plane. That meant about ten hours of flying. We were ordered to fly to northern France, but during the afternoon, not at night when we usually flew. The pilot that day was a Canadian fella called Sidney Wagg. I knew he had a wife and a small baby at home because he carried their photograph everywhere, and whenever he flew he stuck the photograph on the control panel. I can still see their faces. She was a pretty girl and the baby had the chubbiest cheeks you can imagine.

'Before we left, we were given our wakey-wakey pills to keep us alert and the padre said his usual prayer – may you live long, die happy and be in heaven for ten days before the Devil knows you're there.

'I didn't want to die happy. I didn't want to die at all.

'But we flew to France and as we manoeuvred into line to start the bombing, I knew it was going to be the last time I ever viewed the world from the skies, unless I ended up in heaven. I don't know if it was the wakey-wakey pills having a more than usual strange effect on my mind, but instead of the job in hand, I couldn't help focusing on odd little details.

'There was a mole on the back of Sidney Wagg's neck that I'd never noticed before. It had a single black hair growing from its centre. His face was covered in a sheen of sweat, and even though he must have shaved that morning, I could already see a hint of his five o'clock shadow. And I couldn't stop looking at the photograph of his wife and baby. The collar of his wife's blouse had roses embroidered on it. I realised I didn't even know their names. And I didn't know if the baby was a boy or a girl.

'Then the bomb hit us. It came from above and knocked our wing off. I'd always imagined that moment and how terrified I'd be. But it wasn't like that. I was calm. Calmer than I'd been for months. I shouted at Sidney to bail out, but he wouldn't. He kept yelling that he could control it, that he could land the thing. But I didn't want to waste any time, so I ran to the escape hatch and bailed out. And then I was falling; even with the parachute the ground was coming up faster than I could have imagined. I kept hoping Sidney would follow me out, but just before I hit the ground there was a terrific noise and the plane was hit by enemy fire. I kept thinking how they'd all be together now; Sidney and his wife and their baby. But then I remembered that it was only a photograph and that it was only Sidney that had died.

'I was in a bad way when I hit the ground. My parachute was in tatters. And my arm was broken. It didn't hurt then, but I knew it was broken because a bone had ripped a hole in my shirt. But I knew I had to move quickly, before the enemy came looking for me. I wandered into a nearby wood. It was like I was sleepwalking. My body was doing all the work, not my head. I found a barn and I slept and slept and slept. When I woke up there was a young girl looking down at me. I thought I had died and gone to heaven and she was an angel. She went away, but came back later with a man and a woman and they made me take off my uniform and change into some scruffy work trousers and an old shirt. They took me to a safe house and wrapped my arm in bandages and gave me cheese and bread and wine. It was the most delicious meal I had ever had.

'A few days later I got moved to another place; a remote farmhouse in a valley. It was a special place, Violet, and they were special people. They worked for the Resistance and they kept me safe. They looked after me. They reset the bones in my arm and gave me medicine to kill any infection. They fed me and let me rest. And it really was like being in heaven. The war seemed so far away, like it belonged in someone else's life. Like it had all been some horrible nightmare.

'I should have left. I know I should. I should have been smuggled out of France and back to England to report for duty, but I kept finding excuses not to leave. My arm needed more time to heal. I wasn't strong enough to make the journey yet. I made myself useful. I did what I could around the farm and they liked having me there.

'Then, when I did grow stronger, I did more work on the farm and I was good at it. Nobody came looking for me and as time went on it got so that I couldn't have gone back even if I had wanted to. There would have been too many questions. I would have been court martialled, thrown into prison – or worse. Then the war ended and that was that. The decision was made for me. It was too late. I really couldn't come back. And if you want to know the truth, Violet, I didn't want to come back. I'd got a new life that I loved. New people that I loved. And I knew that Dad would never forgive me for what I'd done.'

He swallows a mouthful of cold coffee and pulls a face. 'I deserted the army, Violet. I know it was wrong, but I don't care. I never believed in the war and at least I'm alive and I've had a life.'

'That's where you've been all these years then?' I said. 'At that farmhouse?'

He nods.

'So why have you come back now then, if it was all so wonderful?'

He doesn't answer straight away. Then he says, 'Everyone has to come home at some point, Violet.'

'But why now? How could you have let Mum and Dad think you were dead for seventeen years! Didn't you care about that?' If blood could really boil, mine would be bubbling furiously now.

'Of course I cared.' He shrugs. 'But I suppose I just thought everyone would be getting on with their lives and would have forgotten about me.'

There's something he's not telling me. I can tell by the way his eyes keep slipping away from my challenging stare. 'But I still don't understand. Why now? Why did you come home now?'

'Sometimes,' he says, 'there's no answer to a question. No matter how many times you ask it.' He leans towards me and tries to take my hands. I pull them away and shove them out of reach under the table. He looks embarrassed for a second but then he takes a deep breath. 'Listen, Violet,' he says. 'I'm home now. I've told you my story. Mum's forgiven me. Norma's forgiven me. Dad hasn't yet, but he will. And I'd just like the chance to get to know you. Please. I'll be the best big brother a girl could wish for!'

His attempt at a joke makes me want to spit blood. I clench my fists under the table. 'I've never had a big brother,' I say. 'Not for seventeen years. And I don't need one now.' I push my chair back and stand up to leave. 'Thanks for the coffee,' I say through gritted teeth. Then I zip up my leather jacket and run for the next bus home.

It's late now. It must be gone midnight. I've been in bed for ages, but I can't sleep. I didn't tell Mum that I'd seen Joseph. I didn't want the endless questions that I knew she'd ask or to see a spark of hope in her eyes. And I know Dad wouldn't have cared less anyway. Besides, he was too busy yelling at me.

'Wipe that bloody muck off your face. You're not serving customers looking like that.' And, 'What the hell is that thing you're wearing? Christ, Violet, who the hell do you think you are? You're asking for trouble looking like that!'

I didn't bother to argue with him. Dad'll never understand. Not in a million years. I don't care what he thinks anyway. The only opinion that matters is Beau's. And he'll love my new leather jacket. I know he will.

It's hanging up on the outside of my wardrobe now, taunting me. It's shining in a dazzle of moonlight. I didn't get to wear it again tonight because Beau didn't come. All evening I expected him to walk through the shop door and ask for his six of chips.

Every time the door jangled I looked up with a smile ready on my face. But he never came. And now I feel stupid for thinking he would. Perhaps he thinks he made a mistake, taking me out on his motorcycle that night. Perhaps he thought I was another girl; a fun girl, a dangerous girl, a girl who's up for a laugh.

I want to shout at him. If only he'd bothered to come tonight he would have seen that I *am* that girl now. I look at my leather jacket again and I remember the girl on Chelsea Bridge. The one who asked my name. There's a tightening in my stomach as I try not to imagine that it's her draping herself all over Beau tonight.

French Letters

It's Thursday. Not a good day. It was only last Saturday that Joanne Thomas's body was discovered and now another girl has been found raped and murdered. Her body dumped *outside* the pump house this time. Her name was Pamela Bennett. She was sixteen. She was new to the area, so I didn't know her. I'm glad about that. It's easier to pretend it's not real if something terrible happens to a stranger.

Now everyone's behaving oddly. Hardly anyone's stopping to chat on the streets any more, there's no kids playing outside and there's a horrible silence everywhere. It's like a great machine has come to Battersea and sucked away all the smiles and laughter and replaced them with fear and suspicion.

Dad's been banging on, that it's all the fault of this new pill you can get now that stops you from getting pregnant. He reckons it'll turn all women into fast pieces. But as usual, he's got it all wrong. Only married women can get this pill and Pamela Bennett wasn't married. But even if she was taking a pill that stops you getting pregnant, she should still have been allowed to say no to a fella. Dad's told me he doesn't want to see me all dolled up again either. 'There's trouble enough already,' he said, 'without you going around asking for it.'

And if all that wasn't bad enough, Joseph has moved back home.

He's run out of money for his lodgings and until he finds some work, Mum says he can have his old room back. Dad's not happy of course, in fact he's furious, but Mum's not having any of it. 'He's my son, *our son*,' she keeps saying to him. 'If you don't like it, Frank, then *you* move out.'

Dad has shouted himself hoarse, but Mum won't budge. There's a fierce light in her eyes these days and I think that Dad knows, deep down, that he can't come between a mother and her child. Especially a child who's risen from the dead.

You'd think the Queen was here to stay, the way Mum's been behaving. She's scrubbed the whole place from top to bottom. She's beaten the rugs, washed the nets, polished the furniture and even put a vase of carnations on the kitchen table.

I was in my bedroom when Joseph first arrived. I heard Mum squealing with excitement and Dad slamming out of the house. I heard Mum bringing Joseph up to his room and her telling him, 'There's a clean towel on your bed, love. Have a minute to unpack and settle in, then come downstairs and I'll put the kettle on.'

She's never put a clean towel on my bed.

He was in his room for ages. I heard the sound of his wardrobe door opening and closing and the scrape of drawers. Then, just silence. For the longest time. What was he doing? Was he thinking? Was he sleeping? Was he looking at his childhood toy soldiers and wondering why they were still there on the windowsill? Then Mum called up the stairs, 'The kettle's on, love.' And I heard him sniff and blow his nose and then I realised he'd been crying. Why would a grown man be crying in his bedroom? What is he hiding from us? Why won't he tell us the real reason he's come home? He's not telling the whole truth. I just know it.

I try to stay in my room for as long as I can. I want Dad to know I'm on his side. I'm not going to forgive Joseph for being a deserter either. I can hear them all chattering downstairs; Mum, Joseph, Norma and Raymond. Norma's taken Mum's side of course and she keeps swearing. She keeps calling Dad a hard-hearted bastard and if he doesn't see sense soon, then he's going to lose her as a daughter. It doesn't suit Norma to swear. It's like she's got up in the morning and squeezed into someone else's dress.

They're all laughing. It sounds all wrong. Like they're having a party when there's nothing to celebrate. I pace up and down my room. I can't stay up here for ever and I know Mum's cooked a roast. The smell of pork crackling is drifting up the stairs, making my mouth water. I don't have to talk to Joseph, I suppose. I only have to eat.

As I pass his room, I notice that the door is ajar. I push it with my foot until it swings open. It doesn't look any different. The tin soldiers are still on the windowsill and as I step inside, I can see that the broken piece of mirror is still propped up on the chest of drawers. The only signs that Joseph has moved back in are the fluffy towel on the end of the bed, the empty duffle bag on the floor . . . and a bundle of letters on his pillow.

I edge towards the bed and pick the bundle up. I can still hear them all laughing downstairs, like a pack of hyenas – a cackle of hyenas – so I feel safe for a moment. The letters are held together by an elastic band and there are dozens of them. I pull one out and peer at the envelope. It's edged in blue and red stripes with an ink stamp at the top that says *Par Avion*. The handwriting is all loose and loopy but I can just make out, *Joseph White, Flat 4, 241, Fulham Palace Road, London*. It must be where he was lodging. I pull the letter out and open it up. The paper is tissue thin and smells of something sweet and flowery. The same loopy handwriting, but I can't make head nor tail of it. It's all in bloody French. *Cher Joseph*, it begins. *Dear Joseph* – I know that much. But the rest of it is just wriggles and squiggles of pale blue ink. I slide my eyes to the bottom of the page. It is signed with a big loopy *A*.

Letters in French. French letters. They're not what Jackie was talking about. I know that much. These wouldn't stop a girl from getting pregnant.

I wish there was something to tell me who *A* is. I run my fingers through the rest of the bundle to see if I can feel the tell-tale bulge of a photograph or something. It's hard to tell though – I'd have to open more of the letters and Mum's shouting up at me now, to come down and behave like a reasonable human being.

I carefully fold up the letter and put it back in its envelope. I think about the ring on Joseph's finger and the way he twisted it round and around. He said he'd found new people to love. But there must have been someone in particular. A beautiful

French girl, probably, with a head of dark hair and piercing black eyes. I bet these letters are from her. I flick through the rest of the envelopes. There are a few that look different and when I check the postmarks I see that these ones were posted from London. But it's the same handwriting. Whoever this *A* is, must have come to London too, then. Perhaps she followed him here?

There must be some answers in these letters. Some clues that might help solve the mystery of why Joseph decided to come home after all these years. Something that will shed light on whatever it is he's hiding. It'll be easy enough to find out. All I need is a French dictionary and a few hours in the library.

Norma looks at me disapprovingly as I sit next to her at the kitchen table. 'Good of you to join us,' she says.' I flick the V sign at her and she flushes. 'Just grow up, Violet!' she hisses. 'Just bloody grow up!' Raymond nods at me. He doesn't dare say hello or he'll get a kick under the table from Norma. I don't look at Joseph, and Mum's too busy ogling him to notice me anyway, so I help myself to a plateful of roast spuds and some slices of pork.

'Tell us some more French,' Mum pleads. 'Go on. You've got such a lovely accent.'

Joseph clears his throat. 'Okay,' he says. Strange words dance off his tongue, quickly and elegantly.

Norma claps her hands in delight. 'Oh my goodness!' she says. 'It's amazing. You sound proper French! What did you say?'

'This meal is delicious. Thank you, Mum,' he says.

'Say something else. Say something else,' chants Norma.

Joseph thinks for a moment, then more words fly from his mouth, like dozens of dancing butterflies. 'That means, it's good to be home,' he says.

I nearly choke on a potato. What a creep! Showing off, all pleased with himself. And Mum and Norma gazing at him like he's the best thing since sliced bread.

'So, Joseph,' I say slowly. He looks startled that I've actually spoken to him.

He turns to me and raises his eyebrows.

'Tell us more about France. Who did you live with? What were their names?'

He picks up his cup and takes a sip of tea. 'Well . . . okay,' he says.

I glimpse the hint of a frown crossing his forehead. But then it's gone and he gathers up his face to concentrate on my question. He's had a shave and a tidy up of his hair since I last saw him. He's got Dad's thin-lipped mouth and bum-chin. When Mum's in a good mood she calls Dad's chin his Cary Grant chin; she calls him her very own Hollywood movie star. Trust Joseph to inherit that bit.

'They were called Armand,' he's saying. 'The family I lived with.' He nods towards Mum. 'Mum and Norma know all this already.' He looks back at me. 'It was the grandfather's farm, Eric – Monsieur Armand. He was like an ox. Still working all hours, from dawn till dusk, even in his seventies.' He pauses for a moment to take another sip of tea. 'Then there were Eric's sons, Alain and Leon, and Leon's wife Arabella and their three children, Isabelle, Bruno and Eleta.'

'What were they like?' I ask.

He shrugs. 'They were good people. *Very* good people. They took me in, didn't they?'

'They must have been wonderful,' I say. I spit each word out like they're acid drops. 'You obviously preferred them to us.'

Joseph holds his hands up in surrender. 'It wasn't like that, Violet.'

Mum gives me a warning look.

I ignore her. 'Well, what *was* it like, then? Tell me that, Joseph. What was it like? So bloody wonderful that you couldn't be bothered to let your own family know you were still alive?'

'Violet!' Mum scrapes her chair back, like she's about to stand up and throw me out of the kitchen.

'It's okay, Mum,' says Joseph. He reaches across the table and squeezes her hand. Then he turns to me and sighs. He looks a hundred years old. 'It's hard to explain, Violet. I don't expect you to understand.' He lets go of Mum's hand. 'I don't expect any of you to understand. The war . . . the war . . . it did things to people. Terrible things.'

'More terrible than deserting your own family?'

'Violet!' Mum's voice flies across the table. 'Just stop it! Enough is enough!' But she bites the corner of her lip and it's obvious that she'd like to know the answer to my question as much as I do. She stands up and begins to clear the plates, bashing them together so that gravy and leftover potato shoot from the edges. 'Right, everyone,' she says, through gritted teeth, 'who's for apple pie and custard?'

Norma glares at me fiercely, with her 'I wish you'd never been born' face. Raymond just keeps to himself and quickly spears his last potato before Mum whips his plate away.

126

'Violet . . .' Joseph leans towards me with a pleading look on his face, like I'm five years old and he's trying to get me to eat my greens. But I don't get to hear what he's going to say because there's a knock at the kitchen door, a loud 'Coo-ee!' and Jackie comes breezing into the kitchen.

'Sorry,' she says. 'I didn't know you were having your tea. Just popped round to have a word with Violet, if that's okay?'

'Yes . . . yes, Jackie.' Mum seems relieved by the interruption. 'Come on in,' she says. 'Don't mind us. Would you like some apple pie?'

'No thanks, Mrs White,' says Jackie. She smooths her hands down her slim hips. 'Watching me figure.' She looks around the room. 'Hi Norma,' she says. 'Hi Raymond.' She nods at me. 'All right, Violet . . .' She stares at Joseph and leaves her sentence unfinished with a great big Joseph-shaped question mark right at the end.

It's Mum who eventually speaks. Her bosom swells up at least two bra sizes as she puts her hand on Joseph's shoulder. 'Now, Jackie, you know we had a son called Joseph?' Jackie nods. 'Who we thought for all these years had been killed in the war?' Jackie nods again. 'Well . . .' says Mum, taking a deep breath, 'we didn't want to tell anyone yet, not until he'd settled down a bit, but he . . . he wasn't killed. He wasn't killed at all! This is Joseph. This is our Joseph. Back home with us.' She bends down and kisses Joseph hard on the top of his head.

Jackie makes a show of being shocked. She clamps her hand over her mouth and gasps. She's a good actress, I'll give her that. And a nosey cow. She couldn't wait, could she? She had to come and see the prodigal son for herself. And use me as her excuse.

'Pleased to meet you, Joseph,' she says. She holds out her hand to him and I swear she almost bobs a curtsey.

'Nice to meet you too, Jackie,' says Joseph, as he takes her hand. His eyes sweep up and down her. 'So, you're a friend of Violet's, are you?'

'Yeah,' says Jackie. 'Known each other all our lives, haven't we, Vi?' She edges towards Dad's empty chair, her eyes fixed on Joseph. 'So . . .' she says. 'This is just amazing . . .' She wouldn't dare, would she? She wouldn't dare sit down and have a conversation with him? Of course she would. This is Jackie we're talking about. And she's already forgotten about me, and what she supposedly came here for.

'So, what did you want?' I say quickly, before she changes her mind about the apple pie and takes up residence in Dad's chair. 'You said you wanted a word with me?' I get up from the table and motion for her to follow. 'Come on,' I say. 'We can go to my room.'

'Oh. Right. Yeah . . . sure,' says Jackie. She makes a face at Joseph, as if to say sorry. Then she turns to me. 'Actually,' she says. 'It was only to remind you about the dance tomorrow night. Starts at seven at the Roxy. If you can make it?'

I shrug. 'I don't know,' I say. 'I'm meant to be working.'

'Oh, you'll let her have the night off, won't you, Mrs W?' Jackie smiles her best smile. 'It won't be the same without Violet.'

Norma raises her eyebrows. 'A dance? Violet? Well, I suppose it had to happen one day.'

'But who's going to help in the shop?' says Mum. 'It's Friday. We'll be run off our feet.'

Joseph coughs. 'Excuse me!' he says. 'Have you forgotten that I was once the best fish batterer this side of the Thames? Let Violet have her night off. I'll help in the shop.'

Mum gives me a look that says, see how nice he is to you, even though you're being a horrible bitch. 'Well, there you go, Violet,' she says. 'Your brother has given you the night off.'

'Great,' says Jackie. 'I'll see you tomorrow then, Violet. Best glad rags and all that!' She turns back to Joseph. 'Really good to meet you,' she simpers. 'And I'll see you again, I'm sure.'

'I'm sure you will,' says Joseph, and even though he's old enough to be her dad, he actually winks at her.

V for Vanish

It's freezing this morning. There's ice on the insides of my windows and my breath is frosting in front of my face. I've pulled my clothes into bed with me and I'm dressing under the warm tent of my blankets. Mum's already downstairs cooking a fry up and Dad's in the bathroom, shaving.

They were all up late last night; Mum, Dad and Joseph. They sat in the front room after the shop had shut, with a bottle of whisky. Dad was shouting again for a bit, about how ashamed he was and how he couldn't look people in the eye. Mum was crying again and Joseph was talking softly to them both. I couldn't hear what he was saying, but just before midnight there was a terrible sound. Someone was gasping and choking. I crept down the stairs with my heart in my throat. I prepared myself to open the door of the front room to find Dad standing over Joseph with his hands round his neck. But as I put my ear to the door, I realised it was Dad making all the noise. And he wasn't being throttled, he was crying. He was crying his heart out and it was the worst sound I have ever heard.

'I'm sorry,' he eventually managed to say. 'I'm sorry, son. It's been so hard. It's my pride . . . I know . . . my stupid pride.' His voice cracked. 'When you came back, I couldn't accept it was really you. My son was a hero . . . not a coward.'

'Oh, Frank . . .' Mum said.

'I know . . . I know,' said Dad. 'I should have been overjoyed to have you back. No one could ever replace you. You were my son. My first born.' He took a deep shuddering breath. 'I'm not like your mother. I'll try and forgive you, I promise I will. But I need to know why you left it for so long to come back. How could you let us suffer for all these years?'

'I don't know the answer to that, Dad. Not yet anyway,' said Joseph. 'There's so much stuff in my head. So much darkness . . .'

I didn't wait to hear any more. *No one could ever replace you*, Dad had said. I always knew that. I always knew that Joseph was number one. Even now, after all that he's done, he's still the Golden Boy. He got the biggest slice of their love and Norma got what was left. I was a mistake, and all I got was the crumbs. Hearing it said out loud was like a knife in my heart.

I feel numb now. As cold inside as I feel outside. But I still have to get up. I still have to spend the day peeling potatoes that'll be as hard and cold as frozen rocks. And I'll have to watch as Joseph wheedles his way back into everyone's hearts until there's no room at all left for me. I'll fade away bit by bit, day by day, until I disappear altogether.

V for Violet

V for Vanish

I touch the silver V at my throat. At least there's still Jackie. There's always been Jackie. She can't let me down now.

131

I lay some clothes out on my bed, ready for later. There's an old skirt of Mum's, a shiny peach-coloured thing that swivels loosely around my waist, and a cream blouse with a stain on the bosom that I'll cover with a brooch. It's not exactly belle of the ball stuff but it's the best I can muster from my measly wardrobe. In a few hours from now, I won't care what's happening at home. I'll be at the Roxy. My stomach flips at the thought. Right now, I'd rather stick pins in my eyes than go to the dance at the Roxy tonight. But if I want to hold on to Jackie, I've got no choice. Besides, I tell myself, maybe, just maybe, I might actually enjoy myself.

Mum calls up that breakfast is ready and I hear Joseph – the traitor, the coward – whistling as he makes his way downstairs. Now's my chance to smuggle out the letters.

I creep out of my room and open Joseph's bedroom door as quietly as I can. The room smells different now; of warm breath and clean sweat. He's made his bed and smoothed out the candlewick cover. The tin soldiers are gone and instead there's a pile of books arranged neatly on the windowsill. The bundle of letters is nowhere to be seen. I slip my hand under his pillow, but they aren't there. I look under his bed and through each of his drawers and I check inside his wardrobe. The empty duffel bag is at the bottom of the wardrobe, but there's no sign of the letters. What the hell's he done with them?

'Violet!' Mum yells up the stairs. 'Your eggs are getting cold!'

I groan. They must be here. They must be here somewhere. I stop in the middle of the room and try to think. Where have I looked? Where haven't I looked?

'Violet!'

I pull a chair over to the wardrobe and stand on it. I reach a hand out and search on top of the wardrobe. There's nothing there but dust. I put the chair back in the corner. Think. Think. Think. By now, I know that Joseph hasn't just put the letters away somewhere. He's hidden them.

Where could he hide them in here? Under the floorboards? Then it hits me and I actually slap my forehead. Where does *everyone* hide things? Where's the most obvious place in the whole wide world? I push my hand under his mattress and almost yelp in triumph. I bring out the bundle of letters and quickly stuff them in my pocket.

'Violet! What the bloody hell are you doing?' Mum's shrieking now. Not a good sign.

'Just coming!' I shout. I close Joseph's door and pull down my blouse to cover the bulge in my pocket. Then I run to my room and push the letters to the back of my underwear drawer. They'll be safe there until I get a chance to go to the library. I can't imagine anyone will want to rifle through my knickers. I don't know what Joseph will do if he notices his letters are missing. I don't want to even think about it.

'I'll find out what your secret is,' I say under my breath. *'I'll find out what you're hiding. Then you can say goodbye to being the Golden Boy, for ever.'*

'Did you hear the news?' asks Mum as I shovel cold egg into my mouth. 'Mr Harper's been arrested. They think he might be the one. The Battersea Park Killer.' She shudders. 'I can't believe he can have done those terrible things to those poor girls. And to think I used to say hello to him too.'

'Oh, Mum,' I say. 'Didn't you ever notice there was something not quite right about him? It was so obvious. I've always seen the evil in him.'

Mum snorts. 'Think you're so bloody clever sometimes, don't you, my lady? Perhaps you should join the police force and tell them all how to do their jobs, hey?'

'No need to be like that!' I snap at her. 'I'm only telling the truth.'

'Well, your truth isn't necessarily *the* truth, is it? Just remember that, Violet.'

I don't know what she's talking about. The truth is the truth, no matter what. Two girls are dead and Mr Harper killed them. You can't get more truthful than that.

It's nearly seven o'clock. Mum, Dad and Joseph are downstairs in the chip shop and I'm staring at my reflection in Mum's dressing-table mirror. I look ridiculous. Even I can see that. I look like a five-year-old dressed up in her mother's clothes. Actually, I look like a sixteen-year-old dressed up in her mother's clothes. The lipstick I've put on is too bright, the mascara is already smudged, and my hair looks like someone set fire to it and put the flames out with a bucket of chip oil. Jackie's going to be calling for me soon. I can't let her see me like this. She'll run a mile and never come back.

I run into the bathroom and scrub my face clean with the flannel. Then I tug a comb through my hair and tuck it behind my ears and the arms of my glasses. There's not much I can do with my clothes, apart from taking them off, and I can't go to a dance in my underwear. I run back to my room to fetch my shoes and that's when I see it. My leather jacket. Still hanging on the outside of my wardrobe, gleaming at me invitingly.

I don't give myself time to think. I pull off Mum's skirt and throw it on the floor, then I pull on my old denim jeans instead. I slip the leather jacket on over my blouse and run back to Mum's room. I take a deep breath and carefully paint on a fresh slick of eyeliner and a brush of mascara. I remember the girls on Chelsea Bridge and I keep a picture of them in my head as I use a handful of Mum's bobby pins to secure my hair behind my ears. Next, I backcomb the rest of it and tease it into a giant quiff. Then, before I lose my nerve, I spray nearly a whole can of Mum's lacquer over the whole lot. I squint into the mirror. I can't tell whether I look good or bad, but by now I don't care. I look like the girls on Chelsea Bridge and I feel like the real Violet, and for now that's all that matters.

I shout through to the shop that I'm off and Mum shouts back, telling me to go nowhere near the park, to not speak to any strange fellas and to make sure I stay with Jackie at all times. 'I'll be all right, Mum!' I yell back. 'Don't worry. Mr Harper's banged up now, and I can look after myself.'

'Violet!' Jackie gasps when she sees me. 'What the hell have you done to yourself? It's a dance we're going to, you know.'

'It's what I want to wear,' I say. 'I feel comfortable in it.'

Jackie shrieks with laughter. 'It's not about feeling comfortable!' she says. 'Do you think I'm comfortable in this get-up? My feet are bloody killing me!' She looks amazing. She's all tight skirt, tight jumper and heels. Her hair is stacked high on her head and there are huge gold hoops dangling from her ears. She looks me up and down again and smirks. 'Oh, well,' she says. 'Suit yourself. It's your funeral.'

The Sugar Girls are waiting for us outside the Roxy. They squeal with delight when they see us approaching. They totter up and kiss Jackie. 'Oh, you look lovely! New skirt? Cool earrings!'

'Remember Violet?' Jackie asks them. They nod at me. 'Yeah. Hi.'

'Didn't know she was a Rocker,' says the blonde one. Mary, I think.

'Neither did I,' says Jackie. She wrinkles her nose.

'I am actually here,' I mutter. But already, they've all linked arms and I follow behind as we join the queue into the hall. We're not even in there yet and I'm having second thoughts. I look around at all the other people in the queue. Tight knots of bottle-blonde girls mixed with groups of fellas dressed in shiny suits with tight trousers and pointy-toed boots. Dad would call them a bunch of Nancy-boys if he was here. I stuff my hands into my pockets and try to stay as close to Jackie as I can. As we shuffle further towards the entrance, the music from inside grows louder and louder. Everyone around me starts to jig around as though they're already on the dance floor.

'Ooh, I love this one,' shouts Pauline. I remember her mean blackbird eyes. They're even meaner tonight. They're lined in thick black kohl and are startling next to her pale pancake make-up.

Then suddenly we're inside, the music is deafening and the floor is shaking. It's hot and smoky and there are bodies everywhere. Girls and fellas are writhing, hopping and jerking.

I follow Jackie as she pushes her way into the thickest part of the crowd just as the band on stage strike up another tune.

'Come on, everybody!' shouts the singer. It's like a secret signal passes through the crowd and all of a sudden everyone is moving in the same way. They're twisting their hips from side to side as they lower themselves to the floor and back up again.

Everybody's twisting again, like they did last summer, apparently. The singer on stage belts out the lyrics. I stand there, frozen to the spot, like an idiot. I don't know what to do. Jackie hits me on the arm. 'Like this, Violet,' she yells. 'Pretend you're stubbing out a fag with your toes and drying your back with a towel at the same time!'

I try to do as she says, but my arms and legs don't belong to me. They won't do what everybody else's arms and legs are doing. It feels all wrong. The Sugar Girls start sniggering. I know they're laughing at me. The song goes on for ever. Some fellas have inched their way towards us. They're dancing opposite Jackie and the other girls and they're grinning madly at each other, as though all this twisting around is the best thing in the world.

Come on, Violet, I tell myself. *This is meant to be fun.* I stretch my mouth into a crazy smile, I twist my hips around and shake myself from side to side until I almost believe I've got it right. I'm going round and round and up and down, just as the singer's telling me to. I begin to understand what it's all about and I'm actually enjoying myself and thinking it's going to be a good night after all.

When the tune finishes, I'm as breathless as everyone else and I tag along to the bar with Jackie and the others and stand in line for a glass of lemonade. The fella that Jackie has been dancing with has got his arm around her waist and keeps whispering in her ear.

I tug Jackie's arm. 'You going to introduce me?' I ask.

She can barely tear her eyes away from him. 'Oh yeah,' she says. She clears her throat and tries to pull a serious face. 'Colin, this is Violet,' she bursts into giggles.

Colin smiles at me apologetically, but I can see behind his eyes that he's laughing at me too.

'What's so funny?' I challenge Jackie.

'Oh, chill out, Violet,' she says. 'You're supposed to be enjoying yourself.' She turns back to Colin and they start laughing again at some private joke, except it's not that private, because I know it's me they're laughing at. I sip my lemonade. It's warm and flat, and suddenly that's how I feel too. My blouse feels damp under my armpits and the tiny bubbles of fizz I felt on the dance floor have all burst. I'm a joke. A big, fat joke, and I don't belong here.

I look around the hall at all the heaving bodies. Am I the only one here who doesn't get it? The only one who doesn't think it's fun to gyrate around a dance floor like a demented puppet? I lean against the wall. I wish I could melt into it and disappear. I wish I was back on Parliament Hill with Beau, or on Chelsea Bridge sipping a cup of hot coffee with all the other Rockers. Even being at the shop would be better than this. At least there would be the hope that Beau might turn up.

My bladder pricks. The lemonade's gone right through me. Great. Now I'm going to have to pee. The sign for the Ladies is high on the wall on the other side of the hall. I turn to Jackie to let her know where I'm going, but she's gone. Not just moved from where she was, but proper gone. Now my eyes prick. I blink hard. I can't cry here. I need to pee and I need to cry, and it's urgent. I can't bring myself to push through the mass of wriggling hips, so I walk around the edge of the dance floor with my bladder bouncing to the rhythm of the band's 'bomp bah bomps' and 'rama lama ding dongs'.

It's chilly inside the Ladies and it smells of stale pee, hair lacquer and disinfectant. The damp patches under my armpits turn cold and scratch at my skin. But at least with the door closed, the 'rama lama ding dongs' are just faint memories. There's no one else here; all the cubicles are empty. I choose the cleanest one and pee quickly, before anyone else comes in. I press hard on my eyelids to stop myself from howling. Then I let a few silent tears slip down my face before I wipe them away with the back of my hand. I feel like a five-year-old again, all alone in the school playground without a single friend.

Someone else comes into the Ladies. I sit quietly and let them go about their business. I don't want to go out and wash my hands with some blonde dolly-bird watching me and judging me. The taps turn on and off, there's a moment's silence and I imagine the girl leaning towards the mirror retouching her lipstick and checking her hair. Then her heels clatter away, back out of the door, there's a blast of music, then silence, and I'm alone again. I'm about to open the cubicle door when I have a genius idea. Why don't I just stay here? Nobody'll know how long I've been in here for, and Jackie won't even notice I'm gone. I can sit here and wait it out until it's time to go home. Better this than the torture of the dance floor.

I button up my jeans, pull the flush then settle myself down on the closed toilet lid.

It's okay for the first ten minutes. There's stuff to read on the walls.

Here I sit, broken hearted, spent a penny and only farted
Jenny Loves Paul X
Hitler kaputt
Go home Mother. You're drunk.
Elsie Tanner looks like a spanner.
Johnny Brown wears girls' pants

I wonder who Johnny Brown is and if he really wears girls' pants. If I had a pen with me, I'd write some messages of my own. A poem, perhaps? There's one that I read a long time ago that could have been written about me.

Down in a green and shady bed, a modest violet grew
Its stalk was bent, it hung its head, as if to hide from view.

More voices from outside. 'Lend me your lippy, Sandra.'

'Oh, it's freezing in here. Come on, hurry up and have your pee.'

'You bloody hurry up.'

'Hey, there's no paper in here. Pass us some under the door, will you?'

As they leave, others come in. And then more. One lot after another. They're queuing for the cubicles and I'm just waiting for the awful moment when one of them bangs on the door to ask what I'm doing.

Someone lights up. 'Hey, Jackie, give us a drag.'

'Bout time you bought your own, isn't it? Always poncing off me, you are.'

'Come on. Hand it over. You know you love me really. Ugh . . . you've got lippy all over the end.'

I freeze. They're in here. Jackie and the Sugar Girls. My stomach rolls. They won't know I'm in here, will they? They can't see through doors.

'Where's your little friend, anyway? Haven't seen her for a while.'

'Dunno,' says Jackie. 'Probably practising her dance moves somewhere.' They giggle spitefully.

'Why did you even bring her?'

Jackie huffs out a big sigh. 'Felt sorry for her, I suppose. She's always on her own. Hasn't got any friends. I only know her cos we went to school together.'

'Not surprised she hasn't got any friends. Bit of a strange one, isn't she? And what the bloody hell is she wearing?'

'Don't worry,' says Jackie. 'I won't be asking her again. Your reputation is safe! But you know me and my kind heart. Puppy dogs and kittens and all that. Thought it might cheer her up, coming out. She's got this brother, you see. Killed in the war. Or so they thought. He's only just bloody well come back!'

'No!'

'Yup. And turns out he's a deserter. Been hiding out in France all these years. So me nan says anyway . . .'

'Bloody hell . . .'

Their voices drift away. The music blasts. The door bangs. Silence again. I uncurl my fists. The palms of my hands sting where my nails have dug into the skin, and my throat aches.

Jackie has finally broken our friendship and there's a shard of glass sticking right into the middle of my heart. I always knew it would hurt. But I never knew it would hurt this much. It hurts so much, I think I might die.

But I don't want to die in a toilet cubicle. I want to die at home, lying in bed with *The Country Girls* resting on my chest, open at a page near the end; at the bit where Kate is all alone again after being betrayed by the man she thinks she loves.

Maybe they could read some quotes from the book at my funeral.

I open the cubicle door. There's a cigarette butt on the floor, kissed by a stain of red lipstick. Jackie's lipstick. I crush it under my foot and kick it away under the sinks.

When I step outside the Roxy, the first thing I see is a group of fellas all crowded round their motorcycles. It's so cold that it's hard to tell if the clouds of smoke hovering above their heads are made of cigarette smoke or warm breath. My heart starts banging, bomp bah bomp bah bomp. There are five of them. Five fellas in leather jackets. And I'm sure the one at the back is Beau. I recognise the shape of him and the way he tosses his hair to keep his quiff out of his eyes. He looks this way, and suddenly the worst night ever has turned into the best night ever. It's like I wished him here and he heard me and he came to my rescue. I start to hurry towards him when someone calls my name.

'Hey! Violet! What are you doing out here?' Jackie comes tottering up to me, with Colin following at her heels. 'Wondered where you'd got to. You coming back in?'

I stare at her for a minute. The edge of one of her false eyelashes has peeled away. It looks like a spider with half its legs pulled off. Her lipstick is smudged around her mouth and her jumper has come untucked from her skirt. Colin looks like a dog who's been thrown the Sunday roast bone.

'Didn't think you cared if I was here or not,' I say. 'And anyway, looks like you've been pretty busy. Your nan thinks you're such a good girl too.'

'Don't be a bitch, Violet,' she says. 'It doesn't suit you. Now, you coming in or what?' A bike across the road roars to life and Jackie glances over, a strange look flitting across her face. She turns back to me and opens her mouth to speak. Then she frowns and looks down at my jacket, then back across the road again. She gasps. 'Violet! You haven't been hanging around with them, have you? Is that what the jacket thing is all about?' She starts to giggle. 'Colin,' she says. 'What do you reckon? Violet thinks she's a little Rocker!'

The hot cauldron of rage that's been bubbling around in my stomach suddenly explodes into Jackie's shocked face. 'Just shut up,' I yell. 'Just shut up!'

'What the hell's wrong with you?' she says, backing into Colin.

'I'm going home,' I say. 'I've had enough of all this and I've had enough of you and I'm bloody going home!'

'But you can't!' she says. 'You can't leave me to walk home on my own.'

'I'm sure Colin will sort you out,' I say. 'Or one of your little sugar factory friends.'

'Don't be stupid, Violet. Come on. Come back inside and we'll sort this out.'

'But that's just it, isn't it?' I say. 'I am stupid. Stupid little Violet! Stupid boring Violet. Stupid Violet in her stupid clothes who can't dance to save her life!'

Jackie's mouth drops open.

'Go back inside,' I say. 'Go back to your friends. You're a fake, Jackie, just like your eyelashes. You're not the person you used to be and I don't want to know you any more. I don't want to see you any more. So, just go away!' I rip the chain off from around my neck and throw it, and the silver V, to the floor, then I turn to leave.

'Violet?' she pleads.

'Just piss off!' I yell, over my shoulder.

'Suit your bloody self then,' she shouts back. 'Come on, Colin.' Her heels tap angrily on the ground as they leave.

'Who is she, anyway?' Colin asks her. And I almost laugh out loud. It's a good question. Who am I, anyway?

The bike across the road is still roaring. I can feel it in the pit of my stomach, growling and shaking my insides up; mixing all my feelings together until I'm not sure if I'm angry, sad, scared or excited. But it doesn't really matter any more, because my feet are taking me towards Beau. He's seen me and he's waving me over and I can't get there quick enough.

'Hey,' he says. 'What were you doing in that place? Didn't think that sort of thing was your scene.'

'It's not,' I say.

He laughs. 'Came to find you earlier,' he says. 'At the chippie. But you weren't there.'

'Night off,' I say. The thought that he actually went to the chippie to find me makes me want to explode with happiness.

144

He grins. 'Nice jacket.' He pats his motorcycle. 'Fancy a spin, then?'

I grin back at him. 'Why not?' I say.

I wrap my arms around his waist and press my face against his back as we speed through the streets. I don't care that the cold wind bites into my skin and finds its way under my jeans to freeze my bones. It's good to feel numb. I know that for as long as Beau keeps the bike's engine alive and roaring, all I have to think about is now. All I have to do is watch the pavements and the street lights and the night sky flash by. And nothing else matters.

We stop on Chelsea Bridge again and slot ourselves into place with the rest of the Chelsea Bridge boys and girls. The coffee that Beau buys for me scalds my tongue and throat and brings the blood back to my fingertips with a slow creeping agony. Beau shares his cigarette with me and we stamp our feet as our teeth chatter and we listen to the jokes and the teasing and the conversations that whizz past our ears and over our heads.

'I'm glad I saw you tonight,' I say. 'I wasn't sure, you know, if . . . if I'd see you again.'

'Glad I saw you too,' he says. 'Tell you what, though. That fella who served me my chips tonight wasn't half as pretty as you.' He grins at me.

I imagine Joseph standing behind the counter at the chippie and I wonder how many of our customers will know who he really is. And I wonder if they'll mind being served their suppers by the likes of him. I've half a mind to tell Beau all about him. But I don't, because what if he doesn't want to hang out with the sister of a deserter and a liar? Instead I ask Beau what he's been up to and where he's been, trying to sound as casual as I can.

'Oh, you know, this and that,' he says. He nudges me with his elbow. 'Thought about you a lot.'

I want to believe him. I really do. So, even when a little voice in my head tells me to stop being so stupid, there must be other girls, I ignore it and I catch the eye of the girl who spoke to me last time and smile at her.

'Hey, it's Violet, isn't it?' she says. 'Love your hair. Really suits you.'

I put my hand up to touch it and silently thank Mum for her hair lacquer. At some point I realise that Beau has put his arm across my shoulder. I lean in to him and think about how amazing this all is. It's like I've known him all my life, when I don't really know him at all. And suddenly I know who I am. I'm Violet with a capital V, and this is where I belong.

Later, as Beau is driving me back home, we pass by the Roxy as everyone's all spilling out on to the street. I hold on to Beau as tightly as I can as he opens up the throttle and sends a roar like a Spitfire into the night air. It's a fingers-up to the lot of them. I hope Jackie's somewhere there, watching and listening. And I hope she realises the fingers-up is especially for her.

As we round the corner I catch sight of a figure huddled inside a donkey jacket, hands in pockets, head down against the cold. It's Joseph. I twist my head round to watch the back of him as we rip past. Where's he going at this time of night? I think of the letters, hidden in my underwear drawer, the loopy writing waiting to be unravelled. I can't wait to find out what his little secret is. To find out why he really came home. It doesn't dawn on me until Beau pulls up outside the chippie that perhaps Joseph has gone to the Roxy to meet me and Jackie, to walk us home.

But I don't dwell on the thought because as I get off the bike, Beau puts his arm around my waist and pulls me towards him. 'Ever been kissed, Violet?' he says.

I shake my head.

'Bout time you were then,' he says. He presses his lips against mine. I don't move. I don't know if I'm supposed to. His lips are soft and hard, all at once, and they taste as sweet as toffee apples. Tiny stars burst inside my head. When he pulls away I feel like I've just run up a flight of stairs when I haven't moved an inch.

'See you later, Violet,' he says, his voice all deep and rough. As I wave him off I realise that this might be the happiest moment of my life and that I'll always remember that kiss, even if I live to ninety.

Love Story

I'm at the library before Miss Read has even had time to unlock the door. I've got Joseph's letters and a notebook and pen stuffed inside my jacket pocket. 'You're keen this morning, Violet,' she says as she ushers me inside.

'The early bird catches the worm,' I reply. And I smile to myself as a picture comes into my head of Joseph, transformed into a six-foot long worm, being pecked in half by a sparrow the size of a double-decker bus.

I go straight to the reference section and search the shelves until I find a copy of an English/French dictionary, then I settle myself at a table in the farthest corner of the library and begin my top-secret task.

I open my notebook and pick up one of the envelopes stamped *Par Avion*. I take out the letter and spread it out in front of me. The first bit's easy; *Cher Joseph* = *Dear Joseph*.

I work my way along the first line. The words look all exotic and jumbled and complicated and they are all decorated with little squiggles and dashes.

Anniversaire. Amour. La première fois. Rencontré.

I flick through the dictionary trying to find the same words and their meanings, but it's all so confusing. But then I find that *amour* means love and I know straight away that I was right about one thing – Joseph was in love with a French girl.

I work my way through the rest of the letter, jotting down notes as I go. I can't translate it all exactly, but I think I've got some of the meaning. The French girl writes about remembering the first time they met and how they knew they were meant to be together. And she writes about the time they fell asleep under a tree in each other's arms.

It takes me for ever to work just that much out. I yawn and stretch my legs out under the table. I read through what I've got so far. It's a love letter, that's clear enough. A bloody love letter.

I try to work out the next bit, and I think it's all about nights in a barn with the rain pouring down outside.

I hope they're not all going to be like this. It's like reading the worst kind of poetry. But then there's a sentence that makes me stop. It's about promises and rings and about never taking the rings off.

I put my pen down and I think of the ring on Joseph's finger. She loves Joseph, whoever this *A* is. She loves him very much. But none of her fancy words help to solve the mystery of why he came home. I open the second letter and my heart sinks as I stare at the tangle of words. But I take a deep breath and turn back to the dictionary. After a while I have a new list in my notebook and I stare and stare at the words and try to hear the French girl's voice in my head.

Dear Joseph, I hear her say.

I have done my best. But Papa will not listen to reason. I am afraid that any chance of a reconciliation is now lost for ever. He will not even see me, let alone speak to me.

Do not blame yourself. We both knew the chance we were taking and I for one would not have done anything different. If being with you means losing my family, then so be it.

I will join you as soon as I can.

Yours always,

A

What chance did she and Joseph take, I wonder? And why did she lose her family because of it? I hold my head in my hands for a moment. There are more questions than ever now, spinning round and round in my head.

I start a clean page in my notebook.

1. There is a French girl with a name beginning with A.
2. She loves Joseph very much.
3. They have taken a chance of some sort.
4. She has lost her family because of it.
6. Why??

I don't know what any of these clues mean yet. But I know for certain – the way I always seem to know these things – that Joseph is hiding something, and one way or another I'm going to find out what it is.

I choose another envelope. This one is stamped *Par Avion* too, so I know it was posted from France. As I open it and unfold the letter, I smell the flowery scent again and I half imagine the mysterious French girl standing behind me watching me read her words. I shiver and look over my shoulder. But of course there's nobody there except for Miss Read sorting through the shelves of World History. I turn back to the letter and pick out a couple of words to translate. Then I imagine I hear the girl's voice again, all lilting and sexy with a thick French accent.

Dear Joseph
It was so good to get your letter. I miss you too. I miss you so much my bones hurt. But it won't be long now until we are together again. Try not to go to those dark places too often. I know where they can lead you. There is only despair at the end of that road.
Yours always,
A

Some of the words are difficult to read and according to the dictionary, some of them have more than one meaning in French. But I'm sure I've got it right. I've just got that feeling.

Dark places.
Despair at the end of that road.

What the hell does she mean?

I take another letter out of its envelope. The flowery scent is beginning to give me a headache.

Joseph, her voice whispers in my ear.

Do not talk about those things. Why would you even think about doing something like that? It fills me with horror to hear you talk like that. Please just wait for me. It won't be long now. Promise me you will wait.

Yours always,

A

I pick up my notebook and add to the list.

7. What was Joseph thinking of doing?
8. Where are the dark places that he goes to?
9. Who is she? Who the hell is *A*?

I push my glasses to the top of my head and rub my eyes. And then, just like that, as though someone had posted it through a slot in my skull, the name Arabella pops into my head. Of course. Joseph mentioned her the other day. She was the wife of one of the sons who worked on the farm. Suddenly it all starts to make sense. I glance up at the clock on the wall and see it's nearly midday. I didn't realise I'd been here for so long. Miss Read walks by and taps her watch meaningfully. I need to hurry. She'll be wanting to close for lunch soon and I need to get back before Joseph notices his letters missing.

I quickly sort through them, searching the postmarks for dates. The last letter posted from France is stamped August fifteenth. Two months ago.

I haven't got much time, and I'm getting lost in the dictionary and my head is banging and banging.

Coming soon
On my way
Together again

Then another letter, posted two weeks later. It's the first letter to be sent to Joseph from London. She came, then. She came to be with him.

I'll be there in the park, by the pump house
Seven o'clock
I want you in my arms

And another.

Something has changed
I can feel it

And then the very last letter, posted October fourteenth.

What's happened to you?
I've sacrificed everything for you
You've changed
You frighten me

I scribble it all down in my notebook. And I realise that I've got a story of some sort. A story with huge holes in it. A story book with most of the pages ripped out.

Two people come together in war-torn France. One of them is a deserter from the British Royal Airforce, the other a beautiful French girl called Arabella who works for the Resistance. They fall in love. The deserter loves Arabella so much that he forgets about his own family back in England who believe he was killed in the war. Unfortunately, Arabella is already married, so when, many years later, their affair is discovered, they are forced to part and Arabella's family disown her. The deserter travels back to England and is reunited with his family while he waits for Arabella to join him. When she finally arrives in England, they meet in secret, but something is wrong. The deserter is a changed man. He has dark thoughts and he frightens Arabella. Why won't he tell his family about her? And where is she now? Why have the letters stopped?

That's it. That's where the story ends. But a story never really ends, I know that.

Miss Read coughs. I close my notebook, gather the letters into a bundle and put the dictionary back on the shelf. 'Did you catch the worm then, Violet?' she asks, her cheeks colouring at her attempt at a joke.

'I think so, Miss Read,' I tell her as I head for the door. 'I think so.'

I hurry home. There might be a chance to sneak the letters back into Joseph's room before I have to start peeling potatoes. I'm halfway down Lavender Hill when I stop in my tracks. *I'll be there in the park by the pump house.* That's what she said. That's what Arabella wrote in one of her letters. The pump house. Where Joanne Thomas and Pamela Bennett were found raped and murdered. I swallow hard.

I think I caught more than just a worm. I think I caught a whole bucketful.

My head's in a spin as I open the kitchen door, so the last thing I expect is to hear Brenda's voice. A groan rolls into my throat. So now they'll know all about the argument last night. How I told Jackie to piss off and how I rode off into the night with a dodgy Rocker boy. I don't know what Jackie will have said. It won't be anything good, that's for sure. But I don't care. Jackie was a prize cow to me and she got what she deserved.

I brace myself for the sharp edge of Brenda's tongue. As I walk in the door, she's just taking a sip from a cup of tea. She slams the cup back in its saucer and tea slaps out onto the table and starts to dribble off the edge and on to the kitchen floor. 'Violet! Thank God!' she says.

'What?' I say. I look at Mum, who's grabbed a cloth from the sink to stem the flow of spilt tea.

'Where is she?' asks Brenda. I realise she's still got her rollers in. That's not like her. Brenda would never leave the house with rollers in her hair.

'Where's who?' I say.

'Jackie.' Brenda's voice cracks. 'She never came home last night.'

I'm thrown for a minute. Why wouldn't Jackie have come home? She wouldn't do that to Brenda. She wouldn't let her worry like this. Then I picture Jackie outside the Roxy with Colin, her clothes all rumpled and her make-up smudged. Should I tell Brenda that Jackie probably spent the night with him? That she was out all night with a fella? For some reason, an old feeling of loyalty makes my mouth say one thing when my brain wants to say another. 'She's probably stopped out at one of her friend's. Pauline or Mary or whatever they're called. One of the girls from the factory.'

'It's not like her,' says Brenda. 'She always tells me what she's doing. And she said she was coming home.' She looks me straight in the eye. 'You were with her at the dance. You were supposed to walk home together, weren't you?'

'I . . . I left early,' I say. 'I wasn't feeling right. Had a headache. I thought one of her friends would walk her home.' It's the truth. So why am I being made to feel guilty?

Mum frowns. 'But I heard you come in, Violet. It was late when you got home. Not early.'

'Yeah,' I say. Now it's getting awkward. 'I didn't say I came home early. I said I left the Roxy early.' I hold my head up. 'I met a friend. He . . . he took me for a ride on his motorcycle. To help clear my head.'

Mum's mouth drops open. 'What friend? What motorcycle? First I've heard of this!'

Brenda slams her hand on the table. 'Can we just get back to Jackie!'

'Sorry,' I mumble. 'I don't know what to tell you. When I left she was still with her friends. I reckon that's where she will have gone. Just forgot to let you know, that's all.'

Brenda shakes her head. 'No, no, no. Even if she had, she'd be back by now. Look at the time. It's after lunchtime!' Her chin starts to wobble and she swipes at her eyes with the back of her hand. 'I can't believe you did that, Violet,' she mutters. 'You were supposed to look after each other. Especially after what just happened to those poor girls in the park. How could you? You shouldn't have left the Roxy without her!'

I can't believe she's blaming me. She has no idea what a bitch Jackie was to me. I hear Jackie's voice again. *Felt sorry for her. She hasn't got any friends*, and suddenly, in a breath, those last feelings of loyalty disappear.

'What about Colin?' I say. 'Could she be with him?'

'Colin? A boy?' Brenda's face flushes a deep pink. 'Why would she be out all night with a boy? Jackie's a good girl. You know that.'

'Just a thought,' I say. 'He was there with her last night. He's her boyfriend, I think.'

Brenda's face is almost purple now. 'I'll tan her bloody hide for her,' she says under her breath. Then louder. 'I'll tan her bloody hide, till she can't walk for a week!'

'All right, Brenda,' says Mum. 'Calm down. Come on, finish your tea. Jackie is a good girl. And there'll be a simple explanation, I'm sure. She's probably back home already, for all you know.'

'You're right,' says Brenda, her eyes bright with hope. 'She might be back and wondering where I am. I won't finish my tea. But thanks all the same.'

'Let us know, won't you,' says Mum. 'Let us know she's back safe.'

Brenda scurries out the door. 'If she's not back by teatime,' she shouts over her shoulder. 'I'm calling the police!'

Mum turns to face me. Her hands planted squarely on her hips in battle position. 'You've got some explaining to do, young lady,' she says. 'Riding about in the middle of the night on a motorcycle? What the hell do you think you're playing at?'

'What's your problem?' I say. 'At least I came home.'

She follows me through to the back kitchen.

'So, who's this fella you were gallivanting around with, then? Did you meet him at the dance?'

'He's just some fella,' I say. 'No need to turn in your grave.' I tip some potatoes into a bucket.

'And no need for you to speak to me like that. I'm your mother. Have some respect.'

'Sorry,' I mumble. I don't want to tell her about Beau. I don't want her asking questions. I want to keep him all to myself for now. I shiver slightly as I remember his star-burst kiss. 'He was just a nice fella,' I say. 'Honest. He just brought me home, and that was that. He's not a lunatic murderer or anything.'

Mum's face relaxes. 'Right,' she says. 'Well, just be careful, Violet. You don't want to be getting yourself a reputation, do you?' She pauses 'Maybe,' she says. 'If you see him again . . . this fella. Maybe you could ask him round for tea?'

'Maybe,' I say. I nod at the bucket of potatoes. 'I'd better get on with these if you want chips for the fryer tonight.' I smile to myself. I can't imagine Beau sitting round our kitchen table. I can't imagine it at all. It makes my tummy squirm and my toes curl just to think of it.

'Right. You'd better get on then,' says Mum. She sighs. 'I can't think what Jackie's playing at, worrying Brenda half to death like this.'

I can't think what she's playing at either. But it's none of my business any more, and I shouldn't care. But I do. Deep

158

down inside I want her to be okay. Because it's not easy to stop loving someone that you've loved your whole life, even when they've stopped loving you.

I unzip my jacket before I remember the bundle of letters tucked up inside. I quickly zip it up again. 'Mum?' I say quickly, before she leaves the room. 'Where's Joseph?'

Her eyes narrow. 'Out looking for work,' she says. 'He'll be back in an hour. Why?'

'Oh, nothing. Just wondered.'

Her face brightens for a second. 'It'll all be okay, love. You know that, don't you? I know it's been hard on you, him coming back. He's a stranger to you, after all. But, give him a chance, hey?' She smiles. 'I'm glad you're asking after him, though. It's a good sign.'

A good sign? She doesn't know what she's talking about. But at least I know it's safe now, to nip back into Joseph's room and slide the letters back under his mattress.

Dixon of Dock Green

The police arrive just as we're serving the last of our Saturday night customers. There's one in uniform, all grey faced and sweaty looking. At first I think he's come in for some chips, which is odd, because I'm sure the police aren't allowed to eat or drink on duty. He comes straight to the counter followed by two other men in suits; an older man with a black brush of a moustache and a younger one with red hair and orange freckles spattered across his nose.

The older one, with the moustache, beckons to Dad. 'Mr White?' he says. 'Frank White?'

Dad nods. 'Yes. Can I help?'

'Detective Inspector Gordon,' says the man from under his moustache. 'Sorry to interrupt, sir. We need to have a word with you and your family. Is there somewhere we could go?' The knot of veins at Dad's temple start to throb. That only usually happens when he's angry or stressed. But he doesn't look angry, and he doesn't look stressed. He shuts the door to the hot cupboard and I notice his hand is shaking. He's frightened. Dad is bloody frightened.

Then I realise what's happened. They've come for Joseph.

That's got to be it. The authorities have finally hunted him down. They've come to arrest him for desertion. They've come to take him away to face his punishment.

'Can I at least finish serving these customers?' Dad asks. 'Violet will show you through to the back. Won't you, Violet?' He lifts his eyebrows at me as he indicates for me to go round and let the policemen in through the kitchen door. I look quickly at the inspector and back again at Dad. 'Go on, then,' he says.

Was Dad's eyebrow lift a secret signal? Am I supposed to hurry through to the back and warn Joseph before I let the police in to the kitchen? Or should I just let them take him away? He deserves to be punished. If only for the pain he's made Mum and Dad suffer. But if he does get arrested, I'll never know the truth about Arabella and what really brought Joseph back to Battersea.

My heart's thumping high in my throat. It's like a scene from *Dixon of Dock Green*. I'm one of the actors and I'm about to help a criminal make his get away. I wipe my hands down my apron. 'If you come round the back . . .' I say to the inspector. 'I'll let you in the kitchen.'

His moustache twitches slightly in agreement. It means business.

Mum and Joseph are in the kitchen. Joseph's got a newspaper spread out on the table in front of him and Mum's darning one of Dad's socks. They both look up as I come in.

'The police are here!' I blurt out. I widen my eyes at Joseph. 'The police are here for you!'

'The police?' he says. 'What do they want with me?'

161

'You're a deserter,' I hiss. 'What do you think they want?'

He frowns. 'It can't be,' he says. 'It's not a crime any more . . .' A flicker of fear crosses his face, and for a moment I think he's going to do it. I think he's going to run. But it's too late, there's a knock at the door, and before I can open it and before Joseph can get up and make his escape through the shop, they've let themselves in and we all freeze, as though we've stared straight into Medusa's eyes and been turned to stone.

'Evening,' says the inspector. 'Sorry to intrude. I'm Detective Inspector Gordon, this is Detective Sergeant Jones and this is Constable Durbin.'

'Whatever's the matter?' says Mum, her voice all thin and quivery.

'Mrs White?' asks the inspector.

'Yes, sir,' says Mum, as though she's at school and answering the teacher at registration. Constable Durbin writes something in a little notebook.

'And you are . . . ?' The inspector nods towards Joseph.

'Joseph White,' he replies, looking the inspector straight in the eye. Constable Durbin writes something else down.

The inspector turns to me. 'And you are Violet White? Is that correct?'

I nod.

'Take a seat, Violet,' he says. I pull out a chair and sit opposite Mum. Joseph closes the newspaper and folds it up.

'Would you like a cup of tea or something?' asks Mum. She's wringing the darned sock in her hands like it's a wet dishcloth.

'Thank you, ma'am, but no,' says the inspector. 'We'll just give your husband a minute to get here.'

162

'Can't you tell us what this is about?' pleads Mum.

'It would be better to wait for Mr White to join us. Save going through it twice,' says the inspector.

I slide my eyes across to Joseph. He's tapping his fingers nervously on the table and his face has turned pale. We wait in an awkward silence. I count the seconds in my head, and it's the longest minute ever.

Eventually, Dad comes in from the shop. He bursts through the door, wiping his hands on a cloth. 'Well? What's all this about?' he demands.

'If you'd like to take a seat?' The inspector indicates towards an empty chair.

'No thanks,' says Dad. 'I'm all right where I am. Can you just get on with it, please?'

'Very well, sir,' says the inspector. 'Well, I'm afraid I have some very bad news.' He pauses and pulls at a corner of his moustache. 'I'm afraid I have to tell you that this morning, the body of Jacqueline Lawrence was found in Battersea Park. And I'm sorry to inform you that we are now conducting a murder inquiry.'

Nobody speaks. I'm not sure what he's trying to tell us. Who's Jacqueline Lawrence? Then Mum gasps and lets out a high-pitched whine. Dad rushes over to her and puts his arm around her shoulders. Joseph reaches across the table for Mum's hand and then all three look up at me.

'What?' I say. Then it happens. Somebody, somewhere picks up a hammer and slams it into my head. White hurt flares in my skull and pain shoots through my body.

Jacqueline Lawrence.

Jackie Lawrence.
Jackie.
Jackie's dead.
Jackie's been murdered.

The Big Dipper

I can't breathe. My throat's closed up. I can't get any air into my lungs.

'It's all right, love. It's all right. Come on. Deep breaths. Deep breaths.'

Dad's got his arms around me and is rocking me backwards and forwards. 'Get her some water! Quick!' he shouts.

There's a cold glass at my lips. Cold water in my mouth. It slips over my tongue and slides down my throat. But I can't swallow it. It's choking me. I cough and cough and the water spurts on to Dad's apron. And as I cough my throat opens up and I gasp at the air, and gasp again as my breath returns. 'Good girl. Good girl,' says Dad. He puts the glass to my lips again and this time I manage to swallow a mouthful of water and it hits my stomach with a cold slap of reality.

'Jackie's dead?' I whisper. 'But she can't be. You must have made a mistake,' I say to the inspector.

'I'm afraid not,' he says. 'There's no doubt. Her grandmother identified the body earlier today.'

'Oh God,' Mum murmurs. 'Poor Brenda. Poor Brenda.'

'We understand how difficult this must be for you,' says the inspector. 'But we have to ask you some questions, I'm afraid. And the more information you can give us, the more chance we might have of catching whoever it is that did this.'

'Of course,' says Dad. 'Anything we can do to help. Would you like to sit down now?'

And then we're all sitting around the table like we do on a Friday night. But instead of Norma and Raymond, Detective Inspector Gordon and Detective Sergeant Jones are sitting in their places. Mum has made a pot of tea and someone has put a cup in my hands. I don't realise I'm holding it until my skin begins to burn.

'So, Violet,' say the inspector. 'We understand that you have known Jacqueline for a number of years and that you were out with her last night.'

'It's Jackie,' I say. 'Her name's Jackie.'

'Sorry,' he says. 'Of course. Jackie. Now, can you talk me through last night? Where you went, what you did, who was there? Anyone you may have seen Jackie talking to? That sort of thing.'

I don't know where to begin, but Constable Durbin is still standing by the back door with his notebook and pencil. He's ready to start writing, so I know I have to say something. I take a sip of hot tea and Mum pats my hand reassuringly.

Then I tell them everything I remember. That Jackie called for me at seven o'clock last night and we walked to the Roxy together. She was wearing a tight blue skirt and a matching jumper and had big gold hoops in her ears. Oh, and she had heels on. White patent heels. We met up with her friends from the sugar factory. Pauline, Mary and Sharon. I don't know their last names. We danced for a bit. We did the Twist. There were some fellas there too. One of them was Jackie's boyfriend. His name was Colin. But I don't remember his last name.

Constable Durbin is scribbling all this down. He must have gone through three pages by now.

I didn't feel well, I tell them. I'm not sure what time it was. I went outside. I was going to go home. Jackie came out with Colin and I told her I was going home. She was still with Colin when I left and I presumed he would be walking her home. I can't bring myself to tell them about the argument. It's none of their business and it wouldn't help things anyway.

That's it, I tell them. That's everything. That's the last time I saw Jackie and then I came home.

'You didn't argue with Jackie, then?' the inspector asks. 'Before you went home?'

I hesitate. How the hell do they know about that?

'Only, Mr Trindle, Colin Trindle, says that you and Jackie had an argument. That you shouted at her, threw something at her and then stormed off?'

So they've already spoken to Colin? Of course they have. 'I . . . I . . . yes,' I say. 'It was only something stupid, though. She'd just upset me, that was all.'

'And how had she upset you?' He pulls at the corner of his moustache again.

Oh my God! What is this? Do they think I had something to do with her murder?

'Violet?' he prompts.

'She'd just changed recently,' I murmur. 'She wasn't like she used to be. She had new friends and stuff and started doing

167

things without me. Then . . . then I overheard her talking about me. In the toilets, last night. She was laughing at me. It was like I didn't mean anything to her any more. So . . . so I just blew it, that's all. I told her what I thought and that I didn't want to see her again.'

There's a silence in the room, and my last words hang there. *I didn't want to see her again*. Everyone's looking at me with a strange expression on their faces. 'No!' I say. 'I didn't mean it like that!'

'And then you went home?' Inspector Gordon asks.

I nod.

'How did you get home?' This time it's Sergeant Jones asking the question.

'I . . . I . . .'

Mum cuts in. 'You got a lift from a friend, didn't you?' she says. 'That fella you were telling me about.'

'And what fella is this?' asks Sergeant Jones.

Why has Beau got to be brought into this? It's nothing to do with him. 'Just someone I know,' I say. 'His name's Beau. He gave me a lift home on his motorcycle. But we went to Chelsea Bridge first. For a coffee.'

The sergeant nods knowingly. 'And his surname?'

'Don't know,' I say. I can feel Mum glowering at me.

'Not a good idea to accept lifts home from people if you don't even know their surname, is it?' Inspector Gordon purses his lips at me. 'And what time did you get home, Violet?'

I don't know why I'm being made to feel guilty when I've done nothing wrong. 'I don't know!' I say, louder than I should. 'It was late, okay? But you're wrong if you think I've

168

got anything to do with hurting Jackie.' My voice breaks. 'I love her,' I sob. 'I love her like she's my own sister.'

Mum pulls a hankie out from her sleeve and passes it to me. I push my face into it, but the familiar scents of Lily of the Valley and cold cream make me cry even harder. I want to be a child again, messing about in Mum's bedroom with Jackie. Squirting ourselves with her perfume and rubbing her cream on the backs of our hands.

'Well done, Violet,' says Inspector Gordon. 'I know that was tough for you, so well done.' He asks Mum and Dad and Joseph a few questions. Have they seen anything or anyone suspicious lately? A stranger, perhaps? Someone whose behaviour gave them cause for concern? And were they all at home last night?

No one's seen or heard anything suspicious, Dad tells them. And they were all working in the shop last night – well, him and Joseph anyway; Mum just popped in and out when she was needed. There were just the usual customers, nobody that they didn't recognise, and when the shop closed for the night, they had a bite of supper and then him and Mum went to bed. They can't believe what has happened. When they saw Brenda at lunchtime, they all thought Jackie would be coming home. 'Poor woman. Poor woman,' Mum keeps saying.

'And you, sir?' Inspector Gordon asks Joseph. 'Were you at home all night too?'

Joseph nods. 'Yes,' he says quite calmly. 'I had supper with Mum and Dad, stayed up for a while to read the paper, then I went to bed too.'

And then my heart's banging so hard against my ribs that any minute now, it's going to burst right out of me and splat against the kitchen wall. *Joseph's just lied to the police.* I can't believe what I've just heard. Maybe I made a mistake. Maybe it wasn't Joseph I saw walking towards the Roxy last night. But I can't lie to myself. I know it was. I might wear glasses, but I know what I saw. I feel dizzy and faint and I gulp down a mouthful of hot tea. I try not to think about the mention of the pump house in Arabella's letter and I *really* try not to think about how Joseph winked at Jackie last week, right here in this kitchen.

Inspector Gordon and Sergeant Jones get up from the table. 'Thank you for your co-operation,' says Sergeant Jones. 'If you think of anything else, please let us know. And, Violet?' He turns to me. 'We will need to know some more details about your friend. The one who gave you a lift home. If you could let us know his surname or where he lives, just so we can eliminate him from our enquiries. Okay?' He puts a card into my hand. 'We'll be in touch soon,' he says. Then Constable Durbin closes his notebook with a satisfied snap.

'How did she die?' I blurt out. 'Was she . . . was she . . . ?' I can't bring myself to say the word. I can't bear to imagine it. She hadn't even done it with Colin yet. And to think what her first time might have been like . . . My stomach heaves and the tea I just swallowed rises back into my throat. I gulp it down and try again. 'Was she . . . was she messed about with, like the other girls?'

'Sorry,' says Inspector Gordon. He can't look at me. 'I'm afraid we're not at liberty to go into details about the case just yet.'

'But you arrested Mr Harper,' I say. 'It was in all the papers. Is there someone else now, doing these things?'

The inspector lowers his eyes. 'I'm sorry, Violet,' he says. 'I really can't say.'

Nobody speaks. Not for ages. After the police close the door behind them, we all stare into space. It's like there's nothing left in the world to say. There's nothing that can make any of this any better.

Joseph is the first to move. He goes into the front room and comes back with a bottle of whisky. He takes four glasses from the cupboard and pours a measure of whisky into each glass. Then he puts a glass in front of each of us. 'Can't make it any worse, can it?' he says.

I put my hand to my throat, searching for the V that I know isn't there any more. I couldn't have made this happen, could I? Did I somehow wish for this when I threw my chain at Jackie's feet? When I broke the bond of our matching chains, did I break something else too? Did I want Jackie to be hurt? To be wiped from the face of the earth? Did I want vengeance?

V for Violet

V for Vengeance

I pick up the glass of whisky and drink it down in one go. It burns a thick trail down through my chest and into my stomach. It burns away the guilt and the horror. I pour another glass and no one seems to notice. This one goes straight to my head and wraps my thoughts in a warm, comforting blanket. The next one steals its way into my legs and toes and fingers and makes me hiccough and snort as I try to stop myself from laughing hysterically.

'Violet! Enough's enough!' I hear Dad saying. 'How many of those have you had?' And then somehow I'm in bed and my pillow is the softest thing in the world. I close my eyes and the world inside my head spins round and round. Jackie and me are riding the Big Dipper in Battersea Park. We're holding hands as the wooden train rattles along the rails. It climbs higher and higher until our heads touch the clouds then it plunges us down, faster and faster, and we shriek and yell in delight until our voices get carried away by the wind. Then suddenly, Jackie's hand slips out of mine. I reach out to grab it again, but she's too far away. 'Violet!' she screams. 'Violet!'

I lean over the side of the wooden train and I watch her falling. I watch her growing smaller and smaller and then I close my eyes and clench my fists as the thud of her hitting the ground jars my bones and I wake up suddenly, to the early-morning gloom of my bedroom and a pain in my heart like the devil himself is sitting on my chest.

There are three thoughts in my head.

1. It's my fault that Jackie's dead.
2. Joseph lied to the police last night.
3. I need to find Beau.

Mrs B and Chuck Berry

Jackie's made front-page news. There's a picture of her sitting on the front doorstep of her house. Her hair is scraped back into a ponytail and she's wearing her school blouse. It's open at the collar and her tie is hanging loosely around her neck. She's laughing into the camera. Her face is full of sunshine and hope.

I know where they got the photograph from. It's been sitting on Brenda's mantelpiece these last few months. Brenda got her camera out on the day we finished school for the last time. I was in the photograph too, but they've cut me out. If you look closely you can just see my shoulder resting against Jackie's.

Her body was found in a piece of overgrown scrub, just behind the funfair. Another dog walker found her. She'd been raped and strangled. The same as Joanne and Pamela. I'm glad they found Jackie so quickly. I'm glad she didn't have to lie there all alone for days and nights like poor Joanne.

The police are appealing for witnesses to come forward. Anybody who might have seen Jackie at the Roxy and afterwards.

Norma and Raymond have come round. Norma gave me a hug. I don't think she's ever hugged me before. 'Oh, Vi. Oh Vi,' she sobbed. 'I don't know what to say.' Mum cooked us all breakfast, but only Raymond's managed to eat anything. 'I can't believe it,' Norma keeps saying. 'It's like a nightmare.' She blows her nose and wipes her eyes again. 'It could have been you, Violet. It could so easily have been you.' That sets Mum off wailing again.

There's two of me sitting at the kitchen table. One Violet is looking around at her family, listening to the horrified silence and the tears and the murmurs of disbelief. This Violet is crying too. This Violet has a scream inside her that won't come out.

The other Violet feels hollow, like someone has scooped out her insides. This Violet needs to get out of the house. This Violet needs to go and find Beau. And this Violet can't look at her brother Joseph because every time she does, a creeping fear wraps itself around her brain.

I've told everyone that I need to go for a walk and be on my own for a while. They tried to argue with me. But they couldn't stop me. I had to promise not to go anywhere the park. As if I'd want to. As if I'd ever want to go near that place again.

There's not many buses on a Sunday, so I have to wait a while for one to come along. I don't mind. It's better out here in the fresh air. It's easier to breathe, and doing something, even waiting at a bus stop, helps to ease the pain that's been gnawing at my stomach all morning. I sit on the top deck and huddle down into my jacket. It's weird, watching the world go by; watching people going about their business as though nothing has happened. It's weird that the sun is shining when it should be raining. It feels like I'm watching life happen through a television screen.

I get off at Chelsea Bridge. They're all here, like I knew they would be. 'Hey, Violet!' Beau calls me over when he sees me walking towards him. 'Nice surprise,' he says, as he drapes his arm across my shoulder. 'Hey,' he says. 'What do you reckon?' He points down at his bike. 'Cool, hey?' he says. 'Got me new engine at last.'

'Yeah, cool,' I say.

'Took me months to save for that,' he says. 'You can't beat a Triumph engine. It's the dogs! Take you for a spin, if you like? Buy you a beer?'

I nod. 'That'd be good,' I say. 'That'd be really good.'

We stop at a pub called The Royal Albert. I sit outside on a bench while Beau goes inside to buy the drinks. He brings me out half a bitter while he has a pint. I sip the froth off the top of mine and laugh at Beau when he takes a big gulp of his pint and leaves the froth on his top lip.

'You never told me what you do,' I say to him. 'I mean for work.'

'Electrician's mate,' he says. 'Work for the Board. I don't mind it. Pays for me bike, anyway.'

'And you never told me where you live, either,' I say.

He laughs. 'Why do you want to know all this boring stuff?'

'Dunno,' I say. 'I just do.'

'Well,' he says. 'I got a bedsit. Not far from your chippie, actually. Been there four years now. Ever since me old mum died.'

'Sorry,' I say. 'About your mum.'

'S'all right,' he says. 'She'd been ill for ever. So I was pretty used to being on me own anyway.'

We sip our beer and I think how he's like a book that I really want to read. He's got an interesting cover. It's beautiful and flawed all at the same time. He's not a complicated book,

175

he's open and easy to read and if I want to turn another page I know that he'll let me.

So I tell him about Jackie. I tell him all about it and I don't cry once. But my face goes all stiff from trying not to. His face goes all funny too and I think how nice he is for caring so much when he didn't even know her. He buys me another beer. Then I tell him about the police and how they want to eliminate him from their enquiries, but I couldn't give them his surname because I don't know what it is.

He laughs at this. 'Never told you that either, did I? It's daft really. There's me mum giving me a real fancy first name like Beau when we had the most common surname in the world. Smith,' he says. That's me. Beau Smith.'

He tells me not to worry about the police; that we'll sort it out right now. 'They're always bothering us lot,' he says. 'Just cos we dress in leathers and ride motorcycles. But I've always kept me nose clean, I have. Squeaky clean.' He rubs it against my nose. 'See? Squeak. Squeak.'

We pull up outside Battersea police station and we go inside and ask the desk sergeant if we can speak to someone about the Jacqueline Lawrence case. He looks bored and he shifts his eyes from Beau to me and back again as if he can't quite see the connection. I tell him my name and about the visit yesterday from Detective Inspector Gordon. He sits up straight then and he writes something on a piece of paper and tells us to wait just a minute please. We sit on the hard wooden chairs and Beau makes me laugh by doing an impersonation of the desk sergeant's nervous tick.

After a minute, the door next to us opens and the red-haired policeman from yesterday walks into the room. 'Miss White,' he says. 'Detective Sergeant Jones. We met yesterday.' He nods at Beau. 'And this is . . . ?'

'Beau Smith,' says Beau. He stands up to face the sergeant. 'We've come here cos Violet says you wanted a little chat with me.'

'Indeed,' say Sergeant Jones. 'If you'd like to come this way, please.' He indicates for Beau to follow him back through the door. I stand up, ready to go with them, but the sergeant motions for me to sit back down. 'If you'd like to wait here, Miss White.'

Beau winks at me as Sergeant Jones leads him into the back of the station. As I sit and wait, I pull the zip of my jacket up and down up and down. The desk sergeant glances up at me and shakes his head slightly. I read some of the notes on the notice board. There's a two pounds reward for a missing cat called Charlie and a poster warning people to lock their car doors and windows. I watch the clock on the wall and the minute hand slowly moving around. I remember that a group of policemen is called a posse and a group of thieves is called a gang, but I don't think there's a word for a group of murder victims or corpses. If there was I think it should be a sorrow of corpses.

I'm beginning to wonder if Beau's ever going to come back. Maybe they've arrested him for something and stuck him in one of their cells. Would Sergeant Jones even bother to come out and let me know? I'm about to interrupt the desk sergeant, who's filling out a crossword puzzle, when the door next to me opens and Beau comes striding out. 'All sorted,' he says. 'Come on. Let's go.'

'Why were you in there for so long?' I ask. 'What happened?'

'Nothing much,' he says. 'Gave him my name and address. Told him I gave you a lift home Friday night, then went home meself, then we were talking engines. Turns out that copper's a bit of a motorcyclist himself.' He grabs hold of my hand. 'Anyway, come on. Fancy seeing where I live?'

He pulls me down the steps of the police station and I hear myself laughing. I hear blood pumping through my veins and I feel the emptiness inside me filling up. Being with Beau is like nothing else. He stops my heart from hurting. He makes the world carry on turning.

He drives us to a street with red-brick houses on one side and the remains of a bombsite on the other. He pulls up outside a house with snowy net curtains and a polished front step. I've been on this street before, I think. I picture two girls with liquorice-black tongues skipping home from the sweet shop. I see them stopping at the bombsite to flash their knickers at the boys who are charging through the rubble with guns made of sticks. Two little girls. Now there's only one left. I push the memory away and follow Beau to the front door. He turns to me and puts his finger to his lips. 'You'll have to be quiet,' he whispers. 'Can't let Mrs B know you're here. She's funny like that.'

'Who's Mrs B?' I whisper back. 'Thought you lived on your own.'

'I do,' he says. 'Got me own room and everything. Mrs B's just the landlady. She's all right about most things. But she'd have fifty fits if she thought I'd brought a girl to me room. She likes everything proper you see.' He winks at me. 'Don't look so worried. Come on. It'll be fine.'

He opens the front door and I tiptoe in after him. He points to the stairs in front of us and motions for me to go up. There's a door at the bottom to the left of the stairs and as we walk past it he shouts out, 'Only me, Mrs B!'

I freeze and look at him in horror as I imagine the door opening and a stern-faced Mrs B, all steel-grey hair and threatening bust, catching me in the act of creeping up her stairs. But instead, a wafer-thin voice calls back, 'All right, love! Don't forget to have a look at me wireless, will you? Can't get it to change programmes!'

'No worries, Mrs B. I'll pop in later!' Beau shouts backs. Then he playfully pushes me up two flights of stairs and through a door at the top of the landing.

'What will she do if she catches me here?' I ask. 'Will she chuck you out?'

'She won't catch you,' he says, closing the door behind us. 'There's no way she'll climb those stairs. Don't worry, now you're in here, we're perfectly safe.'

'Well . . . if you're sure . . . ?' I say.

'Sure as sure can be. Come on. Relax. Let me show you my little hide-away.' He spreads his arms wide.

There's not much to look at. The room's no bigger than my bedroom at home. There's posters all over the walls, most of them of motorcycles, and one advertising Chuck Berry, playing in person at the Palladium. Beau catches me looking at it.

'I was there,' he says proudly. 'Saw him for meself.'

There's an old fireplace at the end of the room with a one-bar electric fire in the grate. There's some socks draped over a drying rack next to it. On one side of the room there's a bed and on the other, a small kitchen area. There's a tiny brown-stained sink, a table-top cooker and a single chair.

'Sorry I didn't make the bed this morning,' he says with a grin. 'I didn't know I was going to have a visitor.'

I realise I'm staring at his bed; at the rumpled sheets and the dented pillow and the blanket that's half on the floor. Blood rushes to my face. 'It's all right,' I manage to say. 'It's only a bed.'

'It's good to have some company,' he says. 'Next time you come, I'll make sure I tidy up first. Might even put some flowers in a jam jar!'

'It's nice,' I say. 'It's a nice room.'

'Yeah, well. It's home, I guess,' he says.

We both stand there, an awkward silence prickling the air between us. I wonder what Jackie would say if I told her I was alone with a fella in his bedsit and all I could think about was kissing him again. Then, suddenly, it's like I've been punched in the stomach, as I remember all over again that Jackie's gone. She's dead. She's been murdered. My knees buckle and I just make it to the bed before they give way completely.

'Violet?' Beau's voice is soft and full of concern. 'You all right? Didn't think my place was *that* bad!' He crouches down next to me. 'Sorry,' he says. 'Shouldn't joke. They'll catch him, you know. They'll catch whoever did this to your friend.' He gets up and sits next to me on the bed. 'It's shit, I know,' he says. 'When someone you love gets taken away from you.' He puts his arm around my shoulder and pulls me in.

I lean against him and wait for the waves of sickness that are rolling up and down my stomach to pass. 'The first weeks are the worst,' Beau is saying. 'The pain's so bad you think it's going to kill you. And there doesn't seem to be any point in getting out of bed in the mornings. And you always think it's your fault. That there's something you could have done to stop it happening. And even if you couldn't have stopped it from happening, you could have at least been nicer to them. You could at least have told them how much you loved them.' He pauses. 'But it gets better. I promise you it gets better.' He pulls me in tighter.

I twist around and turn my face up towards his. 'When?' I say. 'When will it get better?' He leans down towards me and his quiff brushes my forehead. Before I close my eyes, I notice how red his mouth is and that there's a tiny white scar in the centre of his bottom lip. He puts a hand on the back of my head and then we're kissing again and he's pushing my mouth open with his tongue and his lips are so warm and the stars are bursting inside my head again. He slides his hand around and under the front of my jacket and then puts it right on my left boob.

I freeze. I'm not ready for this. I haven't even got my head around kissing him yet. Then, it's like he's read my mind. He moves his hand and strokes my back instead. Then he pulls away.

'You okay?' he whispers.

I nod, and press my face back into his shoulder. 'Why me?' I ask. 'Why would you want to kiss me? My sister told me that boys never make passes at girls who wear glasses.'

He laughs. 'You're all right, you are, Violet. I like you.' He pushes my glasses to the top of my head. 'It's not true what your sister said, you know. I think girls in glasses are dead sexy.

Even Marilyn Monroe has to wear them.' He slides my glasses back down on to my nose. 'You're smart,' he says. 'And funny. And you're not like all the others. You never judged me. I reckon we're the same, you and me. We're not like everyone else. We're misfits. I knew we'd get on, as soon as I saw you in the chippie the first time. And you knew it too, didn't you?'

'Yeah,' I say. 'I suppose I did.'

He laughs. 'It's all right to be different,' he says. 'In fact, it's bloody brilliant. We can do what we like, because we're invisible. Everyone likes to pretend that we don't exist.'

It's like he's crawled inside my head and read my thoughts. Except I didn't know that was what I was thinking. I lean closer into him. We might not fit in with everyone else, but we fit into each other. I don't ever want to go home. I want to stay in this room for ever. I'd tidy it up when Beau was out at work. I'd be as quiet as a mouse all day, and when Beau came back from work I'd make him beans on toast for his tea and we'd snuggle up together on his bed. He could bring me some books and I'd read to him when we got bored of the wireless. I could fall asleep with him next to me and every night he would promise me that things would get better.

But after a while, Beau says he should go and sort out Mrs B's wireless and that I should get home before Mum and Dad start worrying about me.

I don't tell him that I want to stay here for ever, that I'm amazed and bewildered by him, but also scared to death that it's all just some horrible joke the world is playing on me.

All the way home, I have to bite my bruised lips so the memory of his kisses stays with me.

* * *

'We need to go and see Brenda,' Mum says, as soon as I get home. 'See if there's anything we can do. Let her know we're here for her.'

I don't want to go. It's too soon. I don't know if I can bear it. What if there's a pair of Jackie's shoes still at the bottom of the stairs where she last kicked them off? Or a scarf on the back of a chair? Or a tube of her lipstick on the kitchen table? How can I bear to see these things and know that Jackie's never coming back for them? And what if I feel the ghost of her? What if she's there, waiting for me? Waiting to take her revenge on me for leaving her at the Roxy and for tearing off our friendship chain and throwing it at her feet?

But I know it's the decent thing to do. I know Jackie would want us to look after her nan and I know that however bad it is for me, it must be a million times worse for Brenda. So I help Mum to pack up a pudding basin full of chicken soup and I carry it carefully around to Brenda's with Mum walking slowly at my side as though we're already part of a funeral procession.

When Brenda opens the door to us, I don't recognise her at first. She's always been old. But now she looks ancient. It's like her whole body has shrunk but her skin has stayed the same size. There's an expectation in her eyes when she first opens the door; a tiny spark of something there. But when she sees Mum and me standing on the doorstep, the spark goes out and her shoulders slump, making her seem smaller than ever.

'I keep thinking it's her,' she says. 'Every time the door goes, I think its Jackie and she's forgotten her key again.' She puts

183

her hand to her mouth and presses down hard as though she's trying to keep something from coming out. A wail of despair, I think or a howl of grief. She takes a shaky breath and looks at us again. 'Violet?' she says.

'Yes, Brenda,' I say, as though I'm talking to a child. 'It's me. We've brought you some soup and thought you might like a bit of company?'

'You?' she says. Her eyes widen and suddenly she looks like the old Brenda again. 'How dare you come here! Get away! Get away now!'

'Brenda?' says Mum. 'Come on, love. It's us. Look. It's me and Violet. Shall we come inside and have a cuppa?'

'You're never stepping foot inside this house again,' Brenda spits. 'Either of you.' She points a finger at me; a wavering, putting-a-curse-on-me finger. 'You killed Jackie,' she hisses. 'If you'd never left her . . . if you'd never left her on her own. If you'd done what any friend would do, and walked home with her that night . . . she'd still be here. My Jackie would be here and not laying on a slab in the mortuary!'

'Brenda!' Mum shouts in shock.

'I blame her!' Brenda finishes, before she slams the door in our faces.

'Well!' Mum breathes out after a moment. 'I know grief does strange things to a person . . . but . . . that!' She grabs the basin of soup from my hands and puts it on the doorstep. 'It's hit her harder than we can have imagined. Obviously. Poor woman.' She leaves the soup on the doorstep and takes hold of my arm. 'Come on, love. Let's go home,' she says gently. 'And take no notice of Brenda. She doesn't know what she's saying. It's just the shock and the grief talking. That's all. She'll come round. You'll see.'

She twitters on, offering me words of comfort all the way home. But they don't make any difference, because I know Brenda's right. It's my fault Jackie's dead. I knew it straight away. And wherever she is, Jackie knows it my fault too. And the only way I can make things any better is to find out who did this dark and terrible thing and make sure it doesn't happen again.

The news of Mr Harper's release is the talk of Battersea, according to Mum. 'Poor man,' she says as she dishes out a plate of cheese on toast. 'He's never going to be able to hold his head high again. People will always suspect him, even though he's innocent. I wonder if he'll stay here. Or if he'll have to move away.' She looks at me all smugly. 'So much for being a Little Miss Know-it-all,' she says. 'Seems you don't know everything after all, Violet.'

Of course I knew as soon as the police came to tell us the news about Jackie that I'd been wrong about Mr Harper. I've never been wrong before. But I don't want to give Mum the satisfaction, so I pretend I didn't hear her and instead I watch Joseph closely as he chews on a bite of cheese on toast. It takes him four chews before he swallows and I follow his Adam's apple as it leaps in his throat. He washes the toast down with a few gulps of tea, then helps himself to another slice. He pauses before he takes a bite and looks over at me.

'You all right, Violet?' he asks. 'Have I got something on the end of my nose?'

I shake my head.

'Only you've been staring at me all through supper. Thought there might be a reason for it?'

I ignore his question and help myself to the last slice of cheese on toast. 'You going out tonight?' I ask.

'Uh huh,' he mumbles through another mouthful. 'Got to see a bloke about some part-time work in a garage. Just a few hours. But it's a start.'

'So you're planning on staying around for a while, then?' I say. 'Shame. I hoped you'd be going back to France.'

'Oh, Violet. Don't start!' Mum bangs her teacup down in frustration.

Joseph sighs and puts his unfinished piece of toast back on his plate. 'How long are you going to keep this up for?' he asks. 'It's all getting a bit boring. But for your information, no . . . I'm not going back to France. So do you know what, Violet? You'd just better grow up and get used to the fact that I'm back.'

I finish eating my toast and brush the crumbs from my hands. 'So where are you meeting this bloke then?' I ask. Because I don't believe him for one second. He's drawn the curtains across his eyes.

'None of your business,' he mutters.

His answer doesn't surprise me. I take my plate over to the sink to rinse. 'Oh, by the way, Joseph,' I say. 'You've got some crumbs on your chin.'

He glares at me and scrapes his chair back from the table. He does it with such force that Mum yelps and her teacup bounces from its saucer and rolls across the table. Joseph grabs his donkey jacket from the back of the door and slams out of the kitchen. The air vibrates and the pots on the draining board rattle. Mum glares at me and presses her lips together into a thin line.

So . . . I think. He's got a temper.

Later, after I've heard Joseph come home and creep up the stairs to bed, the house is quiet. Everyone's asleep. Except for me. I sit cross-legged on bed and open my notebook. I read through all the scribbles on the pages and remind myself of everything I know about Joseph so far.

There's the love letters from Arabella: evidence of their secret affair.

Their affair is discovered and Arabella's family disown her.

Joseph travels to England and Arabella plans to join him.

In the meantime, she is disturbed by some of the things that Joseph talks about in his letters back to her.

He talks of dark places and of things that fill her with horror.

When she finally arrives in England, they meet at the pump house. Why?

Arabella writes that she is frightened of Joseph.

And then there are no more letters. Did something happen to Arabella?

And now there's the other thing too. Why did Joseph lie about where he was on the night Jackie was murdered? He said he was working in the shop all night and then went straight to bed. But I saw him walking towards the Roxy.

Joseph's got a temper. I've seen it with my own eyes. And I remember what he told us all as we sat round the kitchen table on his first night back home. *The war did things to people. Terrible things,* he said.

All I can think is, how terrible is terrible? And all I can see in my mind is Joseph winking at Jackie. And where is Arabella?

The moon's splashed a silvery patch on to the rug on the floor. It's later than I thought. Much later. And suddenly I don't want to think any more. I don't want all this blackness in my head. I don't want to be in this dark place. I just want nothingness. I close my notebook and just manage to drop it by the side of my bed before my head sinks down on my pillow and the next thing I know, Mum is hammering on my door.

'Come on, Violet! What are you doing? Time to get up. It's late.'

All Her Kisses

'You all right, love?' says Mum as I pick at my breakfast. 'You managing to sleep okay?'

I grunt at her.

'Listen,' she says. 'You do know Brenda didn't mean anything by what she said yesterday, don't you?'

I grunt again. Of course Brenda meant it. Because it's true. It *is* my fault that Jackie's dead. Mum leans towards me and kisses me lightly on the cheek. It's as much of a shock as if she'd slapped me. For a second, the world feels better, but then I remember all the other times she could have kissed me, or hugged me and never did. All the times I fell and scraped my knees, the times I was stuck in bed with the measles or the mumps or just a fever, the hundreds of times that Norma was rotten to me. Mum never kissed me then. All her kisses were planted on the face of a dead boy in a photograph frame. She had to wait until my best friend was murdered to award *me* with a kiss. I quickly wipe the greasy mark of her lipstick off my cheek.

Joseph breezes into the kitchen and my heart turns cold. I look down at my plate as he grabs his coat from the back of the door. 'No time for breakfast this morning, Mum,' he says. 'I'll grab something while I'm out.'

I glance up and see him kissing Mum quickly on the cheek; so easily and naturally. And then he's gone.

'Where's *he* going?' I ask.

'To work,' she says. 'He's got some hours in that garage. Heavens, Violet, don't you ever listen?'

'How do you know that's where he's really going?' I say before I can stop myself.

'What are you talking about? Of course he's going to work. Where else would he be going? Honestly, Violet, sometimes I think you live in a different world to the rest of us.'

She rattles on and on. I stop listening to her and think about the French letters again, wondering if I missed something. There might be other clues, something that would explain where Arabella is, and why Joseph doesn't mention her. Something that would stop me thinking he's done something terrible to her.

I leave Mum washing the pots and peer into the shop. Dad's busy cleaning out the fryers, so I run up the stairs and straight into Joseph's room. I push my hand under his mattress and feel around with my fingers. Where's the bundle of letters? I push my hand and arm further under. I search near the head of the bed, all through the middle and down to the bottom. They're not there. They're gone. He's taken them. I pull my arm out and sit back on my heels. Why has he moved them?

I quickly search the rest of his room, but the letters are nowhere to be found. He must have taken them to work with him, or destroyed them. I kick his bed frame in frustration. It

190

feels like someone's stolen a book from me that I've only half read and now I'm never going to know the ending.

I need more clues, I need to know the rest of his story. Because if I don't, then I'm going to be left with this horrible, dreadful, unthinkable thought that's buried deep inside my head, the one that's growing bigger and bigger every day. And I won't be able to live with that.

I wander back to my room, hoping to be by myself for a while before Dad shouts me down to help with the fryers. I open the door and my heart does that thing it does when somebody jumps out at you unexpectedly. It stops for a second. Then when it starts beating again, it's such a shock, it hurts my chest. The bundle of French letters is on my bed. And on top of them is a note.

YOU ONLY HAD TO ASK

I can't settle.

I wash the mud off a load of potatoes and peel the skins off as thinly as I can. I sweep the shop floor and count change into the till. I start ripping up a pile of newspapers. One page after another into a neat pile. Then I stop. Jackie's face smiles out at me from a copy of *The Sunday People*. Her eyes laugh into mine. *We're proper grown-ups now, Vi*, she'd said that day. And it hits me again. Sudden and violent.

Dead.

Jackie is dead. She'll never be a proper grown-up. Never. She'll never go to another dance. She'll never pack another bag of sugar. She'll never get kissed again, she'll never get married, and she'll never have babies. She'll never sit on her nan's sofa again, eating custard creams and watching *Coronation Street*.

The cold air of the back kitchen turns into cotton wool around my head. There's a whooshing in my ears and I stick my head between my knees, like I do if I ever feel faint from period pains. I take deep breaths.

In, out. In, out. In, out.

I stare at the floor. It needs washing. There's potato mud smeared all over the lino and over in the corner there's a collection of dust and fluff and grease stuck to the bottom of the skirting board. There's a coin too, just poking out from under the work counter. I think it's a threepenny bit.

I lift my head. The whooshing has stopped, but my hands are freezing. I look at Jackie's photograph again. I can't add the page to the pile of ripped newspapers. I can't have her smile wrapped around a six of chips. I fold the page carefully and slip it into my pocket.

My stomach jumps. It feels like there's a small bird trapped inside me, trying to find its way out. It flutters frantically around my chest, head and stomach. Every time I hear a door bang, the bird dives into my chest and sits on my ribs like a budgie on its perch, flapping its wings madly.

Mum comes through with a clean apron for me. 'We're opening in a minute,' she says. 'You ready?'

'When's Joseph coming back?' I ask her.

'Don't know,' she says. 'He's not sure how long the garage wants him for today. And anyway, what's that got to do with you being ready for work?'

'Nothing,' I mumble. The bird inside my chest is going crazy. How did Joseph know I'd looked at his letters? Perhaps I'd put them back in the wrong place. And now he's been in my room. Did he read my notebook? Does he know that I'm on to him? Thinking about him being in my room – breathing in my private air, creeping across my floor in his big, black boots, kneeling down to look under my bed – makes my stomach clench and my scalp feel dirty. But I did it to him, so I must be just as bad. Tit for tat.

I serve in the shop over the lunchtime shift. The time passes in a blur of panic. I'm only half aware of how the customers are looking at me, and what they are saying.

'How could she have let that poor girl walk home on her own?' someone mutters. And someone else. 'Poor Brenda. And to think she treated that girl like her own.'

I let the words drift over my head and pretend they're talking about someone else. Finally, the last customer leaves and I sit with Mum and Dad in the kitchen and try to eat a ham sandwich. All the time the hairs on the back of my neck are prickling; waiting for the sound of Joseph walking through the door.

Dad goes to the front room for his afternoon snooze and Mum sits and hems some new curtains for Norma. White cotton with a smattering of cornflowers. 'I know I shouldn't be sewing at a time like this,' she says guiltily. 'But I have to do something. Or I'll go mad thinking about that poor girl.'

The quiet of the house is unnerving; like a Sunday afternoon with nothing to do. I drift from room to room. I tiptoe around Dad, asleep in his armchair. He's got a hole in the toe of his slipper and a button missing from his shirt that makes it gape open around his belly. I can see his string vest. I stare at the mantelpiece and notice that Mum's put a trinket there instead of Joseph's photograph. It's a brown china dog standing on its hind legs with its tongue hanging out. It's an ugly thing and I don't know where she got it from. I wander back to the kitchen and straighten the plates on the dresser. I open and shut cupboard doors and I fill the kettle and empty it again.

'For God's sake!' says Mum. 'Can't you find something to do? Go to your room and read one of your books or something. Moping around's not going to do you any good.'

I think of the letters still sitting on my bed, making a dent in the counterpane. It's three o'clock. Joseph could walk through the door any minute now. The waiting is agony.

I climb the stairs and clump along the wooden floor of the landing to my room. I close the door behind me and take a steadying breath. They're still there of course, glaring at me accusingly from the middle of the bed. I sit down next to them. Maybe they are simply just love letters. Maybe I'm wrong and there is no dark secret to be found. Maybe that's what Joseph's telling me. *I've got nothing to hide. You could have just asked me, if there were things you wanted to know. You didn't have to steal my letters. But, here. Have them anyway, you nosey little cow.*

The light in my room suddenly dims and bullets of rain begin to batter against the window. I shiver and pull my cardi close around me. I pick up the letters and weigh them in my hands. All those words scrawled across all those sheets of paper.

Maybe I've read too much into it. Maybe I translated some of the words wrong. Or maybe Joseph knows I didn't manage to untangle all those foreign sentences. He's been clever. He's bluffing. *Here, Violet. Take a good look. Read them all if you like. You won't find a thing.* But I know I'm not wrong about this.

194

I've got that feeling. Joseph's love story isn't all it seems. It isn't a love story at all. It's a horror story. I know this like I know that Brenda's never going to forgive me, that Beau wishes Mrs B was his mum, that Norma's never going to be happy with Raymond, and that worst of all, Jackie's death is not the last terrible thing that's going to happen to us all. I lie down on my bed and curl up into a ball. I listen to the rain and try not to think about anything at all. I must drift off into a dreamless sleep because the next thing I know, I wake with a start to the sound of voices coming from downstairs.

The rain has eased off and the empty sky outside paints my walls with a sickly yellow light. Joseph's home now. I can hear him laughing with Mum. A door bangs. 'Go and towel yourself off,' she shouts. 'I'll put the kettle on.'

Heavy footsteps up the stairs and along the landing. They stop outside my door. The sound of him breathing. A faint whistle through his nose. Then a knock. 'Violet? Are you in there?'

My heart's banging hard, like a hammer. But I get up from the bed with the letters in my hand. I open the door. He's dripping wet. His hair is flat to his head and his face is flushed and greasy with rainwater. The bottom of his denim jeans are dark and water is pooling around his boots on to the landing. I hold out the letters to him and he takes them.

'Did you find out what you needed to know?' he asks.

I shrug. 'Not really.'

'You only had to ask,' he says. 'You didn't have to snoop around. I know what you think of me, Violet. But you're wrong, you know. I would have liked to have told you the truth. I thought you'd be the one person to understand. But I don't know if I can trust you now.' He waves the letters in my face. 'It's just words, Violet. But they were meant for me, not for you.'

He grips the bundle of letters in both of his hands. They're big, his hands. There's dark hairs growing on his knuckles. His fingers are long and streaked with oil. He's squeezing the bundle of letters and twisting them around. The paper is crackling and creasing. He'll never be able to flatten them out.

'Violet? Are you listening?' he says.

'I've got to go,' I say quickly. 'Dad needs me in the shop.' I don't want to be on my own with him. I don't want to think about his hands squeezing and twisting. I don't want to breathe the same air as him. I push past him and run along the landing and down the stairs.

Sour Milk

It's Tuesday morning. Joseph has just left for the garage. At least, he's taken the pair of oil-stained overalls that he's been hanging on the back of the kitchen door when he comes home in the evenings. I'd follow him if I could, to catch him out in his lie. He could have got the overalls from anywhere and his oil-streaked hands don't fool me for a minute. But I'm a prisoner to the shop and Mum's been watching me like a hawk since Jackie's murder.

There's a knock at the back door. It's the police again. Mum lets them in and then starts flapping because all the breakfast things are still on the table. 'Violet!' she hisses. 'Get those dishes in the sink.' She pats her hair and adjusts her housecoat and offers Detective Inspector Gordon and Detective Sergeant Jones a cup of tea.

'Actually, it's Violet we've come to see,' says Inspector Gordon. 'Just a quick word with her, if that's okay?'

I didn't eat much breakfast. Just a slice of toast. But I have to swallow hard to stop it coming back up. I don't want to puke in front of a policeman.

'Just a few questions, if you don't mind, Violet.'

Mum quickly clears a space at the table and Inspector Gordon makes himself comfortable in Joseph's chair. 'You can both stay,' he says to Mum and Dad. So they sit down too and then we wait for Sergeant Jones to find a pencil. 'Sorry,' he laughs. 'Thought it was in the other pocket.'

'So, Violet,' Inspector Gordon begins. 'You knew Jackie for a long time, didn't you? Most of her life, in fact?'

I nod. He smells of damp wool and importance.

'So you probably knew her better than anyone else, apart from her grandmother, maybe?'

'I don't know,' I say. 'Maybe.'

'Well. These might seem like strange questions to ask, but anything you can tell us . . . anything at all, could really help us in finding who . . . who killed her.' He takes a deep breath. 'So, Violet. Would you describe Jackie as a shy person? Was she outgoing? Friendly? Or did she keep herself to herself?'

It's horrible to think of Jackie like this. Of what she was and not what she is. 'She was friendly, I suppose. She wasn't shy, anyway.'

'Can you think of anyone new Jackie might have come into contact with recently? Did she mention any names to you?'

I shake my head. 'Only the girls from the sugar factory. And that fella she was with at the Roxy . . . Colin.'

'Did she go to the fairground in Battersea Park, do you know? Did she know anyone who worked there?'

'I don't know,' I say. 'We used to go to the fair when we were younger. But I don't know if she still went there.' Sergeant Jones is scribbling in his notebook. 'Do you think the person that killed Joanne Thomas and Pamela Bennett killed Jackie too?' I ask.

'We really can't say,' says Inspector Gordon. 'But, is there anything else you can tell us, Violet?' he asks. 'Is there anybody else she may have met recently? Any places she liked to go? Anything she liked to do in her spare time? Anything at all. Any little detail, even if it seems stupid and irrelevant.'

I shake my head again. 'I haven't seen much of her since we left school. She was . . . she was busy doing her own thing. The other girls – the girls at the sugar factory. They might know more.'

Now Inspector Gordon shakes his head. 'We thought, that as you were her oldest friend, she may have confided in you. She may have told you something that she wouldn't tell anyone else. About boys, for instance? Was there anyone else apart from Colin that she may have been out with?' He pauses. 'And, Violet . . . I'm sorry if this embarrasses you, but do you know if Jackie was a virgin?'

He's right, I am embarrassed. And angry too. What's Jackie's virginity got to do with him? The old perv. And what difference does it make if she was or she wasn't? Even if she was a virgin, before . . . before . . . She's not any more.

'Violet?' he insists, when I don't reply.

'She said she was thinking about doing it,' I mutter.

'I'm sorry?' he says.

I raise my voice. 'She said she was thinking about doing it. And do you know what? I hope she did do it. I hope that at least bloody once she got to know what doing it should really feel like!'

Mum looks like she wants to curl up into a ball and die and Dad doesn't know where to look.

199

Inspector Gordon clears his throat. 'But you don't know if she did or not?' he says as gently as I imagine he can.

'No,' I say. I feel like I've failed some sort of exam. 'She didn't tell me.'

'Okay,' he says. 'And you're sure there's nothing else?'

I shake my head.

'There must be something, Violet,' Dad cuts in. 'Something you can think of that'll help the police.'

'Yes, Violet,' says Mum. 'Come on. Think. There must be something.'

Mum and Dad are glaring at me. It's like I'm shaming them or something. *The useless daughter. She can't even tell the police what they need to know.* But the thing is, there is something I want to tell Inspector Gordon. It's bursting out of me. The words are filling up my mouth and choking me. All those things that have been chewing away at the edges of my mind.

Have you questioned my brother? I want to say. Have you double checked where he was on the night Jackie was murdered? I saw him walking towards the Roxy, but he told you he was working here and then went to bed. He knows Battersea Park. He met Mum there at least a couple of times, and he's met someone else there too, by the pump house, where Joanne Thomas and Pamela Bennett were found. He has these letters you see, from a French girl called Arabella. I think it was her he met at the pump house. In the letters she says that Joseph has dark thoughts and in the last letter I read, she said he frightened her. I don't think she's written to him since. I think she's disappeared and I think my brother has something to do with it.

I want to tell Inspector Gordon all of this and I want Sergeant Jones to write it all down in his notebook. I want them to go and find Joseph at the garage and I want them to ask him all the things I can't ask him. I want them to find out the truth about him. But I can't say any of it. I swallow hard, my mouth dry. I can't say any of it, because if I do I'll break Mum and Dad's hearts.

'She liked to go to the café in town,' I say instead. 'Ruby's Café, the one by the Granada. And she saw *Breakfast at Tiffany's* at the Granada. You know. That new film with Audrey Hepburn. That's all I know. I'm sorry.'

Inspector Gordon runs his fingers down the edges of his moustache. 'Okay, Violet.' He lowers his eyes and waits. He knows there's something I'm not telling him. He's not a Detective Inspector for nothing.

'Sorry,' I say again. 'But like I said, I haven't seen much of her since we left school.'

'Right,' he says. 'Well, thank you for your time, anyway.' He pushes his chair back and gets to his feet. 'But if something does occur to you, please get in touch.' He nods to Mum and Dad. 'Mr and Mrs White.'

Mum hurries to the door to let them out. 'Oh, and by the way,' says Inspector Gordon. 'Thank you, Violet, for bringing Mr Smith to the station on Sunday. It's always best for people to volunteer information than for us to tease it out of them.'

Mum's about to close the door when Inspector Gordon stops it with his hand. He pokes his head back into the kitchen. 'Mr Smith was acquainted with Jackie too, was he?'

'No,' I say. 'He never even met her.'

'Right,' he says. 'Well, thanks again.' And then he's gone and for some reason, I'm left with a bad taste on my tongue, like I've just swallowed a mouthful of sour milk.

'Mr Smith?' says Mum. 'Who the hell is Mr Smith?'

'Just that fella,' I tell her. 'You know, the one who brought me home on his motorcycle.'

Mum says something else. But I'm not listening any more, because there's a rushing feeling in my head, and a panicky shifting in my chest. Why did Inspector Gordon ask if Beau knew Jackie? Like he was double checking something that he didn't believe.

I know Beau never knew Jackie. Of course he never knew her. He would have said if he did. Wouldn't he?

I keep waking up at night. It's like an alarm goes off in my ear and I wake up all hot and shaking between the sheets with my nerves jangling and my heart banging away in my ears. I have to switch the light on just to check there's nobody in the room.

By nobody, I mean Jackie.

I dream about her every night. She's always in a rage. She's always blaming me. *You should have stayed with me, Violet,* she yells at me furiously. It's always raining in my dreams. Hard, violent raindrops pounding down on Battersea Park; every drop as sharp as a knife slicing into the ground. And Jackie's wet through. Her beehive's collapsed around her face and mascara is running down her cheeks in black rivulets. *Don't leave me here,* she cries. *Please, Violet. I don't want to be on my own.*

Then she screams and it's the scream that goes off in my head like an alarm and wakes me up and I have to check that she's not in my room, standing in the corner dripping water all over the floor. She never is. But it always feels like I've just missed her by a breath.

An Orange Sucked Dry

It's Friday morning, and another grey and miserable day. I don't think the sun has shone once since Jackie was murdered. But I'm glad. It wouldn't be right somehow, for there to be blue skies and sunshine when it feels like the world has stopped turning. The week has crawled by, like it's been too tired to even bother trying. Like me, really. All the juice has been sucked out of me. Like the orange I always get at Christmas and eat in my own special way, poking a hole in it and sucking and squeezing until I've sucked out every last drop of juice. When I've finished, all that's left in my hands is a flattened carcass of skin and pith, all empty of sweetness and promises. And, that's how I feel.

I can't stop thinking about Beau either. Every time a motorcycle roars past the shop, I remember the smells of burnt oil and leather and how it felt when he kissed me. It makes my heart twist to think of him sleeping in that room just a few streets away, with his legs tangled in his sheets and an empty bottle of beer on the floor beside him. Or to think of him on Chelsea Bridge, surrounded by the other fellas, all leaning proudly against their bikes.

Every day I pray that he'll come to the shop to find me. I want to look him in the eye and ask him about Jackie. I need him to tell me that he didn't know her. But he never comes. And I can't go and find him, because I'm bloody well stuck here.

The day grinds on. It feels like I'm walking through syrup. Every time I turn around, I expect to see a line of sticky footprints behind me. Even the clock on the wall in the back kitchen doesn't seem to be moving. I wash the floor and scrub the skirting boards and even pick up the threepenny bit from under the work counter. I switch the wireless on to break the silence and Helen Shapiro sings out at me. It used to be my favourite song. I listen to her singing about how the best years of your life are when you are young and how you should run wild and have fun.

The best years of my life? I bloody hope not. I switch it off. It seems a lifetime ago that I last heard that song. Tears fill up my throat. I swallow them down. It *was* a lifetime ago. Jackie's lifetime. And all I can think about now is how she was only just beginning. How her best years were just beginning.

Mum comes through to ask me to go to the shops with her. 'Can't go out on my own,' she says. 'Not until they've caught him. It's not safe.'

I trudge along the High Street, lagging behind Mum as though I'm five years old again. People are hurrying along the pavements as if the shops are about to shut, and its only three o'clock. They look over their shoulders and check their watches. Their eyes dart from side to side, looking out for murderous strangers. Outside the newsagent's there's a blown-up picture of Jackie from the papers, pasted on to a hoarding. Whoever pasted it on didn't do a very good job. There's a crease running right across her face.

In the butcher's, Mr Pitchford wraps up some sausages for Mum. 'Terrible,' he says under his breath. 'Such a lovely girl too.' He doesn't even look at me. I might as well be invisible.

Mum mumbles something and ushers me out of the shop. Out on the street I notice more people staring. Some of them smile sympathetically at Mum and others look at me in disgust, as though it was me that killed Jackie. It's the same in every shop. All everybody's talking about is Jackie. And they're all talking about her as if they knew her. 'Beautiful girl. I always thought she could have been a model,' someone in the greengrocer's says.

'She was always so polite and friendly. Tragic. So tragic,' says someone else.

'I don't know how she can show her face,' I hear someone else mutter.

And in the queue in the bank, they're all whispering. 'They haven't got a clue who the killer is yet, have they?'

'She was supposed to be her friend. But she left her all alone to be murdered.'

'I won't leave the house after dark. Not any more. Not until they catch him.'

Mum virtually drags me home. She's furious. Her feet are stamping holes in the ground. And I know it's me she's angry with. Even she blames me for Jackie's murder.

There's a couple walking in front of us with their Labrador, and in the distance are the treetops of Battersea Park. I wonder if anyone takes their dogs there any more. I wonder if anyone would even dare.

Joseph comes home just as Dad is sliding the bolt on the chippie door. He looks like he's done a day's work with his greasy overalls and dirty face. I'm relieved. At least that's one thing he might be telling the truth about. 'Just going to wash up,' he says to Mum, and he disappears upstairs just as I have to go through to the shop to start the evening shift.

It's a busy night. We're rushed off our feet. Dad says he can't believe how busy it is. 'Where are they coming from? All these people?'

They're queuing outside, right around the corner.

'Ghouls!' says Mum, when I run out the back to fetch another bucket of fish. She's right. All they want to do is stare at me and talk about Jackie.

'Where did she live?'

'Just round the corner, isn't it?'

'Which house?'

'Did you know her?'

Dad calls through for Joseph to come and give a hand. His hair's still wet from the bath and there's a salmon-pink sticking plaster stretched across the back of his hand. As he throws pieces of fish dripping with batter in the fryer, I can't help staring at his hand. As the fish sizzles furiously, my brain's working fast, wondering how he cut himself. Was it an innocent accident at the garage? Or something more sinister?

'Three girls in a matter of weeks,' someone says.

'They're looking for a serial killer.'

'Shocking business.'

'Could be anyone. Could be someone we know.'

A man standing near the front of the queue takes his hands out of his coat pockets and runs them through the slick of black hair on his head. 'Could be any one of us,' he says. 'Any one of us. Standing here. Right now. In this queue.'

That shuts everyone up. The only sound is the loud sizzle of batter crisping in the fryers.

Then someone else shouts out, 'Never would have happened if it wasn't for her.'

Everyone's eyes are on me.

'Enough!' a voice suddenly shouts. I look over my shoulder and Joseph is staring over the counter at the customers, his lips curled in disgust. 'Any of you want a fish supper, feel free to stay in the queue. But any of you want to continue gossiping about a poor dead girl, then I suggest you go somewhere else.'

'Well said, son,' says Dad.

A man and a woman at the back of the shop shuffle out of the door. 'Charming,' the man says. 'I won't be spoken to like that.'

Nobody speaks for a moment. Then the man with the slick of black hair orders a small cod and chips and the silence is gradually filled as the rest of the customers begin to comment on the weather. There's a storm due over the weekend, someone says. Just the weather for banking up the fire and staying indoors.

I watch Joseph pass over the parcel of cod and chips. And something slips inside me. No one's ever stood up for me like that before. And I can't believe how good it feels. It's exactly what a big brother should do for his little sister. I glance over at him as he counts some change out, and I remind myself that Joseph isn't like a normal big brother. He's a fake and a liar and maybe something even more terrible. The good feeling disappears as I remember that I've never had a big brother. And I never will have.

Norma looks awful. 'I can't sleep,' she says. 'Ever since it happened. I haven't been able to get a wink.' We're all sitting around the table for the usual Friday night supper, but nobody's touched their food yet.

'And Raymond can't change his shifts, so two nights of the week I'm on my own all night. You had to put extra locks on the doors, didn't you, Raymond?' Her hair is tugged back into a ponytail and her face is bare. I haven't seen her without make-up for years. She looks like a tired little girl.

'I'll come and stay with you if you like,' I say. 'When Raymond's working. Least you won't be on your own then.'

'She'll be all right, thank you, Violet,' Raymond says. He turns to Norma. 'Won't you, love? I keep telling you, nothing's going to happen.'

'It's all right for you,' she sniffs. 'You're a bloke. You don't know what it feels like to know there's a killer out there on the loose.'

Raymond stabs a chip. Norma chews on a fingernail.

'Come on, everyone,' says Mum. 'Cheer up and eat up.' She looks around at us all and tries to smile. But it's not a real smile. It's an upside down, sad smile. Even her eyes don't crinkle. I know she wants to fix everything and make it all better, but she can't fix this. No one can.

I look across at Joseph. He's picking at the edges of his sticking plaster. 'What did you do to your hand?' I ask.

He jumps slightly. 'Oh . . . nothing,' he says. 'Few scratches from work, that's all.'

There's a pair of thick curtains drawn right across his eyes. What a big, fat lie. 'What did you scratch it on?' I ask.

'What's with you?' he says. 'Why are you so interested in a few scratches?'

'Just making conversation,' I say.

He laughs. 'Well, if you must know, I got it trapped in the bonnet of a car I was fixing.'

'What sort of car?' I ask quickly.

He frowns. 'A Ford Cortina.'

'What was wrong with it?'

'Problem with the timing chain,' he says warily. He shifts around in his seat. 'All these questions. Anyone would think you didn't believe me.'

'Oh, shut up, Violet!' says Norma. 'Stop going on at him. What does it matter how he scratched his hand?' She looks close to tears.

'Listen,' says Joseph. 'I know you've got a problem with me, Violet. But now's not the time, hey? You can see how upset everyone is. Let's just eat in peace.'

He cuts me down with the sharpness of his tongue and he doesn't even flinch. He's so good at being the perfect son that I almost believe in him myself. His knife crunches through his battered fish and as he fills his mouth, everybody else starts eating too.

I watch Joseph's jaw move up and down as he chews. There's a crumb of batter stuck to the corner of his mouth. He catches it with a flick of his tongue. I shudder. A snake in the grass. That's what he is. A poisonous snake, disguised as an ordinary fella, lurking in wait to catch his next victim.

The Pump House

Saturday morning and Joseph is getting ready to leave the house. He's crouched over in his chair tying up his boot laces. Mum's out back hanging up the washing and Dad's in the shop giving the fryers a deep clean. I stand in the doorway and watch as Joseph stands up and shakes down the legs of his jeans. Then he shrugs himself into his donkey jacket and checks through his pockets.

I didn't think he knew I was watching him, until he calls over his shoulder as he's walking out the back door. 'See you later, Violet. Don't do anything I wouldn't do.'

I scowl at his back. What exactly wouldn't you do, Joseph? I want to shout at him. What have you done already? What the hell are you hiding?

I wait a couple of minutes before I follow him. Outside the air is damp and the sky is loaded with fat grey clouds. Joseph has made it to the corner of the street. He's walking fast with his head down and collar up. He's heading towards the High Street. My blood's pumping in my throat. It should be easy for me to hide in the Saturday morning crowds. He turns into the newsagent's, so I hover around outside the greengrocer's, picking up apples and checking them for bruises. When he comes back outside, he takes a cigarette from a fresh packet and cups his hands around a match to light it. He carries on walking and as I follow close behind I taste the remains of the smoke that he's blown from his mouth.

It's only when he stops by the main road and checks the traffic that I realise, with a sickening thud to my stomach, where he's going. I lag behind and wait for him to cross the road, then I watch the broad sway of his back as he walks through the entrance to Battersea Park.

I hurry across the road. But with every step I take the sicker I feel. Despite the roar of traffic and the distant shouts and chatter of Saturday-morning shoppers, a crashing silence fills my ears. It pounds in my head and I have to stop for a minute and rest my hands on my knees and take a few deep breaths. I look into the entrance of the park and my skin crawls. The trees are like sinister giants, their branches like gnarled fingers clawing at the air. The ground is covered in a mulch of rotted leaves and I imagine I can already smell the sweet smell of death rising from the ground. I feel cold sweat breaking out on my forehead. I don't want to go in there. It would be like jumping into Jackie's grave.

But I've got no choice. Joseph's in there. So I need to be in there too.

I clench my fists, grit my teeth and within a few steps I'm in the park and the clammy green air is settling on my skin. There's a figure to the left of me in the distance, walking on the pathway that leads to the funfair. I recognise the sway of his shoulders. I pad along the path after him, slowly and stealthily. I'm the hunter now. A slinky panther stalking its prey.

Joseph's way ahead now. But it doesn't matter. I probably know the park better than he does, so there's no fear of losing him. What good reason could he have to come here, of all places? Is he meeting someone? Is he meeting Arabella? Will I get to see the face of his mysterious French lover?

Joseph walks further and further away from the path and I follow him, keeping as far back as I dare. At least the ground is wet and the leaves are just squishing softly under my feet instead of crackling loudly like screwed-up newspapers. Suddenly, I see it through the trees, the familiar and looming shape of the pump house. It looks more haunted than ever. I stop behind the last of the trees and peer out from behind its trunk. The ground around the building is trampled flat and there's a length of plastic tape, blue and white striped, caught up in the ivy that clings to the crumbling walls. I shiver. I see the ghosts of a dozen policemen, searching the ground for clues and I see stretchers, carrying the covered bodies of Joanne Thomas and Pamela Bennett, being loaded on to a waiting ambulance.

Joseph walks the length of the pump house wall, then he stops and runs his hands over the bricks like he's searching for something. But then his hands drop to his sides and it looks like he's about to turn around. I quickly dive behind the tree. I hold my breath and wait. I strain my ears for the sound of footsteps. But there's nothing. Just the faint smell of cigarette smoke. The wind creeps through the branches above me and a couple of leaves fall silently at my feet. I wait. The minutes pass, and I wait some more. I can't bear it, so with my heart pounding in my throat, I peer around the tree again.

He's still there. But he's leaning against the wall of the pump house now, staring up at the sky. I follow his stare, but all I can see between the swollen clouds is a patch of blue sky and the faint remains of an aeroplane trail. I look back at him and he's checking his watch. He seems to sigh, then he hunches over, puts his hands in his pockets and starts to walk away. I watch him for a few seconds. He drags his feet along the ground like a disappointed kid, like he was expecting to find something, and didn't.

I watch until he reaches the path on the north side of the pump house, then I quickly run to where he was standing. I run my eyes over the wall, searching the brickwork. I brush my fingers over the dusty surface, but there's nothing except cracks filled with spiderwebs, loose flakes of brick and the creeping stems of ivy. My hands are shaking and I can feel my heart beating in my fingertips. But I know I have to check inside the pump house. What if . . . ? What if Arabella is inside there? As I walk around to the front of the building a sudden breeze lifts the back of my hair and I feel the blood crawling through my veins. I almost turn away. But I think of Joanne and Pamela and Jackie and how alone they must have felt and it's like invisible hands are pushing me. And then I'm there, in front of the tall wooden doors. Someone has nailed batons across the width of both doors and there's a large shiny padlock hanging from the lock. I feel dizzy with relief. The police aren't taking any chances.

I look around. Joseph's almost out of sight now. He's walking fast, back towards the park entrance. I wait for a minute and try to make sense of what I've just seen. What the hell was that all about? What was he looking for? Who was he waiting for? I try to imagine calling up Detective Inspector Gordon and telling him that because of a few letters written in French and because my brother visited Battersea Park and because I know he lied about where he was on the night Jackie was killed and because of a terrible *feeling* that I have – Joseph White is the man they are looking for.

They'd think I was crazy. They'd think I was off my rocker. They'd think I was just the jealous little sister, sent as mad as a hatter by the death of her best friend. And maybe they'd be right. Maybe I am crazy?

I look up in a panic. He's out of sight. I've let him get too far ahead. I start to run. My feet squelch into the wet mix of grass and leaves as I pound towards the park's entrance. He definitely went this way, but I still can't see him. I run faster. My breath is coming quickly, in hot spurts. I cut across the lawns, half expecting to hear Mr Harper yelling at me to keep off the grass. But I'm close now. The trees are thinning out and I catch glimpses of rooftops on the High Street.

Then I see Joseph, the back of him, anyway. He's only yards away, but he's out on the High Street before me and just as I think he's going to turn around and see me, all red-faced and breathless, he breaks into a jog and jumps onto a double decker that looks like it's about to pull away from the bus stop. I don't know how I do it, but suddenly I'm flying after the bus with my arm stretched out, my fingers touch the cold metal pole at the entrance, then I'm gripping it hard and pulling myself up on to the platform and I think my chest is actually going to burst open as the conductor shoos me away down the bus to take a seat.

Joseph's not here. He must have climbed up to the top deck while I was jumping on to the bus. People are staring at me like I'm a freak or something and I realise I must look all wild-eyed and panicked. I quickly sit down, next to a teenage boy with curly copper hair and long arms like a monkey that are folded around a rucksack on his lap.

'Where's this bus going?' I ask him.

He looks at me sideways and clutches his rucksack closer to his chest. 'Oxford Circus,' he says. He moves away from me slightly and turns to stare out of the window.

The conductor stands in front of me and rattles his machine. 'Oxford Circus, please,' I say. Joseph might get off before then, but at least I've paid for the whole journey. I keep my eyes on the stairs as the bus bounces along the road. He doesn't get off at the first stop. Nor the next nor the next. He must be going up West, to the very end of the line.

Eventually, the bus judders to a halt at Oxford Circus and everyone shuffles along to the exit. I keep to the back of the queue, my eyes still fixed on the stairs. A woman in a black mac and paisley headscarf comes down first, then two small boys shoving each other and giggling. A man in a suit comes next and then a couple wearing matching suede coats. I'm beginning to think I imagined Joseph getting on this bus. I'm beginning to think I followed a ghost.

But then there's a pair of black boots clumping down the stairs and a pair of blue denim legs and my heart's thumping ten to the dozen as I follow him off the bus and into the crowds of Oxford Street.

He walks fast and with purpose. He's not here to browse the shops, that's for sure. I follow him past Woolworths and Littlewoods and K Shoes. There's a new record shop called HMV. I peer through the door as I hurry past. It's packed with girls and fellas, rifling through stacks of glossy albums or with headphones clamped to their heads listening to their favourite sounds. I should be doing that, I think. I should be spending my Saturdays doing all the fun things that young people are supposed to do, not following my brother to God knows where.

Suddenly, Joseph turns down a road. I look up at the street sign. Berwick Street. There's a busy market up ahead, but before we get to it, he turns down another street, then another and another. I notice how different everyone looks here. The fellas are more like women, with long hair, hipster trousers, and fitted shirts with crisp collars and no ties. It smells different too; of spice and perfume and danger. There's a boy pushing a barrow loaded with cans of film. There's coffee bars, jazz bars, record stores and funny little blacked-out shops. There's narrow doorways everywhere and all of them seem to have a girl sitting on the steps or leaning against the door. They're all dressed up to the nines, even though it's not even lunchtime yet. We walk past one door, painted shiny black, and underneath the door knocker is a sign that says, *This is not a brothel. There are no prostitutes at this address.*

And suddenly, I know where we are. And I know why my tummy's been flipping with a weird excitement, and it's not just because I think my brother might be a killer.

I'm in Soho. Even the name sounds hot and wicked. Everyone knows about Soho. It's where dirty men go to have sex with prostitutes. It's a bad place; a filthy place, as Mum would say. And now I know why Joseph's come here.

He turns down another street. Dean Street. His hands are thrust deep in his pockets and he's zipping along at a pace. I'm not worried that he'll catch me following him. He's too intent on getting to wherever it is he's going. Any minute now, I expect him to turn into one of the doorways and to disappear inside with one of the prostitutes. How will I warn her about what he might do? How can I stop the very worst thing from happening again?

Across from us, on the corner, is a pub. The doors are painted black and the windows have those little diamond-shaped window panes, like they had back in Tudor times. The name, The Golden Lion, is painted in big gold swirly letters on a sign that stretches the length of the wall. Next door to the pub is another doorway with a girl who looks no older than me, standing there, in a skirt up to her bum and with boobs that would make Dad's eyes water. Joseph crosses the road. And it looks like the girl has seen him. She starts to smile and push her boobs out even further. That's where he's heading. I just know it.

I'm about to shout out. Anything. Something.

But then, Joseph simply opens the door of The Golden Lion and disappears inside. And I'm left on the pavement with my mouth wide open and my brain scrambling to figure out why he's come all this way just for a pint in a pub.

'Oi! Violet!'

I nearly jump out of my skin. I turn around and my heart judders. It's Beau. He's walking towards me with a bag in his hand and a stupid smile on his face. 'So . . .' he says. 'This is what you get up to in your spare time, is it? Hanging around street corners. Knew you were a bad girl really.'

I know he's joking, but I can feel a hotness spreading across my face in a mixture of confusion and shame. Joseph is in the pub across the road and Beau is here. Why is he here too, in a place like this?

'Hey,' he says. 'No need to blush. I was only messing around.'

'What are you doing here?' I ask quickly, my voice shaking. 'Have you been following me?'

He laughs. 'Yeah, course I have. I make a habit of following girls around, didn't you know?'

When I don't crack a smile, he shoves me playfully on the shoulder.

'Don't be daft,' he says. He holds up his bag. 'Been to the Soho Record Centre, haven't I? Got the new Chuck Berry. Look.' He opens the bag to show me, but I don't move. He closes the bag and stares at me for a minute. Then he frowns. 'Listen,' he says. 'Sorry I haven't been around for a while, but I thought you might need some space after what happened to your friend and that.' He pauses. 'Doesn't mean I didn't miss you, though.'

I want to tell him I missed him too. I want to ask him if he knew Jackie, and I want him to tell me that, no, of course he didn't. I want to totally trust him. I want to tell him that every bit of me wants to be sitting on the back of his motorcycle with my arms tight around his waist. I can almost feel the wind in my face as I imagine him racing through the streets, and I can almost taste the bitterness of the coffee that he would buy me on Chelsea Bridge. But I can't speak. It's all too much. Joseph in the pub across the road, and Beau standing here right next to me.

'Hey,' he says gently. 'Come here.'

He puts his arm around my shoulders and pulls me close. Then he whispers something to me that makes me think he can read my mind.

'They haven't found him yet, have they?' he says. 'The bloke who killed your friend.'

I shake my head and breathe in the hot, salty smell of him. I didn't realise just how much I'd missed him. He bends to kiss me and this time he pushes his tongue into my mouth and flicks it slowly against mine. He tastes of chips and cigarettes. I freeze for a minute, remembering how Jackie once told me a girl could get pregnant if a boy put his tongue in her mouth. How silly we were. I push the thought away. The taste of Beau and the feel of his breath in my mouth makes my chest ache. He's so close to me, so inside of me, that I'm horrified to feel tears stinging my eyes.

'You okay?' he whispers.

I shake my head and pull back from him so I can push my fingers under my glasses to wipe my eyes. I need to tell someone and I want to tell him. He's the only person I can tell. I take a deep breath. 'What would you do,' I say, 'if you thought that someone close to you had done a really terrible thing?'

'What sort of terrible thing?' he asks.

'The most terrible thing one person can ever do to another.'

He's silent for a minute. 'What are you saying, Violet?' he asks. 'Do you know who killed your friend?'

'I . . . I don't know. I think I might . . . yes.'

He turns me around, takes hold of my arms and looks me in the face. 'Why haven't you gone to the police? You've got to go to the police, Violet!'

'But what if doing that means destroying a whole family?' I can't stop my voice from shaking. 'What if it means destroying even more lives?'

'How will it do that?' He pulls me close again. 'I'll come with you, if you like,' he says. 'We can go to the police together. But you've got to let them know. What if this person kills again? How would you feel then?'

'But what if I'm wrong?' I press my face into his chest. His jumper smells sharp and musty, like a damp flannel. 'What if I go to the police and they come and arrest this person, and I was wrong all along?'

He strokes the back of my hair. 'You can't mess around with things like this, Violet. If you only have half a reason to think you know who might be the Battersea Park Killer, you have to tell the police. For the sake of your friend if nothing else.'

He's right. He's only telling me what I already know. But what he doesn't know is that it's *my* family that'll be destroyed by this. It's my *life* that'll be destroyed by this.

'Thanks for listening,' I say. 'And I promise I'll think about what you've said. But I just need a bit more time. Just to be sure. A hundred per cent sure.'

'If that's what you want,' he says. 'I promise I won't say anything until you've made your mind up what to do. But when you have, let me know. And I'll help you, Violet. You know I will.'

I try to smile, but my lips are all wobbly. He leans down and kisses me again. Just once, on the corner of my mouth. 'Hey,' he says. 'You never told me what you're doing here. It's not to earn extra pocket money, is it?'

He's joking again. But this time I don't mind. I glance behind at the doorway to The Golden Lion and try not to imagine what Joseph is doing inside there. 'Just window shopping on Oxford Street,' I say. 'Walked a bit further than I thought and ended up down here.'

'Got me bike parked up just round the corner,' Beau says. 'Fancy a ride home?'

And suddenly, I'm so tired of it all; of Joseph and the terribleness of everything, of the pain of losing Jackie and of the trying and trying to make things right. And I feel so dirty standing here in this place that I can't think of anything else I'd like better.

There's a police car parked outside the chip shop when Beau pulls up. My heart sinks. I'm not in the mood for more questions or for the looks on Mum and Dad's faces when I can't answer them. I clamber off the bike and turn to say goodbye to Beau. He pecks me quickly on the cheek. 'Better shoot,' he says, and before I know it he's off down the road with a final backwards wave of his hand. I wait until the sound of his engine is like the distant whine of an insect before I turn around and almost bump straight into Inspector Gordon.

'That was Mr Smith, I presume?' he says, looking into the distance after Beau.

'Yeah. What of it?' I say, before I can help myself.

'You two been out somewhere, then?'

'Why do you need to know?' I snap back. 'It's got nothing to do with who killed Jackie, has it?'

Inspector Gordon laces his fingers together and stretches his arms out in front until I hear his knuckles cracking. 'Now, here's the thing, Violet,' he says. 'I popped around to ask you a couple of questions, but you weren't here, and your mum and dad had no idea where you were either. So, I'll ask you again. Where have you been with Mr Smith?'

He's serious. A shiver runs through me, like someone's dropped an ice cube down my back. I knew I'd get into trouble with Mum and Dad for buggering off for the morning but I never thought I'd get in trouble with the police. 'I just went up West,' I say. 'I needed to get out of the house for a bit. You know. I did some window shopping.'

'And Mr Smith?' asks Inspector Gordon.

'I bumped into him up there. He was buying records and he offered to bring me home. Save on bus fare.'

'Uh huh.' He nods, but his face tells me he doesn't believe me. 'But you didn't think to tell your parents you were going out?'

I shake my head. 'They wouldn't have let me go. They'd have been too worried about me.'

'And you can't blame them for that, can you?' he says.

He looks at like I'm a disappointment to him and for a moment I feel like I'm being ticked off by Constable George Dixon from *Dixon of Dock Green*. But if it really was Constable Dixon standing here in front of me, I could tell him about Joseph. Right here, right now. I could tell him everything. He would understand. But then I see Mum, staring at me through the shop window, her face like thunder, and I know that Inspector Gordon is not someone from off the television and I just can't do it.

'I need to ask you something about Jackie,' says Inspector Gordon. 'Her grandmother told us that Jackie always wore a chain around her neck, with a silver J attached, and that you have a matching one, with a V.'

My fingers rush to my throat.

'Only the chain wasn't on Jackie's body when we found her. Do you know anything about it?'

'I . . . I . . . no,' I say. 'I don't know.'

He waits.

'I . . . I took mine off when we fell out that night. Perhaps she did the same.' Not perhaps, I think. I know she did. Of course she did. Our friendship was broken that night for ever. Why would she have kept it on?

'Mmm,' says Inspector Gordon. 'Perhaps she did. Oh, and just one more thing. How long, exactly, have you known Mr Smith for?'

I don't like him talking about Beau. It makes me feel funny inside. Like I'm doing something wrong just by knowing him. But Beau's the only thing making the world turn right now. 'Two weeks, six days and thirteen hours,' I say. 'Is that exact enough for you?'

Mum actually slaps me across the face. I've never seen her so angry. 'Don't you dare do that to me again,' she spits. 'Don't you dare go off without telling me.'

I bite my tongue as tears sting my eyes.

225

'Where the hell have you been?' she asks. 'I've been worried sick.' I can't exactly say, I was following your precious son because I think he's a monster. She'd just slap me again. So instead I say, 'And what about Joseph? You know where he is, do you?'

'That's different,' she says. 'He's a grown man. I don't need to know his every movement. You can ask him yourself later, if you're that keen to know.'

I bloody will ask him, I think. Just to see what lies he'll come up with this time.

But, it is later now, much later. And he still hasn't come home. I'm in the shop with Dad and I can't concentrate. I've splashed my arm twice already with hot oil and I've dropped a parcel of large cod and chips all over the floor. 'What's up with you, Violet?' Dad hisses at me. 'Come on, get with it.'

But I can't get with it. All I can think about is Joseph in The Golden Lion. What was he doing in there? Is that where he hunts for victims? He's good looking for a fella of his age, even I can see that. And he can turn on the charm. I've seen that too, with all his fancy French speak. There's some girls who'll fall for anything.

He'll buy her a drink, whoever it is that he snares in his trap. And then he'll buy her another. Port and lemon, perhaps? I think that's what she'd drink. She'll have just too much. And then she won't think that maybe Joseph is too old for her and she'll forget about what she's read in the papers about the Battersea Park Killer and she'll just be giddy with all the attention.

Then Joseph might tell her about the war. He'll tell her how he flew planes over France, about how he bombed the enemy, about how he is a hero. Then she'll feel safe with him.

She'll perhaps think it will be a feather in her cap if she gets to kiss a war hero. She certainly won't think twice when he invites her to come home with him. They'll get on a bus back to Battersea and she'll giggle all the way as he flirts with her and makes her feel good. We'll just cut through the park, he'll say to her, when they get off the bus. No need to be frightened, I'll look after you. She'll hold on to his arm as they reach the deepest darkest centre of the park. And perhaps she'll start to have second thoughts then. Perhaps the cold night air will sober her up and she'll realise what she's done. But it will be too late by then. Because there's too many places in the park to hide and there'll be nobody there to hear her scream.

'Violet!' Dad's hissing in my ear. 'They wanted pickled onions with that order. What's wrong with you tonight?'

The broken veins on his cheeks have flared up red and there's sweat running in thin trickles down the sides of his face. I could tell him I was having my period, but he'd only die of embarrassment. But it would be better than telling him I was imagining his son taking the life of another young woman. I don't say any of that of course, I just mumble, 'Sorry,' and scoop an extra onion out of the jar, even though I'd rather smash the whole thing on the floor. 'Can I just have a minute, Dad?' I ask.

'I think you'd better,' he says. 'But don't be long.'

I escape through the back kitchen and into the house. Mum's sitting at the table with the shop's account books spread out in front of her and a frown on her face.

'Just getting a drink of water,' I tell her as I fetch a glass from the cupboard. 'I'm not feeling too good.'

She sighs and puts her pen down. 'You and me both,' she says.

227

I fill the glass from the tap and turn to look at her. 'What's the matter?' I ask.

She rubs her temples and sighs. 'It's Norma,' she says. 'I'm worried about her. She was round here earlier, without a scrap of make-up on.'

'So?' I snort. 'No make-up? Well, what's wrong with that?' I lift the glass of water to my mouth.

'Norma's always worn make-up,' says Mum. 'She never leaves the house without it.' She picks up her pen and rolls it around in her fingers. 'I think all this awful business with Jackie has hit her hard.'

The rim of the glass is cold on my lips. I breathe out and my breath ripples the surface of the water. 'You're joking, aren't you?' I say. 'She didn't even know Jackie that well. Jackie was *my* friend!'

'I know. I know,' says Mum. 'Of course it's hard on you too. But Norma's not as strong as you. She never has been. And I'm worried about her. That's all I'm saying.'

I slam the glass down on the table and the water jumps out and slops across Mum's account books.

'Violet!'

'She can't just steal my sadness and pain and make it her own!' I shout. 'That's not fair!'

'Don't be so ridiculous,' Mum shouts back. 'It's not just your pain. It's everyone's!'

She doesn't understand what I mean. I'm not sure I even understand what I mean. I'm just mad at Norma, mad at the world. Mad at Mum. *Look at your precious son*, I want to yell. *Take a close look. Can't you see you gave birth to a monster?*

But I can't bring myself to tell her. I don't want to be the one to rip out her soul again.

I swallow my rage. 'I'm sure Norma will be fine,' I say through gritted teeth. It's obvious what's wrong with bloody Norma. I can't believe Mum hasn't thought of it. She's pregnant, isn't she? Her dream has come true. I wonder if even Norma knows yet.

I leave Mum tutting and mopping up the puddle of water and make my way back to the shop. It doesn't look like I've missed much. There's only a couple of customers left and Dad's almost finished their orders.

'Feeling better?' he asks.

I shrug and start to wipe down the counter, scooping up the spilt salt and dribbles of vinegar in a cloth. The shop door jangles open. I make a wish under my breath that this will be the last customer of the evening. I'm sick of having to plaster fake smiles to my face.

Joseph doesn't come back until gone midnight. My eyes are itching with tiredness. I waited and waited, tossing and turning in bed, listening to the occasional car passing by outside my window, the raised voices of fellas on their way home from the pub and the distant barking of a dog. There were long stretches of time when all I could hear was my own breathing or Mum and Dad sighing and turning over in their bed.

I checked my watch for the thousandth time. Midnight. And then I heard it. The sound of a door being closed softly downstairs. Then footsteps coming slowly up the stairs.

He's on the landing. He's trying to be quiet, but he's stumbling. There's a thud. He hiccoughs. Then his bedroom door closes with a bang. His bedsprings creak loudly, then all I hear are his snores rattling through the walls. He's drunk, I think. And people only get drunk for two reasons; to celebrate or to forget. I pull my blankets tight around my shoulders, because suddenly, I'm freezing cold.

Star Witness

I wake up with a headache. It's like someone's banged a nail between my eyes in the middle of the night. I feel awful. I wrap up in my dressing gown and go to the bathroom to find some aspirin. I swallow two pills, then I wash my face and brush my hair. I stare into the mirror and wonder again what Beau sees in me. It's hard to imagine what I look like through someone else's eyes. All I can see is ordinariness.

On the way downstairs I pass Joseph's room. His door is closed and when I put my ear to it I hear him shifting around and snuffling in his sleep. I pinch the bridge of my nose, but instead of helping, it sharpens the pain in my head. I wince. There's a heavy lump in the pit of my stomach too; like I've swallowed a brick or something. I don't feel right. Nothing feels right about today.

I thud downstairs. For a minute I wonder if Mum and Dad are still in bed. I can't hear the wireless and I can't smell toast or bacon or Dad's fags, or any of the usual Sunday morning things. The lump in my stomach gets heavier.

But they aren't in bed. They're sitting in their usual places around the kitchen table and I know straight away that something is very wrong. Blood drains to my feet and giant fingers squeeze my skull tight. Dad's face is grey and Mum doesn't look much better.

'What's happened?' I ask quickly.

They both blink at me, like they've only just seen me. Mum scrambles to her feet. 'I'll put the kettle on,' she murmurs.

'Dad?' I turn to him. 'What's wrong?'

He nods at the newspaper on the table. 'It's another one,' he says. 'Another girl's gone missing.'

The pain in my head explodes into a million sparks. I slump into a chair.

The kettle boils and steam settles in the air like a storm cloud. Mum bangs around with cups and saucers and when she puts the teapot on the table, she wobbles and tea slops out and spreads in a brown stain across the cloth. 'Oh, God. Sorry,' she says.

I glance over at the folded newspaper.

Concerns grow for missing girl as police continue hunt for Battersea Park Killer

Mum pours the tea with shaking hands. 'I can't bear it,' she says. 'To think, he's close by, walking the streets that we walk, shopping in our shops.' She gasps. 'God forbid we've ever served him in the chippie.' She takes a sip of tea and her teeth rattle on the rim of her cup. 'They're saying there'll have to be a curfew. No female should be out on her own after six in the evening. It's like the bloody Blitz all over again.'

Dad shakes his head in disbelief. 'How many more poor girls?' he says. 'How many more before they catch the bloody monster?'

232

The monster, I think. The monster that's asleep right above your head at this very minute. I gulp a mouthful of tea. It burns my tongue and throat, but I drink some more anyway, because a scalded tongue is nothing next to what I'm about to do. I don't have to think about it any more. I don't have to try and decide what to do. Because now another girl's gone missing it's all been decided for me.

'I'm just going to get dressed,' I mumble. I'm not sure they even hear me. As I walk back upstairs, I realise the pain in my head has gone and the lump in my stomach has melted away. I've just got that feeling instead, the one I used to get when me and Jackie were in the queue for the Big Dipper. That sick, fizzy, stomach-churning feeling that comes before you do something you really want to do, but that you know is going to terrify the life out of you at the same time.

I don't bother knocking on Joseph's door. I barge straight in. He stirs and flips over on to his back. His sleep-ruffled hair is sticking out in damp clumps and his bare arms are flung wide open showing off the tangle of dark hairs in his armpits. His blankets have ridden down his body, and I watch the steady beat of his heart tap-tapping under his naked chest. If I had a knife with me, I could plunge it right into him and stop that tap-tapping before he knew anything about it.

His eyes flick open and we stare at one another for a moment. Then he pulls at his blankets and struggles to sit up. 'Violet?' he says. 'You all right?'

'I know what you are,' I say to him, slowly and calmly. 'And I know what you did last night.'

His eyes widen and he swallows hard. I've never seen anyone look so guilty. 'What are you talking about?' he asks.

'You heard me,' I say. 'I know what you are.'

He narrows his eyes. 'What do you think I am, Violet?'

'A monster,' I say.

His face falls. 'A monster,' he repeats to himself. 'I'm a monster?'

Suddenly, I'm shaking and cold sweat is breaking out on my forehead. I need to get out of here. I've got no idea what he'll do to me now he knows I know. He could kill me this very second with just his bare hands. I turn to go.

'Violet. Can't we talk about this?'

I run from his room and race down the landing to my own bedroom. I slam the door shut and grab my chair to wedge under the door handle. I'm panting hard. What have I done? What the hell have I done? I grab my jeans and try to pull them on, but I'm trembling so much I can't get my feet into the leg holes. I could shout for Mum and Dad. But what if he hurts them too? I shouldn't have spoken to him. I should have just gone straight to the police. I can't believe I've been so stupid.

I eventually manage to get my jeans on, and a jumper and some shoes. What's he doing? Is he planning his escape? Is he packing a bag right this minute?

Suddenly, my door handle rattles. I swear my heart stops. 'Violet. Violet. It's me. Let me in.'

My throat fills with terror and the bitter taste of aspirin. I can't speak.

'Please, Violet. Let me in. Let me explain. Let me talk to you. Please. You've got it all wrong. I'm not a monster. I'm really not a monster.' He rattles the handle again.

'Go away,' I manage to say. 'I don't want to speak to you.'

'Violet.' His voice has gone all high-pitched and pleading. 'You can't just come and say those things to me and then tell me to go away.'

I don't answer him. I can't. I'm trying too hard not to scream.

'Violet! Please!'

I slump to the floor with my back against the chair and my fingers in my ears. *Go away. Go away. Go away*, I whisper to myself.

I'm not sure how long I sit there for, but when I eventually take my fingers out of my ears, there's silence. I stand up slowly and carefully pull the chair away from the door. Still nothing. He's gone. I'm sure of it. I grab my leather jacket from the wardrobe and pull it on, making sure my purse is zipped into the pocket.

It's now or never.

A sudden bang forces a small scream from my throat. But then there's another and another and I let out a breath as I realise it's only the water pipes. Someone's in the bathroom. I inch the door handle down. Slowly, slowly, then I pull the door open a crack.

He's not there.

I open the door wider. The landing's empty. The water pipes are still groaning and I can hear water splashing from the taps. If he's in the bathroom, I'll have to be quick. I tiptoe along the landing and dart down the stairs. *Please don't let him be in the kitchen, please don't let him be in the kitchen*, I chant. I push the door open, and there's Mum and Dad still sitting in silence at the table. Mum's staring into space with her chin resting in her hands and Dad's blowing cigarette smoke over her head. As I walk in Mum straightens up.

'Is that Joseph up and about?' she asks. 'Shall I put some breakfast on now?'

'Not for me,' I say. 'I'm . . . I'm going out.'

'Out?' Mum explodes. 'You're not going anywhere. How could you even think it?'

I don't answer. I look at her face with her eyebrows creased in a terrible frown and at Dad with his cigarette paused halfway to his mouth, and my heart aches for them; for what I'm about to do. 'I'm sorry, Mum. I'm sorry, Dad,' I manage to choke out, and then I'm out of the back door and running, with Dad yelling at my back, 'Violet! Violet! Get back here!'

I run and I run, until my chest feels like it's about to burst. The pavements, the houses, the trees, the shops, the sky – everything's a blur. I race across roads and down back alleys, past boarded-up buildings and old bombsites and pubs that aren't yet open. I run past the west side of the park and I see across the road there's dozens of police milling around outside the entrance. I imagine them all in there, dragging the boating lake and searching every corner, every building, every overgrown piece of waste ground. I don't stop. I run and I run until my feet are burning.

I turn onto Battersea Bridge Road and by the time I reach the police station every breath tears my lungs into shreds. I slow my pace and take deep gulps of air. My heart's rattling along at a hundred miles per hour. I stand on the corner opposite the station. A group of officers are gathered at the bottom of the steps and there are three police cars parked on the pavement. They'll all be in there, working overtime. No Sundays off until they've caught the killer.

I will myself to walk past them all. To walk up the steps and inside and straight up to the desk sergeant. I think about what I'll say. How I'll say it. I'll be calm and matter-of-fact. I'll look directly into his eyes and say, 'I think you should speak to my brother, Mr Joseph White. I think he might be the Battersea Park Killer.' I imagine how his bored expression will turn into one of surprise and panic and excitement. I won't be just some annoying kid. I'll be someone important, I'll be the star witness. They'll usher me into an interview room and offer me tea and biscuits and Detective Inspector Gordon will be called for. They'll send a car or two with flashing lights and wailing sirens straight to the chippie and it'll take at least three officers to get the handcuffs on Joseph.

Then a horrible thought strikes me. They'll bring him here, won't they? And Mum and Dad'll probably come too. I might have to see them. I might have to say what I know in front of them all. My feet are shuffling, my hands are sweating, and suddenly I know I can't do it like this. I can't do it face to face. I need to tell the police what I know. But I need to do it the coward's way.

I set off back towards the High Street, my feet pounding the pavements again. In the distance, the four chimneys of the power station are pouring mauve plumes of smoke high in the sky to join the clouds. I keep checking over my shoulder expecting to see Joseph chasing after me, his arms pumping and his face contorted with rage. I see the telephone box up ahead, sitting outside the bank, its red roof gleaming like a beacon. I run the last few yards, my hand already in my pocket pulling out my purse. I reach for the door, and then groan in frustration. There's someone in there already. A blonde woman, leaning against the window, with a cigarette in one hand and with the phone clamped to her ear with the other.

I walk slowly around the box, making it clear to her that I'm waiting to make a call. She grinds her cigarette out on the floor and scowls at me. Then she turns her back on me and lights another cigarette. There's a pile of pennies next to her on the shelf by the phone. I groan again. She could be in there for ever. Joseph could have packed a bag by now. He could have left the house and be God knows where.

I jiggle around impatiently. Come on, come on . . . She puts another coin in the slot. I start counting under my breath. One . . . two . . . three . . . four. By the time I've reached sixty, I can't bear it any more. I walk to the side of the box and tap on one of the panes of glass. The woman whips her head around and frowns at me.

'Are you going to be much longer?' I ask loudly.

She flicks two fingers at me and turns away.

I bang on the glass again. 'Please!' I shout. 'It's an emergency. I need to ring the police.'

She takes the phone away from her ear and pushes the door open. 'Are you messing me about?' she asks.

'No,' I say. 'Please. There really is an emergency. I just need two minutes.'

'Well, why didn't you say before,' she says. 'Hang on a minute.' She turns back to the phone. 'I'll ring you back in a sec, love,' she says. Then she hangs up and holds the door open for me.

'Thanks,' I say. 'Thanks ever so much.' I step inside the phone box and close the door. The air inside is still thick with the blonde woman's cigarette smoke and the stink of old ashtrays. I dig a penny out of my purse, pick up the phone and dial 100 for operator. The phone rings once and then clicks.

'Hello, operator. How can I help you?'

The woman outside has got her arms folded across her chest. She's tapping her foot and watching me through the windows. 'Can you put me through to Battersea Police Station, please,' I say into the phone.

'One moment, please.' There's a brrr and a click, then I hear the phone ringing at the other end.

'Hello,' says a voice. As the pips start bleeping, I quickly push a penny into the slot. 'Battersea Park Police Station,' says the voice.

I imagine the desk sergeant with the nervous tick; a cup of tea by his side and a half-eaten biscuit. I turn my back to the woman outside and cup my hand over the phone's mouthpiece.

'Hello. Can I help you?' says the voice at the other end.

My mouth's gone dry and my tongue feels three times bigger. I clear my throat. 'It's about the Battersea Park Killer,' I manage to say.

'Yes?'

I imagine the desk sergeant sitting up straight now, grabbing a notebook and pen. 'I think I know who it is,' I whisper.

'Beg your pardon?' says the desk sergeant.

'I said, I think I know who the Battersea Park Killer is.'

'Right. Okay. Can I have your name please, miss. It is miss, isn't it?'

'No! I . . . I don't want to do that. I don't want anyone to know I've called. Just, please listen.' I take a deep breath. 'His name is Joseph White. He lives at Frank's Fish Bar, on Battersea Park Road. I know he's got something to do with it all. He . . . he lied to the police about where he was on the night Jackie Lawrence was killed. He . . . he goes to Battersea Park, to the places where the girls were found. And he was in Soho last night. He has some letters too . . . from a missing French girl called Arabella.'

'Slow down, miss, please. I can't write that quickly. Just repeat what you've just said. But slowly and calmly.'

I grit my teeth. This is the worst thing I've ever done in my life. 'Joseph White,' I say again. 'He practically admitted it to me. Just ask him where he really was on the night Jackie Lawrence was murdered. Ask him about Arabella.' Then I slam the phone down. My hands are shaking. The woman outside bangs on the window. 'You finished, then?' she shouts.

I push the door open and she shoulders past me back into the phone box. The fresh air outside hits me in the face like a slap. But it tastes sweet, and the pure shock of it clears my head, so I feel more like me than I have for days. I shiver and zip up my jacket. The only problem now, is I don't know what to do next. I didn't think this far.

I can't go home, that's obvious. I can't be there when the police come for Joseph. I don't want to see the suffering on Mum and Dad's faces for starters. I wander aimlessly down the High Street, past old Miss Suttie's sweet shop where me and Jackie had our first taste of liquorice and past Ruby's Café where Jackie had her first taste of new friends. It's closed now, the blinds pulled down like sleepy eyelids. I think about Pauline and Mary and Sharon and wonder if the hole that Jackie has left in their lives is anywhere near as big as the hole she's left in mine. But I doubt it. There's nothing that will ever, ever fill the huge Jackie space in my heart.

I walk to the very end of the High Street and around the corner to where Fine Fare is set back from the road in its pale concrete frame. It's got that sad, deserted Sunday look to it. I read the advertisements in the window for green shield stamps and Kelloggs cornflakes. I press my nose against the glass and peer into the darkened interior and wonder which till Norma sat at when she was last working. I stare into the window for so long that I forget where I am and why I'm here.

Then spots of rain start to patter down on to my shoulders, and I know there's only one place I can go now.

An old woman answers the door. She's wearing a flowery housecoat and a woolly hat pulled down over her ears. Wisps of white hair are curling out from around the sides of the hat. 'Yes?' she says. She squints at me. 'Do I know you?'

'No,' I say. 'But I just wondered if Mr Smith was at home. I've got a message for him, you see.'

'A message, eh?' She looks me up and down. 'Well, I'll just go and see if he's available. Hang on a minute.' She totters back down the hall and starts to heave herself up the stairs. I feel guilty. I know there are two flights to get up before she'll reach Beau's room.

241

'Excuse me!' I shout into the hall. 'Would you like me to go up? Save you climbing all those stairs.'

She pauses and shuffles around to face me with her lips pursed. 'Oh no,' she says. 'Kind of you to say, but I don't allow my lodgers to have female visitors in their rooms. It's not decent.' She carries on up the stairs, grunting out loud with each step and I watch her until she disappears from view.

I lean back against the doorframe and look into the street to where a bunch of kids are kicking a ball against the wall of the house opposite. Thud, thud, thud, like the beat of my heart. I think about what I'll say to Beau. He won't mind that I'm here, will he? He said himself, *When you've made up your mind, I'll help you, Violet. You know that I will.* But before I can decide anything, there's footsteps bounding down the stairs inside, and there's Beau walking towards me with a grin on his face and with his quiff all glossy and bouncing.

'Hey!' he says. 'It's you!' He winks. 'Just a minute,' he says. 'I've just got to help Mrs B back down the stairs.'

When he brings her back down into the hall, she's hanging on to his arm and laughing softly at something he's said.

'You're a good boy,' she says, patting his arm. And then she shoots me a warning look. 'He's a good boy, you know.'

'Oh, Mrs B. Don't. You'll make me blush,' he says with a laugh.

'So, are you going to introduce me?' asks Mrs B.

'Course,' says Beau. 'Mrs B, this is Violet. And Violet, this is Mrs B.' We nod cautiously at each other. She looks me up and down, sizing me up, and obviously decides I'm no threat, because she wanders back into her front room and closes the door, leaving Beau alone with me.

Beau joins me on the front step. 'All right, then?' he says. He takes a cigarette out of his pocket and lights it. 'Want one?'

I shake my head. 'No, thanks.'

He nods his head back towards the hallway. 'Can't sneak you up to my room right now,' he says. 'Mrs B will have her ear glued to the door, now she's seen you.'

'S'all right,' I say.

He blows two curls of smoke from his nostrils. 'So, fancy doing something?' he asks. 'Take a ride out somewhere?'

I nod. 'Yeah,' I say. 'That'd be great.' I love that it's all so simple with Beau. It's all about the here and now. No questions asked.

'Wait a sec, then,' he says. 'I'll just go and grab my stuff.' He dashes back inside and I wander down to the pavement where his bike's parked up on the kerb. Maybe I won't have to say anything to him, after all. Maybe I'll just take the day as it comes, and not worry about what comes later.

'See you later, Mrs B,' he calls, slamming the front door behind him. He's zipped up into his leather jacket now, with a scarf wound tightly around his neck. He's got another scarf clutched to his chest and there's a couple of motorcycle helmets hanging from his arm. He tosses me one and then wraps the spare scarf around my neck. It smells of his room. It smells of him. 'Thought we might need these today,' he says, as he helps me fasten the helmet under my chin. 'Got an idea where we might go. You up for an adventure?'

It's like he's read my mind. *I'll go anywhere with you,* I think. *You can take me as far away as you like and never bring me back for all I care.*

'An adventure would be cool,' I say.

He puts on a posh voice and waves his hand towards his motorcycle. 'Well, please do climb aboard then, madam. The road is waiting for us.'

'Thanks, Beau,' I say. 'You've saved my life.'

I haven't got a clue where we're going, but it doesn't matter. Beau is my prince. He's come to my rescue. He sweeps me up onto the back of his trusty steed and I close my eyes as we gallop off into the golden, hazy, happy ever after.

The wind whips past my ears as we speed out of London. I push my face into the scarf around my neck and warm my nose with my own hot breath. The sky is a clear, cold blue, sparkling with white winter sunshine. We're soon on the outskirts of London and the streets and houses and bridges and factories gradually turn into fields and woods and pretty little villages. The air loses its London tang of coal fires and eggy gases and begins to smell of damp grass and cow pats. I press myself into Beau's back and feel the heat of him beneath the leather.

After about an hour, the scenery changes again. It's like someone's rolled out a green velvet carpet over the land. It rolls out in gentle slopes on either side of us and there are hills made of chalk and hundreds of sheep nibbling at the ground. The road winds through the hills, then suddenly the sky opens up ahead of us and there's a steep chalk cliff and the smell of salt in the air.

We drive around another bend in the road and I gasp out loud. I've seen the sea before, of course I have. I went on the bus one summer with Jackie and her nan, to Southend. We'd hoped for a sunny day, but we woke up to grey clouds and spitting rain. When we got to Southend, the sea, which in my imagination would be all greens and blues and sparkles, was black and grey and choppy. Part of the famous pier had burned down the previous autumn and the black skeleton of the pavilion looked like some great sea monster crawling towards the shore and it scared me half to death.

But we walked along the seafront and ate cups of cockles and shrimps and Brenda bought us a tin bucket each which we filled with damp sand and emptied back onto the beach, pretending to have fun as we shivered in our thin summer coats.

But this sea! This sea is just how I imagined it to be. It's huge and blue and polished. And it might not be the middle of summer, but at least the sun's shining today and there's sparkles on the tops of the waves that are breaking into a foamy mess on the beach. There's a pier here too, reaching far out to sea to touch the horizon. And there's not a sea monster in sight. This pier has towers and pavilions, a theatre and ice-cream stalls. There's striped deckchairs running down its length, and it's buzzing with people. Beau drives us along the seafront. The whole place is buzzing with people. There's couples strolling along, arm in arm or pushing prams. There's groups of fellas and girls sitting along the sea wall and gathered under blankets on the beach. And there's children paddling in the sea.

Beau pulls over by some railings, where a gang of bikers are already parked up. We take off our helmets and shake out our hair. 'Welcome to Brighton,' Beau says. The other bikers nod at us in recognition.

'Do you know them?' I ask Beau. 'Nah,' he says. 'But I will do in a minute.'

I follow him as he wanders over. He melts into the group as easily as lard in a hot frying pan. They admire his bike and check out the badges on his jacket and arrange to drive over to Chelsea Bridge one Saturday night. An old couple shuffle past as the fellas are all laughing at something.

'Need a few years in the army, you lot,' the old man mutters. 'Disgusting!'

'Mind how you go, pops!' one of the fellas shouts back. And they all laugh good-naturedly.

'I'm starving,' says Beau. 'Fancy some grub?' He grabs my hand and we head off across the road to a café called Divalls which has the words *Fastest Service on Record* painted in big white letters above its shop window. Beau orders two chip butties and two teas, and true to their word, in less than five minutes we're sitting on the beach biting into the most delicious butties in the world. The bread is cut in thick, soft doorsteps, and the chips are so hot and vinegary that melted butter runs down our chins with each bite. 'Good, eh?' says Beau, grinning at me with a mouthful of bread.

'The best,' I say.

We drink our tea and watch a dog chasing pebbles into the sea, its owner throwing the pebbles further and further out, so eventually the dog is swimming. 'Did you know,' I say, 'that Newfoundland dogs are the best swimmers, because they've got webbed feet?'

'Really?' says Beau. 'How do you know that?'

'Dunno,' I say. 'Must have read it somewhere.'

246

He laughs.

'Also . . .' I say. 'Bassett hounds can't swim at all.'

'You're a card, you are, Violet. A real bloody card.' He lifts my chin with his fingers and kisses the butter from my mouth.

We spend the rest of the day wandering the streets and lanes of the town. There's dozens of pubs and coffee bars. We wander into one and drink mugs of thick, dark coffee while Beau fills the jukebox with coins and we listen to Eddie Cochran and then Chuck Berry's 'Sweet Little Sixteen', which Beau sings along to at the top of his voice.

He pulls me off my chair and spins me round the floor and the other customers clap and sing along too.

Breathless and giddy, we wander back down to the beach and take off our shoes and socks. The sharp pebbles dig into our feet as we walk gingerly to the water's edge and dip our toes into the freezing shallows. I squeal like a little girl and Beau laughs and eggs me on to go deeper. We roll up our jeans and wade in, one step at a time, until a wave slaps over our knees and soaks the bottoms of our jeans. Beau pulls me towards him and our noses bang awkwardly as we find each other's mouths.

The light's fading now, it's getting late. 'Wish we didn't have to go back,' I whisper.

'We don't have to go back,' he says. 'We don't have to do anything we don't want to.'

'Wish that was true.'

He grabs my hands. 'Course it's true! You want to stay here? We'll stay here.'

I bite my cheek, trying not to laugh, as the idea sinks in. Not go home? Stay here with Beau? Not have to face the mess and devastation that'll be happening at home? To stay in this fairy tale bubble for just a while longer?

'Really?' I say. 'Can we really stay?'

In answer to my question, Beau leads the way off the beach and into the town, to a quiet side road where every other house has a *Rooms to Let* notice in its window. 'Which one?' he asks. I pick a house with a sea-blue door that still has winter pansies growing in pots on the doorstep. We walk up the pathway and knock on the door. 'Keep your left hand in your pocket,' Beau suddenly whispers, just before a stern, dark-haired woman opens the door to us. 'Good evening,' says Beau. 'We saw the sign in your window and we wondered if we could have a room for the night?'

A flicker of suspicion crosses the woman's face.

I shove my hand in my pocket. 'Me and my wife,' says Beau. 'Well, we've just had a lovely day out, and we fancy staying over. Can you fix us up?'

The woman smiles, showing off a mouthful of pearly falsies. 'Of course,' she says. 'Do come in.'

The hallway smells of talcum powder and wet dog. The walls are covered in thick red wallpaper and the floor in worn red and black checked lino. 'Money up front,' says the woman, 'if you don't mind. And you'll need to sign the register.' There's a small desk squeezed into a corner of the room. The woman pulls a book out from under it and hands a pen to Beau. 'Name, please,' she asks.

'Mr and Mrs Smith,' says Beau. He keeps a straight face, but I can feel the back of my neck getting hot and I will myself not to blush or giggle.

'Would you sign here please?' says the woman. Beau scribbles in the book as I stare at my feet and at the cracks in the lino.

'Ten shillings then, please,' she says. 'The door will be locked at ten and if you require breakfast it will be served in the dining room at eight sharp.' She passes a key to Beau. 'Any luggage?' she asks, looking us up and down.

'Only my motorcycle,' says Beau. 'It's parked up on the seafront. I'll go and fetch it in a bit.'

'Right you are,' says the woman. 'Well, it's the room to the left at the top of the stairs. Bathroom's right next door.'

We steal our way up the stairs. I can feel her eyes burning into my back. She knows we're not married. She's not stupid. But suddenly I feel stupid. What the hell am I doing? What am I thinking? This isn't the sort of thing a girl like me does. I've never spent a night away from home before, apart from when I slept over at Jackie's, but that doesn't count. Spending the night with a fella is whole different thing. The sort of girls who do this, get pregnant at sixteen and married soon after. They're 'fast pieces', as Mum calls them, and destined to end up on the scrap heap.

Beau opens the bedroom door. 'Ladies first,' he says.

I hesitate. If I step inside, will there be any going back?

'Hey,' says Beau. 'Don't look so worried. I'm not going to eat you. We can go straight back to Battersea if you want. We don't have to do this.'

And that's when I remember there isn't any going back anyway. The police will have Joseph by now. Mum, Dad and Norma will be in bits and none of them will ever want to see my face again. I step into the bedroom and Beau closes the door behind us.

It's late now. But the curtains in the room are thin and the room is at the front of the house so the streetlights are shining in, and I can see Beau's face as clearly as if it were daylight. His head's on the pillow next to mine.

The room is a bit pokey. But it's clean. The walls are painted white and as well as the double bed we're lying on, there's a small chest of drawers with a spare blanket folded up on top, a boarded-up fireplace and a painting on the wall of a girl with eyes as big as saucers.

We've taken our shoes and jackets off, but we've kept the rest of our clothes on. The sheets are the fluffy flannelette sort and they smell of fresh air. We've got them pulled up to our chests.

'You sleepy yet?' asks Beau.

'No,' I say. 'I don't think I'll ever sleep again.'

'I promise I won't snore,' he says.

'I'll poke you if you do,' I say.

'Here,' he says. 'Come over here and have a cuddle.'

I shiver. Is this how it happens? A cuddle first, and then . . . ?

'Hey, you're cold. Come on, let me warm you up.'

I wriggle over to him and he slips his arm under me and pulls me into his chest. I shiver again, but I'm not cold. My stomach is wound up into a thousand knots. He kisses the top of my head.

'Only a cuddle, Violet,' he whispers. 'Not every fella's after only one thing, you know.'

After a while, the knots in my stomach loosen a bit and I let myself relax into him.

'Tell me some more stuff,' he says.

'Like what?'

'I dunno. Like dogs having webbed feet. Some of that weird stuff you seem to know about.'

His sweater is scratchy on my cheek and it smells of sweat and soap. I tell him that there are over a hundred different words for camel in the Arabic language, that people with Moebius Syndrome can't smile and that the word for a group of ravens is an unkindness of ravens. Then I take a deep breath and tell him that earlier on today I shopped my brother to the police.

'Your brother?' He turns on to his side to face me. 'You think your *brother* is the Battersea Park Killer?'

I tell him everything then. About how I have this weird sense about people and that I always knew Joseph was hiding something. About how strange it is that girls only started to go missing when he arrived back in Battersea. I tell him about the letters I read from Arabella, the odd phrases; *dark places, you've changed, you frighten me*. That I think he might have killed her too.

I tell him I saw Joseph walking towards the Roxy on the night Jackie was murdered, but he lied to the police and told them he was at home. I tell him how I followed Joseph to Battersea Park and watched him revisit the scenes of his crimes, and how afterwards I followed him to Soho, where he went to pick up his next victim. I tell him that I'll never forgive myself for not doing anything then. I could have saved the next missing girl. And finally, I tell him how I confronted Joseph this morning, how I called him a monster and how he seemed to know exactly what I was talking about.

Beau is quiet for a long time. 'Yeah, there's some stuff that doesn't add up,' he says, finally. 'But your brother? Your own flesh and blood. Why would he just suddenly . . .' His voice trails off.

'But that's just it,' I say. 'Nobody's seen him for seventeen years. Nobody knows what the war did to his head, and nobody knows what he was really up to in France.'

'God, Violet,' he says. 'I can't get my head round it.' He pulls me closer. 'You're so brave. I don't know what to say.'

'You don't have to say anything, I'm just glad you're here.'

He shifts around onto his back again. 'What's going to happen when you go home?' he asks. 'It'll be madness, you know.'

'That's just it,' I say. 'I can't go home yet. Not until I know they've got him. I can't go back until it's safe.'

'It'll be in the papers,' he says. 'I'll go and fetch one in the morning. If they arrest him today, it'll be all over the front pages by tomorrow.' He slides his arm out from under me and sits up. 'God,' he says again. 'I need a smoke now.' He gets out of bed and opens the window and I watch him as he leans out and blows clouds of blue smoke into the night. 'Hey,' he says. 'Come here a minute.'

I climb out of bed and stand next to him at the window. 'Lean right out,' he says. 'Lean right out and look over there.'

I stretch right out over the windowsill and look towards where his finger is pointing. Far away to left, between the rooftops and chimneys, is a tiny gap, through which the thinnest slice of the sea can be seen. But right at this minute, it's exactly where the moon is shining, like a shimmering silver lining in the middle of all the darkness.

Pits and Bits

Beau is still breathing softly beside me when I finally wake up. His arms are flung out above his head and his quiff has flopped into his eyes. Sunlight is streaming into the room warming the sheets that are tangled around our legs. My first thought isn't, oh my God, I've just spent the night with a fella (even though nothing like that happened), and it isn't, oh my God, my brother's probably going to be in the papers today, named as the Battersea Park Killer. No, my first thought is, I haven't got any clean knickers and I haven't even got a toothbrush.

I cup my hand to my mouth to sniff my breath. Then I remember that a better way of testing for bad breath is to lick your wrist, let it dry for a minute, then if it stinks, so does your breath. So, that's what I'm doing, licking my wrist, when Beau suddenly says, 'What on earth are you doing, Violet?'

'Thought you were asleep,' I say quickly, dropping my arm back onto the bed.

'Don't tell me,' he says. 'There's something you know about licking wrists that I don't, isn't there?'

'Well, actually, yes,' I say. 'Monkeys lick their wrists when they're hot. It helps to bring down their body temperature.'

He laughs. 'And you're just testing out the theory, are you?'

'Might be,' I say. 'It is pretty hot in here.'

'Crazy lady.' He rolls over and nuzzles his mouth into my neck.

I giggle and twist away from him. I don't want him to smell my morning breath. 'I'm starving,' I say. And I am. We haven't eaten since the chip buttie on the beach and my stomach feels like a yawning cave.

He checks his watch. 'Well, we've missed out on one of the landlady's breakfasts. It's gone nine, you know.' Then he slaps his head with the palm of his hand. 'Shit! I need to phone work. Throw a sickie.' He flings the sheets to one side and jumps out of bed. 'Listen,' he says. 'You stay here and sort yourself out while I go and find a phone box. I'll bring us back something for breakfast as well. Okay?'

He shoves his feet into his boots, pulls on his jacket, runs his fingers through his hair and then he's out of the door. 'Won't be long,' he calls. 'Keep the bed warm for me!'

I listen to his footsteps clattering down the stairs and the distant sound of the front door closing. I stretch and yawn and rub my eyes. Then I reach down for my glasses that I put under the bed last night.

The room's so quiet and empty without him. There's nothing of his in here and for a minute I worry that he might not come back at all. I still don't understand what he sees in me. Perhaps if we'd done more than just kiss last night, I would understand more. I thought that all every fella wanted to do was to get into a girl's knickers. But not Beau. 'I'm not like that, Violet. I wouldn't want anybody to do anything they didn't want to.'

Thinking about knickers, I hurry out of bed and into the bathroom next door. Luckily there's a scrap of soap stuck to the side of the sink. I quickly strip off and give myself a once over. Pits and bits, Mum would have said. I dry myself off on some sheets of cheap, slippery toilet paper, then turn my knickers inside out.

Back in the bedroom, I tidy the bed then open the window and look out on to the street, waiting for Beau to come back. It's another dry day, and although the air is cold, there's enough blue in the sky for me to pretend it might be summer. I imagine what it would be like to never go home. What it would be like to stay here in Brighton with Beau. He could get another job with the local electricity board and I could find some work in one of the fish and chip shops. I'm an expert at wrapping fish suppers, after all. We could rent a room somewhere and every night after work, I'd cook us our tea and then afterwards we could ride along the seafront on Beau's bike and we'd get along just fine, just the two of us.

I can see him now, strolling back down the street with an armful of paper bags. I lean out of the window and wave to him. It takes him a minute to see me, but when he does he lifts his free arm and blows me a kiss. I feel better now I know he's back, and I run to the bathroom again to rinse my mouth out with water and to scrub at my teeth with my finger.

I'm sitting cross-legged on the bed when he comes in and dumps the bags next to me. He bounces onto the bed and starts to tip out the contents. 'Breakfast,' he says, as two bottles of Coca-Cola, a loaf of bread and a packet of ham roll across the blanket. 'Toothbrushes,' he says. 'Pink for you, blue for me. And lastly, a newspaper.'

I stare at the newspaper, then at Beau, my heart banging in my throat. 'Have you looked?' I ask. 'Is he in there?'

'I don't know,' he says. 'I wanted us to do it together.'

I pick up the paper and slowly unfold it. It's a copy of the *Daily Mirror*. I spread it out on the bed. Joseph hasn't made front-page news. There's a story about a strike at London Airport and a picture of Queen Elizabeth visiting Ghana. I turn the page. Still nothing. Just an article about toys – 'Only Six Weeks to Christmas'– an advert for diamonds, a story about London Fashion Week. I turn more pages, faster and faster. The football and rugby results, an advert for Qantas – Fastest Jets Around the World Service: London to New York in 7 hours – crossword puzzles and the television programme guide.

'I don't understand,' I say. 'Why isn't it in here?'

'Maybe it's too soon,' says Joseph. 'Maybe they're still questioning him. Don't forget, they thought it was that other bloke at first.'

'Mr Harper,' I murmur.

'Yeah,' he says. 'They were wrong about him, weren't they? Maybe they just want to be sure this time?'

'Or maybe they haven't caught him yet,' I say, the horrible possibility dawning on me.

'Or maybe,' says Beau, quietly. 'Just maybe, he's really not the Battersea Park Killer.'

I shake my head. 'Of course he is! It all adds up, doesn't it?' I glance up at him, but he quickly looks away and starts to unwrap the bread and ham. 'You don't believe me, do you?' I ask. 'You think I'm making it all up?'

'Course I believe you. But there's a chance you could be wrong, you know.' He shoves some ham between two slices of bread and takes a bite. 'Sometimes,' he says, with his mouth full, 'it's like you really *want* him to be the killer.'

Suddenly, I'm not hungry any more. I watch Beau finish his sandwich and shake my head when he offers me a bottle of cola.

'Hey,' he says. 'Don't be like that. I didn't mean to upset you or anything.'

'I'm not upset,' I say. But I keep my head down so he can't see that I'm lying. 'But I can't go home today. I can't go home until I know they've got him.'

'Well, I won't go home either, then,' he says. 'Bout time I had a holiday!'

'But what about your job? Won't they mind?'

He grins at me. 'Don't give a toss if they do. Besides, I just phoned in sick. As far as they're concerned I'm stuck indoors with a bad case of the runs!'

I pull a face at him.

He laughs. 'Yeah, sorry. But it was the first thing that came into my head. Anyway . . .' He rummages around in his pockets and pulls out a handful of coins and a couple of pound notes. 'Reckon we've got enough here for another day or two.'

I pull out my purse and tip the contents out on to the bed. 'More than enough.'

He rubs his hands together. 'Riiiight,' he says slowly. 'Holiday here we come. I'd better go and tell the landlady that Mr and Mrs Smith would like to stay at least another night.' He winks at me and grins excitedly.

I stick out my tongue and then grin back at him. Suddenly, I'm starving again. I grab at the ham and push a whole slice into my mouth. 'Greedy cow,' says Beau. But he's laughing and so am I, and even though it's November, the sun is shining into the room, and just for that single moment, everything is perfect.

We dance to the jukebox and drink coffee, we stuff our faces with ice cream and candyfloss, we walk to the end of the pier and back again, I have my fortune told by a gypsy. *You will meet a tall, dark stranger*, she tells me. *Be wary of him*. We sit on the beach and share a fish supper. The hot cod slips through our fingers and the salty grease burns our lips. We stand in the sea until our legs are numb and we suck on sticks of gaudy, pink rock until our cheeks turn inside out. When Beau runs into a newsagent's to buy more cigarettes, he comes out with a toy gem ring, the kind that are meant for little girls. This one is plastic gold with a ruby-red gem glued on top. He slides it on to my little finger.

'There,' he says. 'Now, you're my girl.'

We spend the evening in a pub by the seafront. Beau teaches me how to play pool and darts and we drink glass after glass of warm beer until the world turns soft and fuzzy, and I love being Beau's girl so much that I want to run to the end of the pier and scream my happiness into the wind.

We stumble back to the boarding house and just make it up the stairs before we hear the landlady turning the key in the front door. For some reason this is the funniest thing in the world. We fall on to the bed and our kisses are wet and spitty with laughter. Then, by some unspoken signal, we are pulling off our socks and shoes and wriggling out of our jeans and sweaters until we're down to just our underwear and I'm not even the tiniest bit embarrassed. We pull the bed covers back and tumble under the sheets.

The shock of his skin touching my skin makes my mouth go dry. He holds me close and strokes my back from my shoulders to my waist and back again. I shudder, because it feels so nice and because my head is full of beer and the scent of him. His mouth is on my neck and he's kissing me so gently that I start to ache inside. Then his mouth is on mine and I feel like I'm floating away somewhere on a huge, soft cloud. If I believed in heaven, this is what it would be like.

'Violet,' he whispers. 'Do you want to?'

I know what he's asking me and it would be the easiest thing in the world to say yes. But it's the biggest thing in the world too. And what if I get it wrong? And what if I don't know how to do it? And what if I get pregnant? I imagine how different it would be for me than Norma. She could be proudly pregnant, but I would be hidden away like a dirty secret.

'I've got some French letters,' says Beau. 'So don't worry about that.'

He kisses me again and touches me down there. And it feels so special that I forget to ask what a French letter is. I can't pull away from him now. I want to go the whole way. Whatever that means and whatever it does to me, I want my first time to be with Beau. 'Okay,' I whisper. 'Let's do it.'

He keeps his arm around me as he reaches down and takes something out of his jacket pocket. It's a small packet which he tears open with his teeth. I watch in fascination as he pulls out a small rubbery circle.

'Is that a French letter?' I ask.

'Yeah,' he says. 'You never seen one before?'

I shake my head.

'I'll look after you,' he says. 'Don't worry.'

And then he's pulling it on to himself, down there, and suddenly I understand, and then he pulls me close again and closer and closer, as close as I've ever been to anybody, and it hurts a bit but he kisses me and kisses me and my heart actually bursts with happiness.

He strokes my hair and for a long time I listen to the boom of his heart gradually quietening down. His hand falls away from my hair and the air around my head is filled with the fruity smell of beer as his breathing gets deeper and deeper. When I'm sure that he's asleep, I let myself give in too and I run through the pictures in my mind of all the wonderful things we've done today and I try not to think about tomorrow.

Two Pennies

Tuesday morning and it's back to being winter again. Rain is hammering at the window and our little room which seemed so cosy and bright only yesterday, now looks shabby and gloomy and smells of damp and strangers. Beau groans and pulls the sheets over his head.

'Is that our little holiday over then?' he says.

I curl into the warmth of him. 'Don't know,' I say. 'Depends what the papers say.'

He groans again. 'That means you want me to get up, doesn't it?'

'I'll go,' I say. 'If you tell me where the paper shop is.'

'No way,' he says. 'You stay here and keep the bed warm.'

He heaves himself up and sits on the edge of the bed. There are freckles splashed across his back and a thin white scar just below his left shoulder blade. I run my finger over it. 'How did you get that?' I ask.

'Bike accident. Got another one here, look.' He lifts his leg onto the bed and points to the only part of his thigh that's not covered in dark hairs. The scar there is thick and twisted like a length of bleached rope. 'Only you and me mum ever seen that one,' he says. My heart jerks, and as I watch him get dressed and leave the room to go and find a newspaper, I realise that I've probably fallen quite a lot in love with him.

Beau throws the newspaper on the bed and it lands in my lap. He's still panting and the rain has plastered the hair to his head. There's something wrong, I can see that straight away. Beau's face has turned white and his lips are pressed together in a thin line. He closes the door and sits on the end of the bed.

My hands are shaking as I try to unfold the paper. It's wet from the rain and I have to peel it open. I ready myself to see Joseph's face staring out at me with the word *Killer* emblazoned above it in thick black letters.

But instead of Joseph's face on the front page, there's another face. One that's even more familiar than his. It takes a minute for my brain to catch up with my eyes. But when it does, I realise with a horrible sinking feeling that the face staring out at me is *my* face. It's from the same photograph they used for Jackie's picture in the paper, the one of us sitting on Brenda's doorstep. But this time it's Jackie that's been cut out. There's just the faint smudge of blonde where the end of her ponytail rests against my arm.

PANIC GRIPS BATTERSEA AS YET ANOTHER GIRL GOES MISSING

'We've got to get you back home,' says Beau. 'Right now.' He looks so grown up all of a sudden; with his collapsed quiff and with his eyebrows all knitted together in a frown.

I don't move.

'Come on,' he says, urgently. 'We'll have the police here in a minute if the landlady's read the paper. 'She'll think *I've* kidnapped you. She'll think I'm the bloody Battersea Park Killer.' He paces around the room, as I gather up my jeans and sweater and shoes. 'I didn't know we'd get into trouble for this,' he says. 'I didn't know your mum and dad would report you missing.' He glares at me. 'What were you thinking, Violet? You could have called them any time. Didn't you realise how worried they'd be? Are you really that stupid?' He pulls a pack of cigarettes from his pocket and lights one without even bothering to open the window

I can't speak. I'll just end up crying if I open my mouth. And I can't bear him looking at me like that either; as though he's wasted his time on a stupid, good for nothing little girl. I swallow hard and turn my back to him while I get dressed. 'Come on,' he says. 'We'll go straight to the police station here, tell them you're okay, tell them you're safe. Or do you want to phone your mum first? She'll be going out of her mind.' He pushes his hand through his hair and groans, 'Shit. Shit. Shit. I feel like such an idiot!' He kicks the side of the bed.

'I'm not going back!' I shout. 'I'm not going. And you can't make me!'

He grabs hold of my shoulders and shakes me. His eyes have gone all glittery and hard. 'Listen, Violet,' he says. 'I never wanted to tell you this. But I have to now.' He takes a deep shaky breath. 'I did know Jackie.'

He might as well have punched me in the stomach with a sledgehammer.

'It was only the once,' he says. 'I got chatting to her at Ruby's Café and she seemed like a nice girl. I took her for a quick spin on the bike.'

I feel sick.

I can't believe I let him touch me.

I can't believe I did it with him.

I don't know him any more.

'It was just that once,' he says. 'I never saw her again. She wasn't my type. But the police got wind of it. They've been giving me a hard time, Violet. And if they know I'm here with you now . . . Well, can't you see how bad it looks?'

I'm shaking. My teeth are chattering. 'I . . . I just need to pee,' I manage to say. 'I won't be a minute.' I hurry out of the room and straight past the bathroom. I run down the stairs, keeping my fingers crossed that the landlady is busy in the dining room polishing spoons or something. And she must be, thank the stars, because the hall is empty. I'm out of the front door, at least two streets away and soaked through to the skin before I realise I've left my jacket back at the boarding house. But it's too late now. I'm not going back. I don't know where I *am* going, but I know I can't go back there.

Jackie and Beau. Jackie and Beau. I clutch my stomach, but it won't stop hurting. I remember that night at the Roxy. Jackie laughing at me for being a little Rocker. But she'd already been there. She'd already been with Beau. She'd been there first. Like she did everything first. I push away the other thought. Because it's too unbearable. But it's there all the same, prodding at my brain. *What if it was Beau? What if it was Beau?*

I keep my head down as I wander through the tangle of lanes and streets behind the seafront. I walk blindly, my mind a blank. The rain keeps pouring down and the only thing I really think about is that luckily, no one will recognise me, because I must look more like a drowned poodle fished out of the sea than anything like the picture in the paper. I want to go home. But I can't go back. Not until Joseph is behind bars. I'll sleep on a park bench if I have to, I'll go begging on the streets, I'll do whatever I have to do until someone believes me; until someone takes me seriously.

I stop and rest for a minute in the doorway of a bakery. Someone pushes past me into the shop and shakes the rain from their brolly all over my feet. Not that it makes any difference. My socks are already squelching around in my shoes. I haven't got a clue what to do next. I feel around in my jeans pocket and pull out a couple of pennies. That's it. The rest of my money is still in my purse in my jacket pocket.

I rub the two pennies together in my hand. I'll call Norma, I suddenly think. It's the obvious thing to do. I'll tell her I'm safe and then I'll tell her all about Joseph. She won't believe me at first, she'll think I've gone funny in the head; that I need to be taken away by the men in white coats and be locked up in a padded room. But somehow I'll have to make her believe me. I'll tell her that if she doesn't convince the police to arrest Joseph, then I'll walk out to sea and drown myself and she'll have to live with the guilt of my death for the rest of her life.

I wander down a few more streets until I find a phone box. It's empty, so I quickly step inside, grateful to be out of the rain at last. I stand for a minute dripping on to the floor and squeezing out the ends of my hair. There's nothing to wipe my glasses on, but I do my best with the cuff of my sweater. Norma's the only person I know with a telephone at home, so there's only ever been one number to memorise. I cross my fingers that it's still early enough to catch her at home before she starts her shift at Fine Fare, or even better, that today is one of her days off. I pick up the phone and dial BAT7654, then chew my lip as I wait. One ring, two rings, three rings . . . *please answer* . . . four rings, five rings . . . then at last, a click, and Norma's voice, 'Hello, Battersea 7654. The pips cut in and I fumble with the pennies in my hand to get one in the slot.

'Norma?' I say. 'Norma, is that you?'

There's a long silence. 'Hello?' I say. I check to see the penny went all the way into the slot and that I am actually connected.

But then Norma's voice explodes into my ear. 'VIOLET! OH MY GOD. IS IT YOU, VIOLET?'

'Yeah, Norma, it's me. Listen . . .'

'Oh God, oh God. Violet, where are you? We've been out of our minds. How are you calling me? Oh God. We thought . . . we thought he'd got you. We thought you were dead.' Her voice breaks into loud sobs.

'It's okay, it's okay,' I say. 'I'm fine, Norma. Really, I'm fine. But you've got to stop crying a minute and listen to me. I haven't got much money and the pips are going to go in a minute.'

She sniffs loudly. 'Oh God,' she says again.

'Listen to me, Norma, I've got to tell you something about Joseph . . .'

266

'Joseph!' she says. 'Oh, Violet . . . it's so awful. You know about Joseph? What do you know? What's he done to you?'

'What do mean, what's he done to me?' I'm puzzled now. What is she talking about?

'The police have got him, Violet. Don't you know? They came for him yesterday. They're questioning him about the murders, and then you were missing, and we all thought . . . we all thought. We didn't know what to think.' She's gabbling now. Her words are falling over themselves. 'But you're alive. They've got it all wrong. Oh, Violet, you've got to come home.'

Now it's my turn to be silent. My thoughts are jumping around in my head. They've got him. They've got him. It's all going to be okay. I can go home now. I can tell them all everything I know. They'll lock him up. And it'll all be over. This awful nightmare will all be over.

'Violet? Violet? Are you still there?' Pip . . . pip . . . pip . . .

Shit! I push my last penny into the slot. 'Norma! Listen, I'm in Brighton . . .'

'Brighton? What the hell are you doing there?'

'It doesn't matter,' I say. My brain's clicking and clicking. 'Can Raymond come and fetch me in his taxi? If I wait by the entrance to the pier, can he come and pick me up?'

She hesitates. 'I . . . I suppose so, yes. Of course he can. Of course he will.'

'Is he there now? Can he leave now?' All I can think about is getting home. Getting out of these wet clothes. Getting into a hot bath. Seeing Mum. Seeing Dad.

'I'll run round to Mum's,' says Norma. 'She'll have to let the police know . . . I'll tell Raymond now . . . oh God, Violet.'

And then the pips go again. And then the line goes dead. And I stand there and listen to the soft purr of the dialling tone until my hand goes numb and I'm shivering violently in my wet clothes.

It'll take Raymond about an hour to get here. And it feels like the longest hour of my life. I pace up and down outside the entrance to the pier, anxious that at any moment someone's going to recognise me. *Look! It's the girl from the newspaper. The one that's missing!* Luckily, there's hardly anyone around. The weather's seen to that. The rain has stopped hammering and has turned into a cold and miserable drizzle. There's a few people braving the walk along the pier with their brollies bouncing above their heads. The tide's high and the water's all black and grey and choppy. I watch waves crash onto the beach and listen to the roll and clacker of a million pebbles as they're pulled back into the sea. It feels like Southend all over again.

Every time a black car hisses past on the wet road, I think it's going to be Raymond. I sit on the sea wall and try to hug myself warm. A green car, a blue car, a bright white Mini. And then, at long last, a black shape at the end of the road, growing bigger and bigger. And instead of hissing past, this car begins to slow down. It crawls to the kerb and stops.

I never thought I'd ever be so glad to see Raymond, but it just shows how wrong you can be. When I jump into the passenger seat, I can't stop myself from leaning over and giving him a quick hug. He's all stiff and awkward, like hugging a gravestone.

'Thanks for coming,' I say.

He shrugs and pulls the car away from the kerb. 'S'all right,' he says. 'You haven't half stirred it up. Couldn't you think of a better way of getting yourself in the papers?'

'I never meant that to happen. I wasn't thinking,' I say.

'You had the entire Met out looking for you. Good one, Violet.'

I don't know if he's trying to be funny or what, but I'd rather he didn't point out the obvious. 'So what's going to happen to Joseph?' I ask, ignoring his remark. 'Have the police said anything?'

'Not to us,' he says. 'But I reckon now you're back, that's one less murder they can do him for.'

He almost sounds disappointed. I start to wish I'd hitchhiked home or even bloody walked. I've forgotten what a total bore Raymond can be. But luckily he's not the talkative type, so when I decide not to carry on the conversation, he lapses into silence too.

I look out the window and watch raindrops chasing each other across the glass. I watch the sea disappear around a corner. And then I watch the chalk hills and the velvet-green slopes and all the hundreds of sheep slide by. I rest my head against the cold glass. The car engine thrums through my bones. Cars pass by on the other side of the road. There's a farmhouse. A river. A small wood. A field of cows. My head empties. My eyes begin to droop. I'm sliding into a blissful nothingness.

Then suddenly. 'Violet. Pass my fags, would you. They're in the glove compartment.'

I lift my eyelids. They weigh a ton. Raymond's put the heating on and I'm too hot. And my head hurts. I sigh and lean forward to find his fags. I pull open the glove compartment and dig around inside.

'There's a packet of Camels in there somewhere,' he urges. 'And me lighter.'

I find the cigarettes first, and slide one out of the packet to hand to him. Then I rummage around some more until my fingers close around the metal square of a lighter. I pull it towards me just as the car turns a tight corner. I fall back into my seat and the lighter drops to the floor. 'Sorry,' I murmur, and I reach down to pick it up. I can't see it anywhere; it's obviously slid under the seat. So I lean forward even further so I can get my arm under. I feel around blindly with my fingers, but it must have slid back further than I thought. I stretch my arm back as far as I can and then my fingertips touch something. Something metal, I think. But not the lighter. I scrabble my fingers along the floor until I get a better grip. Something thin and cold and delicate. I close my hand around it and bring it out from under the seat.

'You find it?' asks Raymond with the cigarette between his lips ready to be lit.

'No,' I say. 'But I've found something else.' I uncurl my fingers and there's a silver chain pooled in my palm. I pick it up and it unravels and stretches out. As it dangles from my fingers, the silver J swings in front of my eyes like a hypnotist's charm.

French Sky

I've never heard silence like it. Even though the car engine must still be thrumming and even though the windscreen wipers must be squeaking across the glass, the silence in the car presses down on me like a ten-ton rock. And then I say the stupidest thing I've ever said in my life. 'What are you doing with Jackie's necklace in your taxi?'

Even as the words leave my mouth, terror is filling me up from my toes to the roots of my hair.

Raymond sniffs and wipes the back of his hand across his nose. 'Oh, Violet,' he says. 'You've really gone and done it now, haven't you?'

I flick my eyes sideways. We're still in the middle of nowhere. We haven't hit the outskirts of London yet. I can't jump, we're going too fast.

'You're not going anywhere, Violet,' he says, as though he's read my thoughts. 'Well, not yet anyway.'

It feels like there are hands around my throat already, pressing down hard, squeezing the voice out of me. I can't breathe and then I'm breathing too fast and all I can think of are the haunted walls of the pump house in Battersea Park and the screams of four girls as they are lost to the world.

I want to die right now. And I don't want to die at all.

Raymond bangs the steering wheel with the flats of his hands. 'One thing you need to know, Violet. I love your sister. I love Norma. I'd never do anything to hurt her.'

For some reason, those words frighten me more than anything else.

'You can't kill me,' I say. 'They'll all know it's you. Norma knows you've come to pick me up.'

'Think you're so clever, don't you,' he spits. 'You always were a stuck-up little bitch. Always thought you were better than the rest of us, with your books and your fancy words. But you're not that clever, are you?' He turns to glare at me and his lips are wet with spit. 'Don't have to say I actually picked you up, do I? Got to the pier and you weren't there. I waited around, but you didn't show up. No choice but to drive home, did I? Who's going to know any better?'

'Why, Raymond?' I ask, my voice a tiny, scared creature. 'Why have you done these things?'

'I like it,' he says, giving me the worst answer of all. 'Gives me a kick.' He turns and grins at me. 'You know what it feels like on the rides at the funfair, Violet? How exciting? How the Big Dipper makes your stomach roll? How you feel on top of the world? Well, imagine that, only a thousand times better. And those girls, Violet. They were so stupid, you know. They deserved everything they got. They should've known better than to get in a car with a strange bloke. But just because I drive a taxi, they think it's safe, you see. And your little friend Jackie . . . she was the worst. So trusting . . . so trusting.'

'Please, Raymond. Please don't hurt me. Just take me home and I promise I won't say anything about the necklace.' I'm crying now. I can't help it. I'm V for Violet, not V for Victim. This can't be happening. I just want to wake up. I don't want my picture to be on the mantelpiece because I'm dead. Then, before I can stop it, there's hot liquid spreading across the crotch of my jeans, and I remember a playground long ago and a little girl scared out of her wits. But this time Jackie's not here to help me.

'Have you pissed yourself? You dirty little cow.'

And then I'm screaming and screaming and screaming and Raymond's yelling at me to stop. He's punching me in the face to shut me up. And I'm grabbing at his arm and trying to bite him. He elbows me in the mouth and there's a sickening crunch and bright white pain and the metal taste of blood. And then I don't care about me any more, I just want him to die. So I fling myself at the steering wheel and he yells and claws at my face and the car is swerving wildly, but I won't let go. Then my stomach leaps into my mouth as an explosion of metal and glass slams into me. I try to scream again as the car skids and judders, but my voice has been ripped from my throat. I imagine I'm flying high in a clear blue French sky and then spiralling down, down, down, and the last thing I see before darkness closes around me is a thousand glittering fragments of broken glass.

'Violet. Violet. Help me. Please help me.'

I slowly open my eyes. Who's calling my name? I twist my head to one side. It hurts. It hurts so much. There's stuff on my face. I try to brush it off. Pieces of glass scratch my cheek.

I try to focus. I'm still in the car, but the window's all smashed and the sky is in the wrong place. I try to move again but a pain shoots through my leg and all I can see for a minute are thousands of dazzling stars. My legs are where my head should be and I realise the car is upside down. I try turning to look the other way.

And then I see him. He's right next to me, all scrunched up under the steering wheel. His shoulder is touching mine. I try to scream but there's no sound left inside me.

'Violet,' he says again. 'Help. Please.'

And then I see the blood. Thick and red and oozing from his chest, around a jagged slice of metal. I dare to look at his face. His eyes are half closed and sticky with more blood that's pouring from a black gash on his forehead. 'Please,' he says. 'Please.'

I don't even have to think about it. I lean towards him and whisper in his ear. 'Hey, Raymond. Violet here. You know, V for Violet. V for Victory. V for fucking Vengeance.' Then I pull as hard as I can on the jagged slice of metal until it slides from his chest. I watch as the blood pumps thick and fast from the wound and I wait until his screams stop dead.

Then, with my last bit of strength, I crawl through the smashed window and collapse onto the road with the silver J still clutched in my hand.

Grapes and Magazines

I like to sleep. I like to sleep a lot. The nurses say it's good for me. It'll help me to recover. Luckily, I don't have nightmares or even dreams. There's always just a soft nothingness to sink into. I reckon it's all the painkillers they've been feeding me. When I'm not sleeping, I'm reading. There's a stack of books on the bedside cabinet that Miss Read brought for me.

Not that there's much time for reading. What with all the visitors. Inspector Gordon was one of the first, once the doctor had said I was well enough to talk.

'We wouldn't have caught him without you, Violet,' he said. 'Nobody can believe how brave you were. It's a shame he died at the crash scene. There's plenty of people who would have loved to see him hanged.'

I don't think he knows what I did. But even if he does, I don't think he cares.

Mum comes in every day, of course. She brings grapes and magazines and bustles around the bed, straightening the covers. She never says much. I don't think she knows what to say. But every time she leaves she says, sleep tight, watch the bedbugs don't bite and tells me that she loves me. I think she's trying to make up for lost time.

Beau's been to see me too. I didn't want to see him at first. I couldn't forgive him for Jackie. For not telling me that he knew her. But he pestered the nurses so much, that just for their sake I let him visit. He won me back straight away when he plonked a great bunch of violets down on the bed.

'I miss you so much,' he said. 'And I'm so sorry for everything.'

He reckons I only made the car crash so I could get a set of scars that are better than his and he won't stop teasing me about how wrong I was about Joseph. 'You'd better work on your detective skills next time you fancy solving a crime,' he said. It hurts when I laugh. But it would hurt even more if I couldn't.

And then there's Joseph. It took a while for him to come. But now he can't keep away. He talks and he talks and the least I can do is listen.

'Hey, Violet,' he said. He sat in the chair next to my bed and plucked at the edges of my blanket. 'I'm so proud of you. You're a plucky little thing. Much braver than I ever was.'

I wanted to say sorry to him, but I didn't know where to begin. Luckily he had enough words for both of us.

'I understand, you know,' he said. 'Why you thought it was me. I know you put the police on to me. But I want you to know I don't blame you. You always knew there was something I was hiding, didn't you? You just added it up wrong.' He shrugged, like it didn't matter to him any more.

'We're strangers really, aren't we? You and me. A brother, more than twice your age, who you never knew – can't blame you for being wary. They told you I was a hero, didn't they? And you had to live all your life with them mourning me. But then I came back and it was all a lie. I was a lie. Why wouldn't you hate me?' He stopped and took a deep breath.

'And I am a lie, Violet. But I don't want to be any more.'

I reached out and took his hand then.

'I thought you'd found me out when you called me a monster,' he said. 'Everyone thinks we're monsters. I'm used to that. Even when the police took me in for questioning, I still thought that you'd reported me for being 'one of them'. But then they started to ask me about the girls, about Jackie, and about some letters from a French girl called Arabella. I knew then that you'd really got it wrong. You'd really cocked up. The Arabella that I knew never wrote to me. She was only glad to see the back of me.' He cleared his throat, like he was trying to get rid of another piece of sadness.

'You asked me once if I was married. If there was someone special. I told you there was someone, that it was complicated. And I would have told you the truth then, if you'd given me more time. If you hadn't been so ready to judge me. I needed to tell someone, and I thought you might understand, being from this new generation, where you all seem to think so differently. But then you stole my letters. You sneaked around behind my back, and I was angry. I couldn't trust you after that.'

He squeezed my hand. Only a tiny movement, but I knew it meant that he'd forgiven me.

'I want to tell you the truth now,' he said, 'because I'd rather you thought I was a monster than a murderer.'

He took his hand away then. But only so he could rub his face. He looked so tired.

'I always knew I was different, Violet. Right from when I was a little boy. I didn't know what or why or how. I just knew. I couldn't put a name to it or anything. But as I got older – well, there were one or two occasions – it seemed like other people had no problem in putting a name to it. I didn't want to be different. I didn't want the shame of it. I thought the army would knock it out of me. At least I hoped it would.

'But then, oddly, after my plane was shot down, that was when it all got better. That was when everything started to make sense. That was when I met him, you see. It didn't happen straight away. It wasn't love at first sight or anything. He was just Eric's surly son. I didn't even see much of him to begin with. Not while I was recovering from my injuries. But then, once I was better, I began to work on the farm. And we kept finding ourselves alone together out in a field somewhere; fixing fences, mending walls, clearing the ground. One day I smashed my thumb with a hammer and he made me hold it out to him so he could see what damage I'd done. He was so gentle. And then suddenly we were kissing and it was like I'd been on a long, long journey and I'd finally come home.'

He stopped talking and glanced at me to check the expression on my face. I nodded at him to continue.

'His name is Alain. He's the son of Eric Armand, the farmer who had taken me in. So you can imagine how careful we had to be. And we were. For years and years and years. He was why

I never came back, Violet. At first I couldn't, for fear of prison, and then . . . and then, it just seemed kinder to leave you all thinking I was a dead hero. Better that, than for you all to find out what I really was.' He got up from the chair and started to pace around my bed.

'But then, we were discovered. One tiny slip. One careless night. We'd fallen asleep in the barn, wrapped in each other's arms, and it was Eric who found us. It was a terrible time. None of them understood. Not Eric, not Alain's brother Leon or his wife Arabella. They were sickened by us. Eric kicked me off the farm. I had nowhere to go. I blamed Alain. He blamed me. Our life together in France was over.' He stopped pacing and sat down carefully on the edge of the bed.

'That's when I came back to England. Got some lodgings in Fulham. Alain planned to join me. But being back here, being back where I came from, made me confront myself again after all those years. I couldn't accept who I was. I couldn't live with the stigma of being a homosexual. I couldn't live with the thought that I was doing something wrong, when it felt like the most right thing in the world. When Alain got here, he tried to help. But we had to meet in secret. Sometimes at a pub in the evenings, or when we wanted to be closer we would meet in Battersea Park, by the old pump house. Sometimes we would leave notes for each other, pushed into the cracks of the walls. It was exciting at first, like falling in love all over again. But it got harder and harder. And the constant fear of discovery did something to me. It messed with my head. It made me want to end it all. I wanted to kill myself. Why couldn't I live my life like everyone else? Why did we have to sneak around? Why

279

did falling in love for me mean I was branded a criminal or a degenerate, with the fear of prison or drugs; doctors trying to make me into something I'm not?

'I told Alain I didn't want to see him any more. And that's when I came home. To try once again to be "normal".

'I thought I could forget him, but true love can never be forgotten. Remember that, Violet. I've been looking for him, you know. He's here, in London somewhere. That's why I went back to the pump house. To see if he'd left me a message in the walls. That's why I was in Soho. That pub, The Golden Lion, it's the one place we used to be able to meet in peace. It's one place where people don't judge us.

'I haven't found him yet. But I'm going to keep on looking. Life's too short, isn't it? I could have been killed in the war like all those thousands of other young men. But I cheated death.

All those girls that have died. They've been cheated out of a life. So I should make the most of mine, shouldn't I? I should live it how I want to. And be who I want to be.'

I look at my brother sitting on the end of my bed and I think about his picture on the mantelpiece and how much I hated him, when I didn't even know him. The brother that I'm looking at now, I don't hate. I don't love him yet, but I think it will come. And although he's not a hero in the usual sense of the word, I've got one of my feelings that because he is who he is, he's going to end up being *my* hero.

The End

The sun is warm and buttery. There are even fluffy story-book clouds in the sky. I'm glad. It makes the graveyard seem friendlier. Joseph pushes me along the path in my wheelchair. It'll be a while before I can walk again. My left leg was broken in two places and my right leg suffered a compound fracture; that's when your bone breaks through your skin. I also fractured my skull. But I'm healing nicely. The doctor warned me that I might become over-emotional at times and have problems with my memory. It's called neuropsychological dysfunction. But I seem to be okay so far. I'm not having any trouble remembering my studies anyway. I start evening classes next week. I'm going to take my A levels. English, maths and biology. If I work hard, which I will, by the time I'm nineteen I can join the police force. Inspector Gordon says he'll give me a recommendation. I can already imagine the photograph of myself on the mantelpiece, all dressed up smart in a silver buttoned uniform and peaked cap. Beau says he's always had a thing about girls in uniform. Just as well, I reckon. (I haven't told him yet. But one day I'm going to get into detective college and I won't have to wear a uniform then.)

The churchyard is packed. I don't think we'll be able to get near the graveside. But Jackie won't mind. We've got to stay at the back anyway. Keep out of sight a bit. Brenda won't want to see me here. I don't think she'll ever forgive me. But that's okay. I'll never be able to forgive myself either.

Jackie would be thrilled that so many people have turned up for her. Joseph stops and puts the brakes on my chair. I've got a bunch of violets resting in my lap. I'll put them on the grave later, when all the fuss has died down.

I put my hand up to my throat to touch the silver J that's resting warmly against my skin. Detective Inspector Gordon brought it back to me yesterday, after they'd finished using it as evidence against Raymond. Not that it was the only piece of evidence. They found a pair of Joanne Thomas's earrings too. Raymond had given them to Norma as a present. And there was a purse belonging to Pamela Bennett and other things in a suitcase under his bed. The police don't even know who they belonged to yet. God knows how many others there were.

Poor Norma. I was wrong about her being pregnant. She was just terrified of her husband. Six years married and he never had sex with her. And she was too proud and too ashamed to ever say anything. She always knew there was something not right. But she never, in her worst nightmare, dreamt it would be anything like this. She's moved back home for the time being. Sharing my room. I cuddle her in the night when she starts to shake and cry. We all thought she was really going to lose it. Especially when they found the body of the fourth girl, and it was someone she worked with at Fine Fare. Well, she did lose it at first. But she's surprised us all. It's like she's getting some of her fizz back. Little by little, day by day. She's more angry than anything else. And I think that's a good thing.

The churchyard's gone quiet now. The vicar is starting the sermon. I look up at Joseph, standing next to me, and slip my hand into his. He never left my bedside when I was in hospital. We talked and talked and we haven't stopped since. I told him things are changing. People don't think like they used to any more. I told him it was about time he stopped hiding away. It was time he stopped being a coward. I told him that I know loads of brilliant stuff. And one of the things I know is that the world always needs a hero. Someone to change things. Someone to lead the way. Someone to help change people's minds.

I'm meeting Alain tomorrow. And I can't wait.

The vicar's voice rises above our heads.

May the road rise to meet you,
May the wind be always at your back.
May the sun shine warm upon your face,
And the rains fall soft upon your fields.
Until we meet again.

Author Note

Reproduced below is a letter that I stumbled upon when I was searching for stories from soldiers who had deserted during the Second World War, and before I really knew what this book was going to be about. It really touched me and I kept coming back to it again and again. It proved to be my inspiration to write about gay love in the 1960s, about the war, about desertion, about choices and about Joseph and Beau and Violet. It was written by an American Second World War veteran called Brian Keith to Dave, a fellow soldier he met and fell in love with while stationed in North Africa in 1943. It was reprinted in the September 1961 edition of *ONE* magazine – a groundbreaking pro-gay publication.

Dear Dave

This is in memory of an anniversary – the anniversary of October 27th, 1943, when I first heard you singing in North Africa. That song brings memories of the happiest times I've ever known. Memories of a GI show troop – curtains made from barrage balloons – spotlights made from cocoa cans – rehearsals that ran late into the evenings – and a handsome boy with a wonderful tenor voice. Opening night at a theatre in Canastel – perhaps a bit too much muscatel, and someone who understood. Exciting days playing in the beautiful and stately Municipal Opera House in Oran – a misunderstanding – an understanding in the wings just before opening chorus.

Drinks at 'Coq d'or' – dinner at the Auberge – a ring and promise given. The show for 1st Armoured – muscatel, scotch, wine – someone who had to be carried from the truck and put to bed in his tent. A night of pouring rain and two very soaked GIs beneath a solitary tree on an African plain. A borrowed French convertible – a warm sulphur spring, the cool Mediterranean and a picnic of 'rations' and hot cokes. Two lieutenants who were smart enough to know the score but not smart enough to realise we wanted to be alone. A screwball piano player – competition – miserable days and lonely nights. The cold, windy night we crawled through the window of a GI theatre and fell asleep on a cot backstage, locked in each other's arms. The shock when we awoke and realised that miraculously we hadn't been discovered. A fast drive to a cliff above the sea – pictures taken and a stop amid the purple grapes and cool leaves of a vineyard.

The happiness when told we were going home – and the misery when we learned we would not be going together. Fond goodbyes on a secluded beach beneath the star-studded velvet of an African night, and the tears that would not be stopped as I stood atop the sea-wall and watched your convoy disappear over the horizon.

We vowed we'd be together again 'back home,' but fate knew better – you never got there. And so, Dave, I hope that

wherever you are these memories are as precious to you as
they are to me.

Goodnight. Sleep well, my love.
Brian Keith

Alison Rattle

Alison grew up in Liverpool, and now lives in a medieval house in Somerset with her three teenage children, her husband – a carpenter – an extremely naughty Jack Russell and a ghost cat. She has co-authored a number of non-fiction titles on subjects as diverse as growing old, mad monarchs, how to boil a flamingo, the history of America and the biography of a nineteenth-century baby killer. She has worked as a fashion designer, a production controller, a painter and decorator, a barmaid, and now owns and runs a vintage tea room. Alison has also published three previous YA novels with Hot Key Books – *The Quietness*, *The Madness* and *The Beloved*. Follow Alison at www.alisonrattle.com or on Twitter: @alisonrattle

ALSO BY ALISON RATTLE . . .

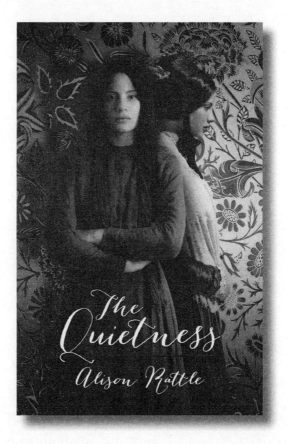

When Queenie escapes from the squalid slums of nineteenth-century London to become a maid, she has no idea about the dangers of the dark world into which she is about to become embroiled. She soon comes to realise that something is very wrong with the dozens of strangely silent babies being 'adopted' into the household . . . and when lonely Ellen comes to the house, the girls' lives soon become irrevocably and tragically entwined.

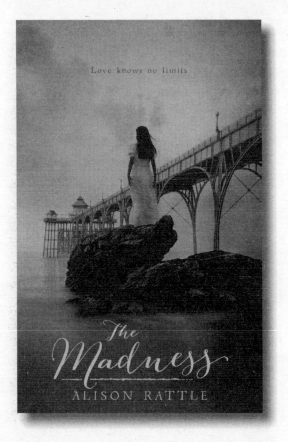

Love knows no limits

The
Madness

ALISON RATTLE

When Marnie develops a passion for charming and handsome Noah, it threatens to consume her. How can love between a cripple and a son of a lord ever become a reality? As Marnie's infatuation turns to fixation she starts to lose her grip on reality, and a harrowing and dangerous obsession develops that seems certain to end in tragedy . . .

Alice Angel has known only a life of rules, restriction and punishments as she strays from the rigid path of Victorian propriety that her mother has set out for her. After a chance encounter with a charming stranger, and narrowly escaping being condemned to the madhouse, Alice sees her opportunity to run and grasps it with both hands. But she runs straight into the clutches of a mysterious religious sect, and an apparently charming man called Prince. Instead of freedom, is Alice in fact more trapped, alone and in danger than ever before?

HOT KEY BOOKS

Thank you for choosing a Hot Key book.

If you want to know more about our authors
and what we publish, you can find us online.

You can start at our website

www.hotkeybooks.com

And you can also find us on:

We hope to see you soon!